ALIVE IN THE ATTIC

Sitting down with the doll cradled in her arms, the little girl examined it slowly, from its bent toes to its dented, one-eyed head. The beaded eye gazed blankly at her face. The girl looked closely at the eye, then down at the mouth where she noticed a tiny round hole, placed perfectly between the doll's lips.

That's so you can breathe and eat, she thought. *I'll give you breath.* Leaning down over the doll's face, she pushed her breath into the hole. Finally, she stopped.

"Live, dolly, live," she said hopefully, but the doll remained lifeless in her hold.

Trying again, the girl slowly straightened the doll's twisted legs and arms, running her fingers over its limbs. Her hands began to tingle and grow warm with the doll, and—to her mild astonishment—one of its tiny legs *moved.*

The girl's excitement grew, distracting her from the glowing eye that now boldly returned her stare. . . .

MORE FANTASTIC READING!

MaMa

BY
RUBY
JEAN
JENSEN

ZEBRA BOOKS
KENSINGTON PUBLISHING CORP.

ZEBRA BOOKS

are published by

KENSINGTON PUBLISHING CORP.
475 Park Avenue South
New York, N.Y. 10016

Printed in the United States of America

ONE

"My daddy is dying, my daddy is dying," the child crooned softly as she rocked in her small chair. She stopped rocking and gazed at the opposite wall, the colorful bedroom paper with the funny characters that told stories of elves and woodland sprites and cows that jumped over the moon, and asked softly aloud, "What is dying?"

Dying is changing. A daddy going from a big, big man who laughed a lot and carried her on his shoulders, to a shriveled person who lay in his bed and held out to her a hand that had turned pale and thin, that had shrunk to bones. A hand that trembled. It was changing all over. From a face once full in her small hands and warm to a face that was different, with no flesh anymore. Bones, again, like his hands. Skin the color of the cloudy sky. Cold. A terrible kind of cold.

Mama hadn't told her that Daddy was dying, nor had Daddy, not even the day when he no longer got out of his bed and she asked him, "What's wrong with you, Daddy? Why don't you get up anymore?" He said to her, "I'm just tired, baby." It was Stephanie, her big sister, who had finally told her. And her brother Tommy. Stephanie drew her to the end of the hall, with Tommy following, and Stephanie bent down as though she were angry about something and whispered shrilly into her ear, with Tommy watching, his face showing no sympathy for her. She stood cornered by them and heard the words she didn't understand but which had a terrible meaning that brought up from some corner of her nightmare world this new feeling of fear. "Daddy is dying, Dorrie. Dying. He's got leukemia. Don't bother him. Don't ask him why he doesn't get up!" And then, with tears in her eyes that showed she wasn't angry after all, Stephanie went running away into her room and slammed the door. Tommy remained, staring at her with the same unsympathetic eyes as though daring her to repeat her mistake, as though she had taken one of his toys, or one of his model airplanes down from its shelf. He finally spun on his toe away from her with disdain, saying, "You're just a little kid. You don't know anything. Don't ask any more questions."

That was a long time ago. At Christmas time.

She began rocking again, crooning singsong, her voice close to a whisper. "Don't ask. Don't ask. Daddy is dying. Daddy is dying."

She listened to the silence in the apartment, so

6

high above the street below that not even the traffic sounds came to her ears. Daddy was gone now, taken away yesterday morning on a kind of bed by men from the hospital. And gone with him was Mama. *Was Mama dying too?*

Her door opened, and the newly familiar face of her grandmother looked in at her. "What are you doing, dear?" she asked in a soft voice that grandmas used. "Wouldn't you like to bring one of your books and let me read you a story?"

Grandma was another of the changes that Daddy's dying had brought. She had come to live with them for a while. A while? That was what her grandma had said when Dorrie first asked. How long was "a while"? No one seemed to know, not even Stephanie, who knew everything. Or Tommy, who wouldn't have told her even if he had known. She hadn't dared ask Mama, for Mama had changed too, going from a laughing and playful person to someone who never noticed her anymore. Their home had changed also. The house was gone, and so was most of the furniture she had known all her life. Instead, they lived in an apartment high off the ground and she was never allowed to go down to the playground by herself.

"Dorrie?" her grandma said, as though trying to wake her gently.

Dorrie got up from her chair and drew one of her books from the shelf. She didn't care about the story, not this morning when she felt so deeply the silence in the apartment, but Grandma would hold her on her lap, and there was a warm comfort in that, in being close and cuddled, that Dorrie needed now.

7

They sat in the small living room and Dorrie lay her head against her grandmother's shoulder and listened to the voice of the storyteller.

"Once upon a time there lived . . ."

The side railings had been raised on Vern's hospital bed and surrounded him like horizontal prison bars. At times his hands gripped weakly at the bars as he attempted to raise himself, but weakened and drugged, eyes closed, he fell back, unable to escape. Elsea stood at his bedside, knowing that the end of his life was here, at last, after all the months of suffering. Anytime, the doctor had said. He would not be returning home again. She had adjusted to losing him and was facing his death tearlessly. The tears and the denials had come earlier, when together they had lain in each other's arms and faced their eventual separation. Yet her muscles were permanently tensed, it seemed, her entire body held together only by the fragile skin that contained her.

Blood, dark, angry red against his paleness, trickled from his nose and she used the dampened washcloth in her hand to wipe it away. The cloth, rinsed frequently in the tiny sink in the corner of the hospital room, had turned pink again. Blood ran slowly from each ear and each nostril and from the corners of his mouth. She wiped it away, trying to cleanse the pink tinge from his gray skin, but each time she rinsed the cloth and turned back to him the blood was trickling again, slowly, from every opening in his body. His eyes were closed, but he was only partly asleep, for he stirred restlessly and reached out for her. She clasped his hand, already growing death cold. A faint groan came with the blood from his mouth. She wiped the blood away.

One nurse was silently checking the flow of the IV and the tangle of tubes that ran from other parts of his body. Another nurse came in as quietly with a needle on a tray. She spoke softly to Elsea.

"Why don't you go down to the cafeteria for a cup of coffee, Mrs. Marsh. I'm giving him an injection now that will give him an hour or two of sound sleep."

"I can't—"

"You should. You've been in this room since yesterday, and you need to relax awhile. We'll take care of him."

Elsea backed away, the pink-tinged, bloody washcloth knotted in her hand. Vern stirred slightly in the bed, but didn't open his eyes and appeared not to feel the pierce of the hypodermic needle. His head tossed from side to side, his body too weak now to respond to whatever wishes might be left in him. A nurse's aide came in and removed the bloodied pillow from beneath his head and replaced it with one that was bleached white as the winter snow that iced the mountain peaks far beyond the hospital window.

With the soiled pillow case bundled in her hands, the aide paused in front of Elsea and smiled faintly. "Can I take that?" she asked.

Elsea wondered what she was talking about. She remembered suddenly the washcloth in her hand and held it out to the aide. The girl nodded, wrapped it in the case and slipped softly from the room.

Outside in the hallway was the clatter of the lunch truck being moved and stopped, moved and stopped, and the cheerful sounds of the voices of the aides who were serving the lunches to those patients able to eat. They passed by the door that stood open only a couple of inches and Elsea glimpsed the white of their uniforms.

Vern's head now lay still on the pillow, turned with one cheek against it. Already the stain of red was growing, spreading slowly below his nostril. A nurse slipped a clean towel between his head and the pillow.

One of the nurses glanced again at her. "He's sleeping now. Why don't you go get a cup of coffee? You must be exhausted. Coffee will help."

Elsea nodded. She wasn't sure whether she had slept last night. Maybe for a few minutes in the uncomfortable chair in the corner during one of his quiet spells. She wasn't sure if she was tired. How could she know when her mind seemed so stilled and waiting, so separated from her body?

She got her handbag from the corner chair and with a last glance at her husband went out into the second world of the hospital hallway. Here people walked along slowly, in robes, holding the handrail against the wall. They smiled at her. Surgery patients on the mend. People with hopes left. Others, dressed in street wear, went purposefully in one direction or another, bringing flowers, small gifts, boxes of candy. There was subdued conversation and bits of laughter. Nurses at the circle station in the fourth floor lobby laughed and talked. Elsea felt as though she observed all this from a different

10

planet. Don't you know, she thought, how it feels to have your husband lying in one of those closed rooms dying? Do you have any idea how it feels to watch someone you love, someone so important to your life, drift away in pain and terror, losing the battle against which he fought so hard? No, you don't know. I hope you don't. She felt isolated by her experiences. This was something incommunicable. For the first time in her life she understood how one's experience can separate human from human, so that you're aware of nothing but your own aloneness. Even when she had held Vern in her arms, when they had tried to comfort each other, she had become terrifyingly aware of the loneliness that experience can cause. He could not communicate to her his total fears; she could not share them. She could not tell him of her feelings of helplessness, of the inner strain to hold him back from death, nor of the future in which she felt she faced a coldness more intense than outer space, a vulnerability to life itself and all the dangers it might bring. He worried about her and the children, about his aborted plans to make a secure future for them. She assured him they would be all right, while within her the knot of fear grew as their savings dwindled. And deep inside was the tremble, the dread of facing life without him, with the responsibility of a thirteen-year-old daughter, a ten-year-old son, a five-year-old daughter, and no job skills of her own. *What would they do?* What so many others have done before you, a voice inside her said, and yet that didn't help. For they, like her, were isolated by their own experiences, each one different from the others.

11

The gentle fall of the elevator brought her at last to the basement, and arrows on the wall and along the polished floor pointed the way to the cafeteria. She entered a large, warm room in which there was a clatter of trays and tableware and a mixture of food odors, none of which tempted her failed appetite. She bought a mug of coffee and sought the privacy of a corner booth. She had started smoking again, and she lit a cigarette with her first sense of pleasure of the day, a fleeting sensation, as briefly come and gone as the flame on her lighter. She leaned back against the booth and closed her eyes. Perhaps she was tired, after all, and just hadn't noticed. A deep exhaustion she hadn't faced.

The future she had dreaded for all the months since she had learned of Vern's illness was imminent, she knew. As though she stood on the brink of a chasm into which she must step, she looked down upon it, at its bottomlessness, its deep fall. Into her life again had come her parents, ready to help in any way they could. They held the lifesaving net at some point in the dark beneath her. A week earlier her mother had come down from her home in northern California, the small town in and near which four generations of her family had lived, the town Elsea had left after high school when she came to Los Angeles to attend the university. She had never expected to go back to stay. Her marriage to Vern had planted her firmly in a suburb of Los Angeles, where life had been good until six months ago. Now, her grandmother's house, vacant for many years, was going to be their next home. Rent free, it seemed a kind of unwanted haven. On the market for five years, but unsold, she had the feeling that it had been waiting for them. The conversation with her mother returned to her, fragmented in her memory. It was as though her mother had come specifically to tell her the house was hers, if she wanted it.

"I can't take it, Mother. It would be like taking your dreams away. You and Dad have wanted to travel, and its sale would give you that. I can't take it."

"It doesn't seem to be marketable. Not in these times of financial stress, or of more modern tastes. It's too old, too big. Much too old-fashioned. There's no reason why you and the children can't live in it. It would eliminate having to pay rent. That would help you, wouldn't it?"

"Help me? At this moment our income wouldn't be enough to continue paying rent on this apartment. Of course a rent-free house would help. But I'd agree to move into Grandmother's house only if you agree to leave it on the market. When it sells we can find another place to live."

Her mother had finally complied, mainly, Elsea was sure, because there seemed little chance of the house going now after five years.

Elsea's thoughts drifted to the house, and the vague memories of childhood visits there. It held a treasure of three generations, an attic filled with everything from broken furniture to every toy every child in the family had ever owned. None of her three children had seen the house. During their visits to the small northern town they had stayed in her parents' house, Grandmother then in a nursing home nearby, the old family house closed since

Stephanie was three years old. She wondered if her own kids would like it there. It would be like moving from the twentieth century to the nineteenth. The furniture hadn't changed in her own lifetime, nor, as her mother said, even in hers. "I'll have a cleaning crew go in and get it in shape," her mother said, but Elsea disagreed. "No, I'll do it. It will give me something to do." The dust that her mother warned her of seemed almost welcome. What was dust? Such a minor problem.

She hadn't discussed their next move with her children. To tell them would be like burying Vern prematurely. The time would come too soon.

The loudspeaker droned in a monotonous feminine voice the names of various doctors, sounds that followed one in all areas of the hospital and which become an almost unnoticed part of the background movement. She dozed, and came sharply awake as she realized it was now her name being spoken. "Mrs. Vern Marsh. Mrs. Vern Marsh, would you come to Nurses' Station Four, please. Mrs. Vern Marsh."

She ran, leaving her cigarette burning in the ashtray, a drooping, long, gray ash indicating that it hadn't been touched since it was lighted. When she found the elevators at upper level floors she ran on to the stairway and began the climb to the fourth floor.

A nurse was waiting for her, and touched her sympathetically on the arm. "Your husband has died, Mrs. Marsh. But we would rather you not go in just yet—"

Elsea was already pulling away, running on

toward the closed door to his room. The nurse came quickly behind her, but didn't stop her from pushing open the door.

He lay still now, flat on his back, his arms placed at his sides. A doctor and two nurses stood by the bed. The sheet was being pulled up. The blood had stopped flowing.

Elsea stopped just inside the door. She thought she had adjusted to his death, but now she knew her adjustment was only beginning. She turned away, her eyes closed, and felt the arms of the nurse go around her in a vain attempt to comfort.

Dorrie was wearing her prettiest dress, but she found small pleasure in its pink ruffles and full, short skirt. Her legs felt naked without her jeans. Her white shoes with the straps across the tops of her feet were stiff, not soft like her favorite ragged sneakers. In front of her, Mama too was dressed up, and on either side of her walked Stephanie and Tommy. Tommy was wearing a suit, and he looked so odd she had stared at him when first she saw him. He hadn't noticed her stare. With solemn eyes he hadn't noticed she was anywhere near. Neither did Stephanie.

Grandpa had come down from his home and joined the family yesterday. But it was Grandma's hand that clutched hers so tightly. Dorrie wanted to ask where they were going, but the people around her were too distant, in some way she didn't understand. She had overheard a softly spoken argument before they left the apartment between her

mama and grandmother. "I don't want Dorrie to go
to the funeral, Mother." And Grandma answered,
"I'll stay here with her if that's what you want, but
consider this—she'll always wonder what happened
to her daddy. She may feel he simply deserted her."
A moment of silence, then her mother speaking
again, "Then maybe she should see him at the
funeral home. Before the funeral. I don't want her at
the services, or the cemetery. She can see him only at
rest."

What's a funeral? Dorrie didn't ask. It was then
her grandmother had come to help her into her
prettiest dress-up clothes.

Now her grandma was leading her into a room
that smelled of flowers, along a carpet that silenced
all footsteps. Her mother turned and picked her up
and carried her, leaving the others standing in a
group. Dorrie saw a beautiful arrangement of many
flowers, their colors subdued beneath soft, low lights
that came from somewhere hidden behind folds of
draperies. And in front of it all she saw a silvery gray
box, long and narrow, with rounded corners and
half of the lid raised. Then she saw her daddy was
lying in the box, in the quilted satin that lined it. His
eyes were closed. His lips were closed. He was as still
and unmoving as a wax doll. Dorrie stared down
into his face.

*Wake up . . . wake up and speak to me . . .
Daddy.*

"Dorrie," her mother whispered, "Daddy is—is—
He's—"

Dorrie leaned forward suddenly, so that her
mother's arm had to clutch her tight to keep her

from falling. She reached down to his face and touched it, moving her hand slowly along his cheek before her mother pulled her away. But the feel of him was with her, permanently, his total coldness, his unyielding flesh.

She began to struggle in her mother's arms. She wanted to touch him again, to rub his face with her hands until she brought back the warmth and woke him and made him open his eyes. She needed only to touch him, she knew, to make him rise from this strange, narrow bed with the lid that was, like the rest of it, lined with quilted satin. She wanted to bring him out of there, to scream at her mother to let her reach him again. But her voice was silent. There were anxious movements around her, as soundless as in a dream. Arms were reaching for her. Grandpa's. Then she was being passed on to Grandma and hurried out again from the room that smelled of flowers.

The door closed behind her, leaving her daddy in his terrible, beautiful bed.

TWO

The changes continued. Dorrie watched for them, accepted them in silence, and confined her questions to her teddy bear, the only one of her toys she clung to. Now they had left the apartment, without her daddy. No one told her anything, offered her any explanations. She kept wanting to ask what a funeral was, but the faces around her were still closed away from her, not smiling, not even talking very much. Stephanie and Tommy had stopped going to school, and then the packing of their clothes had begun. Then they were in the cars traveling into the mountains far north where they stayed for a while in Grandma and Grandpa's house. Now, with her teddy bear clutched in her arms, they were in Mama's car again and going to another house. Pressed into the corner of the back seat, Dorrie tried to straighten the dent in Teddy's nose, whispering under her breath, "Once upon a time there lived . . ." A princess, the story had said, but Dorrie didn't know what a princess was. ". . . A teddy bear. Live, Teddy, live." She lifted one of its stubby arms, the arm that had no hand, just a lighter brown fur on the end; but the arm fell back when she released it.

She glanced up at the tall, green pine trees along the sides of the narrow, curling road along which the car moved, and back down at her teddy bear. One side was squashed out of shape from all its years of sleeping with her. One ear laid back and flopped when she tried to adjust it forward to match the other. The bad ear was on the side of the head that was flatter than the other. Its black plastic nose retained its dent no matter how hard she tried to press it round again.

"Once upon a time there lived—"

Tommy, who sat in the back seat as Stephanie had gotten the choice up front with their mother, growled suddenly, "Shut up, Dorrie. I'm tired of hearing that."

"I was talking to Teddy, not you."

Their mother said, "Leave her alone, Tommy. Here we are, kids. The driveway was built for Model T's. Stephanie, watch that side to make sure I don't get that trailer in the ditch."

Stephanie rolled down her window and stuck her head out. The graveled drive joined the blacktop road by means of a bridge across a deep gulch running downhill from the mountains. A drainage ditch, it carried melted snow water and was now, in spring, almost a small creek. The rented U-Haul

20

trailer at the rear of the car, with Elsea's slow maneuvering, barely missed the ditch.

"It's okay," Stephanie said, drawing back in from the misty air and rolling her window up.

The car crunched along the packed gravel of the drive.

"Here's the house," Elsea said and sat back against the seat as though she had just brought them safely across a canyon on a swinging bridge. She let out a long breath.

Silence. The car had stopped, and its engine cut off when Elsea turned the key.

Stephanie said, "Hey, it's neat." She sounded surprised.

Dorrie looked up. She saw a tall house, green like the trees that formed its background, with strange porches and a round tower at one corner. She leaned forward. It was almost like a castle shown in one of her storybooks, only not so big. But perhaps just as big, for how could she tell about pictures?

With her teddy bear tight under her arm she followed the others and got out of the car.

"Who lives here?" Dorrie asked, reaching for her mother's hand. She didn't want to go into this strange house without the security of her mother's touch.

"Nobody lives here. But we're going to be living here now, Dorrie, isn't that nice? You'll find all kinds of interesting things here. This is the house where my mother was born and lived until she grew up, and where her mother was born and lived all her life."

"That," said Tommy, "was our great-grandmother."

21

Great-grandmother? "Was she a witch?" Dorrie asked.

"What a dumb question!" Tommy said, scoffing.

Elsea looked down at Dorrie. "What on earth made you say that?"

"It's like the witch's house in the woods."

Tommy said, "Oh, it's not either. That house was made of gingerbread and stuff like that."

Elsea kept out of it, but she looked at the trim on the porches and along the eaves, and thought of the coincidence. Gingerbread trim. For a strange and unnerving moment she saw the house through the eyes of a child who had never seen it before. The green wood shingles, warped and twisted, that covered the exterior walls of the house became rectangular cookies crusted with green mold, or frosting. The round tower at the corner of the house, with its conical rooftop, looked like a stick of candy with a topping of chocolate ice cream, frozen in time. The reddish brown brick chimneys, so many of them, were old peppermint sticks jutting out from the chocolate roof. The backdrop for it all was the deep, dark forest of conifers, silent and mysterious and dangerous. She remembered her grandmother, who had grown cantankerous and almost witchlike in her later years, demanding querulously of her, "Don't be going into the attic and disturbing things. I don't want the toys broken and misplaced." But now Elsea said to her children, "Grandmother was a really nice person until she got old. And then I got on her nerves. Perhaps I didn't visit her often enough for her to know me. Her name was Dorothy too, Dorrie. You were named after her."

"My name is Dorrie," the child stated firmly.

"Yes, we call you Dorrie, but your legal name is really Dorothy Rae. Dorrie is just a shortened form of Dorothy. Let's all go in now and look the house over. I haven't been here in a long, long time."

Five long, wood steps led up to the porch, and each of them squeaked in a different musical pitch, like rusted bass strings. The old key went into the front door lock with difficulty, and Elsea had to use both hands to turn it. The door opened, groaning. Inside, the front hall was narrower than she recalled and the ceilings much higher. She pushed the ancient button that turned on the hallway light.

"Ah," she said with a breath of relief. "I see the electric company got the power turned on."

"Grandpa said they did. And the water too," Stephanie said.

"Yes. Good."

Tommy asked, "Was Daddy ever here?"

"Yes, he was here once. Not long after we were married we came up and visited Grandmother."

"I'm glad he was here," Stephanie said.

Tommy said, "Then he knows all about it, doesn't he?"

"Yes, he does," Elsea said, not really sure what Tommy meant. But she had a sudden warm feeling that he was there now, at her side, entering into the house that was to be their home now, at least until they could make better arrangements. A few months here and she would be ready perhaps to face the future in different surroundings, go back to school, get a job, create another home for their children.

She opened the door on the left. "This is what

23

Grandmother called the sitting room. See, the round corner is part of the tower." It was filled with windows and window seats, jutting out from the corner of the room, and the same old cushions were still there, lying still and dusty beneath the yellowed lace curtains.

"Golly!" Tommy said. "Two fireplaces?"

"Yes. In the beginning there was no furnace, so there had to be quite a lot of fireplaces to keep the house warm."

"Is there a furnace now?"

"Yes, in the basement."

"Let's turn it on," Stephanie said, hugging her arms against her chest. "It's cold and damp in here. And it smells funny."

"We'll turn it on as soon as we get that far. First, let's look at the rest of the rooms."

A wide doorway at the rear of the sitting room opened onto the library, and immediately Tommy said, "Another fireplace! Golly, look at all the fireplaces."

"And the books," Elsea pointed out. "We'll have a lot of dusting to do."

Stephanie pulled one of the books out of the shelves and opened it. "It's old," she said. "Published in 1898. I wonder if it's a romance? I like romances."

"It probably is," Elsea said, "and suitable for you to read."

Tommy opened a small door on the right and found a dark little closet. He closed it immediately. Just to the left of that door another led into the central hall. They filed through. At the left was a narrow, sharply twisting stairway that disappeared into the second floor gloom, but Elsea passed it by and showed them through another room, with another fireplace.

"Is this another sitting room?" Stephanie asked, then immediatley corrected herself. "No, there's the dining table. But it's got an awful lot of chairs and lamps and things."

"Yes, people lived differently in the old days."

They entered the kitchen, the pantry, the breakfast room and then went down into the basement where Elsea turned on the heat. Tommy ran back up the narrow basement stairs and Elsea could hear him opening and closing doors. When she was ready to go on to the second floor she called him. Dorrie was still at her side, clutching her hand in silence.

The second floor was laid out much like the first. The area above the sitting room, with the round, tower corner and two fireplaces, was the master bedroom. A sunroom, matching the one beneath, was across the hall. Above the dining room was another of equal size, with slanted corners, and a central fireplace flanked by windows. A bathroom took up the space above the pantry. Two more bedrooms opened off the twisting, narrow hallway. Tommy found another small door, closed, and opened it. Stairs, as steep and narrow as all the others, reached upward into dim space.

"And that's the attic," Elsea said. "Would you like to go up now?"

Both Stephanie and Tommy said yes, and Tommy led the way, pushing aside an old and dusty spider web that threaded like a barrier from wall to wall in the stairwell.

At the top of the stairs Elsea pulled the dangling string that turned on the single ceiling light in the almost windowless attic. The floor was of boards, with an occasional rug laid down here and there, their patterns long gone under the dust cover. Old furniture cast deep shadows the light couldn't dispel, but the glass cases of treasures stood out, placed along the right wall, filled with tiny porcelain figures, with old dishes and knickknacks and odds and ends that looked worthless, but had been important to someone once upon a time. Boxes of toys scattered among the shadowy piles of furniture and trunks of old clothes drew Dorrie from Elsea. The small hand pulled away from hers for the first time. Elsea wandered around the large unpartitioned attic, looking at things she vaguely remembered while Stephanie and Tommy exclaimed over one thing or another.

Elsea slipped back in memory, to times when she had sneaked up here silently and guiltily, afraid to touch anything lest her grandmother hear her and shout for her to come down. She had the same feeling now, that she shouldn't be here. The rest of the house was open and welcoming, but the attic was closed off from her once very young and curious hands and eyes.

"Did I show you the view of the creek?" she asked suddenly, remembering the one window from which it could be seen.

"No," Tommy said. "Is there a creek?"

"There certainly is. Come on downstairs. We can see it from the bedroom that Grandmother called the chamber."

They went down from the dusty attic, Elsea leading the way into the large chamber with the high canopied bed, the red plush settee, the velvet draperies. She pulled the draperies aside and stood back. Below, like a ribbon of light through the dark trees, was the creek that rushed in a boulder-filled bed down from the mountains. Tommy made a sound of delight deep in his throat.

Elsea told him, "The salmon come up that stream of water to spawn every year. During salmon season, the water is literally swarming with large fish."

"Can we go fishing for them?"

"I don't know. There are times when it's against the law to catch a salmon, and I think it's when they go upstream to spawn. We'll have to find out about it."

"I remember once when Daddy took me fishing in the mountains down home."

"Yes," Stephanie said dreamily. "We camped out. I remember that, too."

"That was a good summer," Tommy said.

Elsea listened to them for a few minutes, recalling with them that wonderful summer, just two years ago. But the thought became painful. It was a part of their lives that was gone forever, left only in memory.

"We'd better get to work, kids. We've got to unload the U-Haul and get our things in, and our beds made, and some cleaning done before dark."

Tommy said, "Can I have this room?"

"That's between you and Stephanie."

"Okay with me," Stephanie said. "I'll take the

27

sunroom with all the windows. I kind of liked it."

"And I'll take the master bedroom," Elsea said. "With the double fireplaces. I guess I can put potted plants on the hearths. We'll set Dorrie up in the room next to the bath."

"That's a good idea," Tommy said. "Then she can get her own glasses of water."

They went back downstairs again, this time with Stephanie leading, and out across the groaning old porch and steps to the car. Elsea opened the trailer and handed a load of sheets to Stephanie.

It was then she noticed that Dorrie was not with them.

She paused, looking around the front yard, and seeing the fog rising from the area of the creek and deepening the shadows beneath the trees. "Where's Dorrie?" she asked.

Both Tommy and Stephanie wore looks of puzzlement. Neither of them knew; they shook their heads silently, their blue eyes wide now and wondering.

Elsea called, "Dorrie?"

There was no answer. The sound of her shout, falling away, left a deep silence in which not even a bird called. Far down the hillside came the faint roll of the creek rushing toward the valley.

She shouted again, louder, "Dorrie!"

Stephanie said softly, "She must have stayed in the house."

With a sudden rush of panic, Elsea ran back up the steps and yelled through the front door, "Dorrie!"

The house sent back a faint echo of her own cry and nothing else. After a pause in which Elsea listened and heard only the faint creakings of wood and the pulse of her own blood, she walked down the hall to the stairway and looked up. "Dorrie, where are you?"

The answer came faintly from far above. "Here, Mommy."

Behind Elsea, Stephanie said, "She must be in the attic."

Elsea stood still, looking up. Of course that was where a five-year-old child would be. They had gone off and left her there, thinking she was following. But, drawn as she herself had once been, Dorrie's eyes and attention had been taken by the toys in the attic and she had remained behind. Elsea would never call her down from that treasury of old toys. She recalled too well her own yearnings to be allowed to play there to her heart's content. It had once been the world's most fascinating place for her. If Dorrie could find pleasure there, no one would stop her.

She turned away from the bottom of the stairs. "Let her stay as long as she likes. She can't get hurt up there."

"She'll get dirty," Stephanie said.

Tommy agreed. "I'll say!"

"A little dirt won't hurt her," Elsea said as she went back down the hall toward the front door and all the work that had to be done. "It will keep her busy while we're getting the house in shape and our dinner cooked. We'll leave her alone until then."

Dorrie sat on the floor, her teddy bear forgotten by her side. In her hands she held a small, bent, dented celluloid doll dug out from all the toys and dolls in an old wood box. She rubbed her hand along the twisted legs, and over the thin shell of the head that had only one bead eye left. Her fingers worked at a fruitless attempt to straighten out all the dents in this dolly that were far worse than the one dent in her teddy bear's nose. She whispered softly as she worked with the naked doll.

"Once upon a time there lived a dolly. A long, long time ago. But a bad thing came and made the dolly start dying, and one of its eyes fell out, and its head got all mashed up. . . . I'll see if I can find your eye."

She got up and went to the toy box. It was filled to the brim with small carved animals made of wood, others of a harsh material and stuffed, seams splitting and bits of straw sticking out. She sat each one carefully aside, lined up. The wooden horse stood on its little blunt feet, but the stuffed cat with the straw sticking out its broken seams fell over although she put it on its feet several times. She turned her attention back to the smaller items in the box. A leg, detached from something, lay alone. She searched in the bottom for the eye that belonged to the doll, but did not find it.

Her eyes turned toward the glass case against the wall. It too had seams, these made of wood, holding the glass together. She opened a glass door and reached in where dust had not collected and carefully drew out a figurine, a bird perched on a limb. She looked at it a long while, then replaced it. She found a tiny cradle decorated with fat babies that had wings. Inside was a doll covered by its carved blanket. She replaced it also. In a cup were buttons, and she brought one out and tried to fit it into the eye of the celluloid doll on the floor, but it was the wrong size.

She sat down again and cradled the doll in her hands. Her fingers examined it slowly from its bent toes to its dented, one-eyed head. The beaded eye gazed blankly upward toward her face. Then she noticed something she hadn't seen before. In its mouth was a tiny hole, round, just the right size for the nipple of a doll bottle.

"That's so you can breathe and eat," she said. "I'll give you breath."

She had watched mouth to mouth resuscitation on television and had been fascinated by it. She had seen a drowned child brought back to life by the medics that rescued it from the swimming pool.

She put her mouth over the face of the doll and pushed her breath into the hole in its mouth, again and again. She paused, breathless, saying, "Live, Dolly, live. Now you will live."

She watched it, but it lay still in her hands. Her palm moved slowly over the legs of the doll. They were curved slightly at the knees, like a baby. Its arms twisted grotesquely in odd directions. Dorrie straightened them, laying them close against the round little protruding stomach. She rubbed, palm flat against the body and legs of the doll. Her hand

31

began to tingle, as though a million tiny needles had come alive in the doll and were sticking into her flesh. She kept rubbing, excitement building and causing her breath to quicken, her lower lip bitten against the discomfort in her hand. She felt a warmth begin, and then to her mild astonishment one of the tiny legs moved.

Moved.

Writhed beneath her hand like the worm she had once touched, the worm she had thought was a bit of plastic someone had dropped.

She jerked her hand away and held it poised above the doll.

The leg moved again, below the strain of her gaze.

She smiled.

Dorrie touched the doll's leg with a finger that tingled, and felt the movement. The smile curved the corners of her mouth.

"Nourishment," Dorrie whispered, remembering that her mother had said that to her daddy when he lay weak in his bed. "That's what you need, and then you'll not be dying anymore."

She lay the doll aside, watching it closely. The glass eye gazed at her, the other empty socket pink and blank. As she watched, the leg moved again, struggling weakly, like an insect that had lost its wings.

Dorrie reached down and touched the doll's stomach tenderly. "I'll feed you," she whispered. "I'll find your bottle and give you milk. Be patient now, and I'll be back."

She rummaged again in the toy box, and found in the debris of broken toys on the bottom a tiny doll bottle with a perfectly formed little nipple. Intent now on feeding the doll she didn't look back at it.

It was moving toward her, wriggling with slow strokes of the one leg, leaving in the dust spiderlike tracings.

Its one eye gleamed as though lighted from within, staring at the back of the child.

THREE

The man stopped at the edge of the trees beyond the driveway of the house and, half hidden by shrubbery, looked at the woman going out of the front door toward the car and trailer. Long, dark hair, parted in the middle, had separated over her shoulders so that thick strands hung forward against her breasts. She was wearing a leather jacket that came to the waist and denim jeans. But it was her profile that stopped him so suddenly. *Barbara*. Barbara had come home to him. But no, it wasn't Barbara after all, and of course he had known it wasn't. But the resemblance was shocking.

Another figure came out of the house, a young girl about twelve or thirteen. The voices of the woman and girl were low, too far away for him to hear distinctly. He had no interest in what they were saying. He had stopped because of the woman's appearance, halted in his tracks to stare at her unseen, and to delude himself into thinking for a moment that Barbara lived again. Even the car was similar, except this one was without the shattered windshield of the other, the bent top and hood . . . and the blood.

He began to move toward them, but stopped again as a young boy came running out, yelling loud enough for his words to carry clearly.

"Hey, Mom! Do you know this crazy old house has got 28 doors, 105 windows, 6 banisters, 4 cupolas, 15 dormers, 8 bay windows, 289 stairs, 3 porches, 56 doorknobs, 6 fireplaces, 17 cupboards and 9 closets? And only one bathroom!"

The woman's face turned and, full view, the man saw the resemblance to Barbara lay only in her size, her coloring, and her profile. This one had an oval face, with even features and a rather small, full mouth. Her eyes were large and dark. Barbara's mouth had been large, balancing her high cheekbones. The woman he watched now smiled indulgently at her son.

"Is that what you've been doing? Counting things? Well, come on and make yourself useful for a change."

She handed both kids boxes from the opened trailer, and then, as they disappeared into the house, stood for a moment with her face raised toward the sky so the man could see that she had closed her eyes. The pain, he knew it well. He could almost see the sudden grip of loneliness, of grief. She bent then, over the opened trailer.

Elsea was trying to lift out a box of dishes. Stephanie and Tommy had gone into the house with their arms full. The box of dishes was heavier than she could easily lift, and she grunted with the effort of trying to extricate it from among the other boxes. When the voice spoke directly behind her it came as a violent surprise. It was a soft, masculine voice, materializing from the silence that was disturbed only by the wind in the pines. She nearly fell into the trailer before she caught herself and whirled, her startled heart a rush of hammering in her chest.

A man's hand touched her arm and steadied her. She looked up into a bearded face. She had an impression of black eyes, black hair and white teeth. He was tall and broad across the shoulders, and wore faded jeans and a mountain man's red-and-white-checked flannel shirt.

"Sorry, I didn't mean to scare you into jumping into that trailer," he said. "I should have come down the road whistling. Except, of course, I came through the trees."

She glanced at the thick background of trees that surrounded the house on three sides. "Of—of course," she repeated, thinking he must expect her to know why it was natural that he approach from among the trees. She hadn't known that anyone lived within miles back in the mountains behind the house. The road in front rose from a small town about a mile away, and she couldn't recall seeing very many houses in that mile. What had she here? A mountain man who camped out on her back step? Or perhaps someone who had lived without asking in the old carriage garage or one of the other buildings in the trees behind the house.

The man was nodding on up the road that climbed toward Mount Shasta. "I have a trailer house just around that first corner of trees. I've been a kind of overseer of this house for Mister and Missus Sammons for almost three years. Didn't your dad tell you about me?"

"I—" She was beginning to get her breath again and her heart was going down to nearly normal, no longer trying to escape from her body. She remembered, yes, her dad and mother saying something about a man who had been keeping an eye on the place. Even in this sparsely populated mountainous area there might be vandals after a house no longer inhabited. And there were some rather valuable antiques in the house. But she couldn't remember his name, or anything else they might have said.

With an obvious attempt to put her at ease, he stepped back a few paces and said, "Maybe I'd better introduce myself. I'm Corey Stapleton. Just a kind of bum that doesn't like crowds and cities." He smiled. "Maybe I shouldn't leave it as just 'bum'— there's more to it than that. I'm what I call a writing bum. I live in my trailer and write articles for wild-life magazines, and I also write western novels. Don't apologize for never hearing or seeing my name. I'm used to anonymity. I don't ever expect to be famous. Or rich."

"Oh. Yes. Now I remember. In fact, that was one of the reasons Dad was finally persuaded not to make the twenty mile trip up here to help us unload and get settled. He said Corey would look in on us.

38

I'm sorry. I'd forgotten all about it." She pushed one side of her hair back behind her ear, and for the first time in many long months really thought of her appearance. She hadn't done anything to her hair but shampoo it since Vern's sickness began. And she had completely stopped wearing makeup.

He was no longer looking at her. He had moved forward and was reaching down into the trailer. "I'll do the unloading and carrying for you, Mrs. Marsh, while you unpack. If you'll just show me where you want these things we'll have you settled in a short time."

"Thank you, Mr. Stapleton, but the kids and I can manage. We don't want to disturb your work." She had never felt so awkward and self-conscious. She wished he hadn't come. Or that at least she had been expecting he might. Had her father told her he'd be around to help her out? She wasn't sure . . . yet he might have. The two weeks since Vern's funeral had become a blur of movement and pain and shock, even though she had thought herself prepared to face that part of his dying.

"You're not disturbing my work. My hours are too flexible for that. I've been expecting you today. I came down earlier this morning, but you hadn't gotten here yet." He lifted the box of dishes with no effort and went toward the house with it balanced in both hands.

Elsea grabbed a smaller bundle that was marked "towels" in Stephanie's large artistic print and rushed ahead of the man to open the door. Her son and daughter were coming along the narrow hallway and both faces registered briefly the surprise she had known earlier. They had similar eyes, blue as indigo, long-lashed, slightly slanted. Tommy was tall for his age, almost as tall as Stephanie, who was still childishly slender with only a faint budding of breasts. Both of them also had their father's light brown hair, which, in the southern California sun where they had lived, had developed bleached highlights of true blond. Only Dorrie was different. Small, with dark hair and eyes like Elsea's, a quiet little thing who kept mostly to herself. Of the three children, Dorrie was the one whose presence was easiest to forget, who least intruded on Elsea's thoughts and time. For hours Dorrie would stay in her room playing, or sit in front of the television with her chin propped in her hands totally absorbed. Before Vern's illness Elsea had tried to keep Dorrie more occupied by other things. But after his illness began, Dorrie's habit of staying alone had become a comfort. At least she was protected, Elsea felt, more than the other children. Less affected by his sickness and his death. If Dorrie had ever asked one question about her daddy, Elsea had not heard it.

With a warm feeling of pride, Elsea said, "Mr. Stapleton, this is my son, Tommy, and my daughter, Stephanie. I have one more, Dorrie, our baby, who's up in the attic looking at all the toys."

Tommy's eyes showed a sudden and expressive friendliness. Stephanie's remained more reserved.

The man said, "Corey. Just call me Corey, please. Hi, Tommy and Stephanie. I'm your next door neighbor. I'd shake hands with you, but they're full."

"Hi," Tommy said, with a quick, wide smile. "That's okay. Golly, I'm glad you're here. I thought we were all alone up at this house."

Elsea saw Stephanie was now smiling. Both of them had immediately accepted this stranger into their lives, and Elsea had a sudden premonition that he would be, in some way, a permanent force. But she wasn't sure she was comfortable with the idea.

She led the way to the kitchen, listening to Tommy and Stephanie's overlapping chatter of conversation with their new friend. The three of them went out again while Elsea began unloading food from the sacks on the counter. At one end of the room, the ancient refrigerator was clacking and hopping on its six-inch metal legs, trying hard to work at modern standards. It must have been at most a 1930 model. As old as Elsea's mother. Elsea opened its door and felt cool air surge forth. She put into the skimpy interior the gallon plastic bottle of milk, two cartons of eggs, bacon, sausage, lunch meat, cheese. She kept out the roast. Next would come her fight with the equally old stove with the oven perched on one end like the tail of a creature long extinct. The least she could do was prepare a decent meal for a change, and invite Mr. Stapleton— Corey—to stay and eat with them. It was he who seemed now to be doing most of the work.

Two hours later, the trailer was unloaded, the beds were made, the linens, towels and kitchenware were put away, and the kitchen was warm and pleasant with the odors of dinner nearly ready to serve. Corey had accepted Elsea's invitation and was seated at the table with a cup of coffee.

As Stephanie finished setting the table, Tommy stood on one foot near Corey, still talking as though he'd been forced to be silent for months and was trying to make up for lost time. They were into wildlife now, with Tommy brimming with excitement. Corey had promised to take him and Stephanie along the next time he went into the forest to shoot pictures for a new wildlife article. Elsea had to interrupt Tommy's flow of chatter.

"Tommy, excuse me, but it's time to go upstairs and get Dorrie."

Tommy hopped out of the room on one foot, then broke into a run that caused the old floors of the house to tremble. His footsteps clattered up the stairs, sounding as though he leaped three or four risers at a time.

Going from the upstairs hall into the attic stairway was like going into a dark and musty tunnel. Tommy stopped, feeling something he hadn't noticed the other time he had climbed these stairs. He hesitated, and the hair on the back of his neck rose like the hackles of the wild creatures Corey had told him lived in the forests. Far above, at the end of the dark tunnel, a pale, yellow light revealed something floating in the still, suffocating air. Dust motes. That was all it was. But he had an eerie feeling that something was stirring silently there, causing the dust to rise, and that Dorrie was gone.

Swallowed by whatever it was that moved in the dust of the attic. That it had taken her, and she would never be seen again.

He backed down one step. Then he called out, his voice faint and timid, "Dorrie?"

The dust floated, the silence remained.

He thought of running back downstairs for the strong and comforting presence of Corey. But then he thought of his own cowardice. Corey would never be afraid to go into a plain old attic like this just because dust floated in the air. Corey would go on up. Tommy didn't want his new friend to know he was afraid, more afraid than he'd ever been in his life.

Slowly, trying to make no sound, he climbed the steep stairs until his head was above the attic floor and he could look from one shadowed end to the other. Above him, dangling on its cord like a bloated spider lighted from within and hanging down from its dust-coated web, was the one light bulb. Blurred by dust, it left most of the attic in deep shadow.

And Dorrie was not there.

Tommy held his breath and stared at the piles of furniture, at the glass cases of figurines and old dishes, at the row of boxes that held so many different old toys.

Nothing moved, unless it had hurried to hide behind something.

He had started to back down when he saw her. A small lump curled at the side of a long wood toy box, she looked as though she had lain there so long that the dust had covered her too. *Was she dead?*

Terror tight in his throat, Tommy climbed the rest of the steps and went slowly toward his little sister. She was lying on her side, and she had something sickeningly pink and naked-looking clutched to her face.

Tommy swallowed, his voice incapable of sound.

With stiffened knees he went closer to Dorrie.

It was a doll against her face. A small doll about eight inches long, all dented and bent, with only one eye. And that eye caught the light and threw it back at Tommy, as though there was in it a kind of life that wasn't really life, but worse, much worse.

He bent down and touched Dorrie's shoulder. Then he clutched it hard and shook her. There was warmth there under his hand, reaching out from beneath her striped pullover. Her little blue jeans, with the elastic at the waist, were dirty and dust smeared her face.

His voice came frantically alive. "Dorrie! *Dorrie!*"

She stirred. Her hands opened and the doll fell aside, between her and the toy box. She sat up and blinked at him, widening her eyes the way she always did when she first woke. A terrible fury covered the fear in Tommy's tight, dry throat.

"Darn you, Dorrie, why'd you pick this place to take a nap?" He jerked at her arm. "Get up!"

She shrugged away. "Don't. You're hurting me." Her fists rubbed her eyes, streaking the dust even more.

"Well, come on, we're ready to eat. We have to go wash you up before we go downstairs so Corey won't see you in a mess like this." He grabbed her by the hand and forced her to her feet. She came behind him, almost dragging.

"I got tired," she said.

She didn't ask who Corey was, and Tommy was too mad now to tell her. He hurried her toward the stairs and thought of the light as they passed beneath the string that turned it off. He knew they must conserve energy, for not only was it patriotic, but they didn't have money anymore to leave lights burning. He couldn't turn out that light, though, and let the darkness in the attic have power over them. Quickly he urged his sleepy little sister down the stairway and into the hall. He shut the attic door firmly.

"I got tired," Dorrie said again. "I got so real tired, and so I just went to sleep, even though I didn't know I was going to."

Behind him, as she came along, Tommy heard her draw a long, slow breath. It was the kind of breath his daddy had begun to draw before he died. As though all energy was being drained away.

FOUR

Tommy brought Dorrie into the kitchen, pulling her along with her hand in his. She lagged at two paces behind him, her arm stretched by his, her pullover hiked up so that the elastic waist of her jeans and a strip of white flesh was revealed. Her face had a full moon washed from the dust that still clung to the edges of her hairline and her neck. The seat of her pants was fairly dust-free, showing where Tommy had tried to spank her clothes clean. He had washed her hands, but dust clung to the elbows of her sweater. She was yawning widely.

Elsea, sitting at the table waiting, held out her arms, and Tommy shoved his little sister to her. Elsea lifted Dorrie and held her on her lap, arms tight around the small body that still had baby plumpness. She brushed the long, dark hair back from her half-clean face.

"This is our baby, Mr. Stapleton. Dorrie, can't you speak to our guest? He came over and unloaded our things and carried them in, and he's going to eat with us."

Dorrie looked at the stranger, then laid her head against her mother. The dark eyes gazed intently, but rather than speaking, Dorrie yawned again.

Tommy took his place at the table and apologized for Dorrie. "She doesn't talk much. But she likes you, anyway."

Corey said, "Beautiful child."

Elsea smiled. With the smile came a gentle light that Corey watched, eyes switching from the child to the mother. It was a smile of deep love, coming for a moment beyond the still composure that covered the sadness in her face. It must have been that kind of smile, Corey thought, that had prompted an artist to create a painting he called Madonna.

Elsea released Dorrie after another hug and helped her onto the chair that had a book and a cushion on it to raise the small girl to table height. They began to eat one of the best meals Corey thought he had ever tasted. Compared to the meals he cooked for himself, it was a banquet.

More changes, Dorrie thought, staring at the strange man. Was he going to be living with them? She couldn't keep her eyes off the black beard long enough to use her fork to pick up her food, so she quietly lay the fork aside and began eating with her fingers, hoping neither Tommy nor Stephanie saw. Mama was not as apt to criticize her now as her sister and brother; since Daddy got sick, Mama stopped

48

noticing her table manners and Tommy and Stephanie began to act as though they were her parents. But now the black-bearded man was telling a story about a mountain lion, and no one saw her picking up her green peas one by one with her fingers.

"Beautiful," the man was saying, just as he had said about her. "There's nothing more graceful than a mountain lion in his prime, not even a deer. He lay there on the cliff watching me. I got several shots of him—pictures—then he got up, stretched, and leaped about twenty feet to the top of another cliff and disappeared into the forest."

Stephanie asked, "But weren't you scared?"

"No. I didn't crowd him."

Elsea said, "But aren't they dangerous? Weren't you at all nervous?"

"They're dangerous when they're cornered, of course, and will defend themselves as long as they can, just as any living creature will. Even man. Especially man. But except to the prey it goes after, they aren't dangerous."

"Ranchers don't care for them, I've heard. They kill domestic animals."

"Certainly. They kill to eat. If the rodent population drops, they go after whatever they can get in the animal category. Calves, lambs, whatever they can catch. Isn't it the same with humans? The roast you buy in a grocery store doesn't grow there, cut and packaged. All meat-eating predators get their food however they can, but without the benefit of guns or slaughter houses, and certainly without the permission of ranchers who own the animals."

Elsea was looking at the roast beef on her plate as though she had never considered before where it came from, or that in her civilized way, she too was a predator. Corey, watching her, smiled apologetically.

"Don't worry about it. The world isn't a perfect place, but it's all we have, and its laws of nature were set before our time." He started to say more, changed his mind and said instead, "Not a very good subject for the dinner table. I'm sorry. I've lived alone so long, I've forgotten how to act."

Excitement had brought Tommy up so that he was using his chair with only one knee. He was still back in the forest with the mountain lion. "Would you let me go along sometime, Corey? When you go to find wild animals? I can be real quiet. I'd sure like to go along. Would you take me?"

Stephanie leaned forward against the table, her eyes as eager as Tommy's. "And me! And me?"

Elsea interfered quickly before their guest could answer. "Hey, kids, settle down. He can't be bothered with you when he's working."

Corey said, "We might try it sometime. But most of my trips into the woods don't round up more than a few squirrels. The larger animals aren't that plentiful anymore. They're slowly disappearing. I feel that eventually the only animals outside of man will be in zoos or in cattle pens. As man multiplies, he takes over the world, and the habitats of the so-called lesser animals are destroyed. Another thousand years and there won't be much left but mankind."

Tommy said, "A thousand years!"

50

"Yes, I know, we'll never see it, will we? But somewhere down the line we'll have descendants who will."

Elsea asked something she had been wondering about, but which she had so far found no appropriate place to mention, "Do you have a family, Corey?"

"Children? No. I have brothers and sisters scattered across the country, and a mother living near one of my sisters in the East, but my wife was killed in a car crash four years ago."

Elsea looked at him again, feeling surprise at herself for thinking this man so removed from everything but his interest in wildlife, removed from the tragedies that can enter one's private world. "A car crash," she murmured, thinking of the slow death of her husband. "That's . . . so sudden. It must have been a terrible shock to you."

"Yes." Now he was looking at his plate and saying no more.

Elsea noticed that Tommy wasn't sitting in his chair and that Dorrie was staring at the man, eating with her fingers, putting into her mouth whatever those fingers happened to find handy.

"Tommy, sit down and finish your dinner," she said. "And Dorrie, watch what you're doing and use your fork, please."

Dorrie looked at her mother with widened, dark eyes. Surprised. She picked up her fork. Her mother was seeing her again.

Subdued by the mention of death, Tommy and Stephanie settled down to finishing their dinner. Elsea regretted having inadvertently brought up the

51

subject. She had seen that Corey Stapleton wore a plain, gold wedding ring, and assumed he had a wife somewhere. Of course, she too wore her wedding ring yet. She flattened her left hand on the table, palm down, and looked at the ring. It was set with five small diamonds. It was the symbol of marriage to someone. And Corey, after four years alone, was still married to a dead wife. Death did not end a marriage. She had not yet imagined herself, or her life, four years from now. She had lived a day to day, hour to hour existence for too long.

She wanted suddenly to be alone, to have the day ended, the kids bathed and in bed so that her thoughts could form into some kind of cohesion. She felt them struggling, separated in the depths of her mind, like a flock of birds trying to rise into a pattern of flight, to form and grow and come together to disclose her future. Possibilities for her future.

But later, when at last she was alone, the first day's work finished and the kids settled in their rooms for the night, she stood at her window looking out into the darkness and all she could think of coherently was the faint light she saw through the trees. It was the light in Corey's trailer home, she was sure. And her struggling thoughts remained unformed in her subconscious. She was still living hour to hour.

Stephanie went to sleep almost immediately, tired from the long day that had brought them from her grandparents' house down at Redding to her great-grandmother's house in the mountains. She had

52

helped with all the work, washing and putting away all their dishes, as well as washing and replacing some of the old, dusty dishes that were in the cupboards. She had grown accustomed to helping her mother during the past year since her dad's illness had become the dominant force in their lives. And now, tired, but relaxed in a way she hadn't been in a long time, she snuggled into the warmth of the blankets and fled into the comfort of sleep.

Tommy lay wide-eyed in his bed. He kept thinking of the attic just beyond his ceiling and he wished there was no attic at all. In the apartment where he had lived, there were other people above his ceiling. In the house where he had lived before that, the attic was shallow and filled with insulation, thick, pink cloudlike batting that he had seen once when Dad let him stick his head through the opening in the hallway ceiling that was covered by a kind of flat, trap door. The attic was the only thing about this new home that he didn't like. Everything else was great. Especially their neighbor, Corey.

He thought of Dorrie. He had kept a close eye on her all evening, when he thought of it. He saw that she ate a lot of food and he had finally decided she wasn't dying after all, for when his daddy had started drawing those long, tired breaths he had stopped eating. He decided Dorrie was just a lazy little twerp, and he was still mad at her for scaring him. It was something he was too proud to talk about, even to his mother. So he hadn't told her Dorrie was asleep up there, on the dusty floor. And of course Dorrie hadn't told. She never told anything much.

If you didn't see her, you'd never know she was around.

Had she always been so quiet, or had she started being quiet when Daddy got sick? Tommy couldn't remember, it seemed so long ago now.

She was just his little sister, that was all, someone who sometimes messed around with his model airplanes and cars and other stuff he didn't want her touching.

He guessed maybe he yelled at her too much. Maybe that was why she liked to play alone. Tomorrow he would try to be nicer to her, for it had been terrible when he thought she, like Daddy, was dead.

Dorrie, too, lay awake, suddenly remembering. She hadn't fed her doll. She pushed back her covers and searched the floor at the side of her bed for her house shoes. A tiny nightlight plugged into an electrical outlet cast a glow like a moon half-snuffed by clouds or fog. It kept her from being in complete darkness, but didn't help much in finding her shoes. The air in the room was cold, much colder than the air in the apartment where she had last lived. She thought of the doll upstairs, growing colder and colder again, and needing the nourishment of milk Dorrie had promised her. Now that the doll was no longer dead, it needed her. There in the attic before she had fallen asleep in the afternoon, while she was finding the bottle, it had crawled to her, and Dorrie knew it recognized her as being the one who had brought her to life.

Dorrie found her shoes and pulled them on. They were soft and furry inside and came past her ankles, past the warm flannel of her pajamas.

She had many things to do. First, the doll, the bottle and its milk; then the other toys, dolls, animals of wood and animals of straw, she would bring them all back to life.

She whispered in the stillness of the house, "Once upon a time there lived all the dolls, and all the animals in Great-grandmother's attic."

She went out into the dark hallway, silently, leaving her door open for the faint light it gave. Slipping past the closed doors of the other bedrooms, she came at last to the end of the hall and the attic door.

The light in the attic was still on, shining faintly down through the cloud of webs that hung from the low railing at the top of the attic steps and trailed from the ceiling far above. Dust on the steps gritted beneath her feet. It was very still in the attic, as if no one had ever lived there or moved there, and when Dorrie's head came above the floor she looked with growing anxiety toward the toy box and the little celluloid doll.

It lay crumpled and still, face down, one arm twisted back, one leg askew.

Dorrie began to hurry, her voice crooning in soft sympathy, "Oh poor little dolly. Don't be to dying again, little dolly, don't." She went down on her knees in the dust and scooped the doll up into her hands, cradling it, pressing it against the warmth of her face. Tears edged hot from her eyes and trickled into the corners of her mouth. "Don't die, dolly, don't, please. Come back. Live, Dolly, please, please? I'll feed you. Right now. I'll be right back."

She dropped the doll back onto the floor and ran, and then she remembered the doll bottle, and turned back for it. The little celluloid doll lay on its back on the floor, its one eye staring at her, glittering in the light, baleful, glaring, but when Dorrie ran with the doll bottle back to the stairway the eye lost the small figure of the child and gazed in impotent intensity at the cobwebs that swayed in the movement of air caused by Dorrie's passage.

The attic door at the bottom of the stairs closed softly.

The cobwebs hung still.

The celluloid doll struggled to move. The scrapings of the tiny half-formed toes against the floor were feeble, and growing more feeble, and at last stopped, leaving the attic without sound. But the eye of the doll grew stronger and glared toward the ceiling with malevolent brightness, fed by the fury of its helplessness.

Dorrie found her way through the darkness down the front stairway and along the hall toward the kitchen. She wasn't afraid of the dark, but it slowed her steps, and all she could hear was her own breathing. She had to hurry, to keep the dolly from dying again, yet she couldn't see where she was going.

She found a doorway at the back of the house and saw triangles of deep gray in the blackness of the room. Windows. She went forward slowly. The smell of food was still in the air, and she knew she had found the kitchen. She put her hands out, feeling for a chair, and when she found one she dragged it back to the doorway. Climbing onto the seat she ran her hands along the wall until she found what she was looking for. She moved the light switch, and suddenly the room was no longer dark.

She hurried.

She dragged the chair back to the table, brought a carton of milk from the refrigerator and climbed onto the chair so that she could handle the milk carton without spilling. With the tiny doll bottle sitting upright, she carefully poured milk into it. But the milk spilled anyway, and she had to take time to wipe it up. It took so long. She could see the dolly upstairs, no longer moving, needing her, needing to be fed. And it made her hands clumsy, so that milk spilled, and dribbled on the floor when she carried it back to the refrigerator. She had to wipe the floor, too.

She put the nipple on the bottle and looked at it with satisfaction. It was filled with nourishing milk, and ready for the dolly.

She ran out of the kitchen and up the stairs, and only when she had reached the top of the stairs did she remember she had not turned out the kitchen light. But she didn't pause. The dolly needed her. She could feel it needing her.

And she had to hurry . . . hurry . . . hurry.

She closed the attic door behind her carefully.

Dorrie's steps grew slow as she crossed the attic to the doll. She stared at it, watching for signs of movement. The doll lay still, its tiny face with the glass bead eye turned upward toward the ceiling.

Dorrie knelt beside it and lifted it. She put the milk-wet nipple to the mouth.

Nothing.

The doll was cold and dead in her hands.

It did not want the milk.

Dorrie dropped the bottle and cradled the doll in her hands, bringing it closer to her face, watching for signs of the movement she had seen earlier. She drew a long breath, and let it out slowly, and it touched the doll's face, and the eye changed, brightened, gleamed with an inner light. And Dorrie's eyes brightened, too, in response, and a tiny smile turned up the corners of her mouth.

She put her lips against the face of the doll and blew softly.

In her hands the movements began. The doll's tiny fingers twitched. The legs jerked.

The doll came alive in the child's hands.

FIVE

Elsea woke to the sound of rain. A gentle slipping of water down the window, a rhythmic drip, drip against the window sill. She wanted to pull the covers over her head and lose herself in fragments of leftover dreams, for the day ahead had too many demands on her time and her energies. She had to go to the post office and make sure the mail would be delivered properly to the old box out at the roadside. New tenants. New names on the box. She had, before that, to take Stephanie and Tommy and enroll them in school, and she didn't even know where the school was located. However, the town was small. The school was probably the largest building it contained. After that . . . after that. . . . She couldn't remember.

First, I get up.

She smiled wryly as it occurred to her what she had just done, what she had been doing for months. Within her mind she told herself each action, as though without those instructions she would be incapable of acting.

She went down the hall to the bathroom with her clothes over her arm, but on the way she looked in on the kids. Dorrie was sleeping soundly, her teddy bear hugged in her arms, her dark hair almost hidden by the blanket she had pulled up over the back of her head. Tommy was sprawled on top of his blankets. He was wearing heavy flannel pajamas. A good thing, she told herself as she touched his shoulder.

"Up, Tom," she said. He blinked and frowned and tried to twist away from being awakened, and she told him, "You've got a few minutes to wake up. I'm using the bathroom first, and since there's only the one you can wait until after Stephanie." She saw his smile as he arranged himself to continue his nap.

She went into Stephanie's room and awakened her before she went on to take her shower.

"Breakfast," she told herself aloud in the spray of water that felt warm and pleasantly stinging on her face. "Eggs? Or cereal? Cereal, maybe, hot."

If anybody heard her talking to herself, she thought as she dried and dressed, they would think she had lost her mind. So perhaps she should try another method of planning her day.

She waited until breakfast was ready and both her older children had come downstairs before she went after Dorrie. The child was still sleeping, and when Elsea picked her up, she was limp and heavy, leaning against her as though exhausted.

"Dorrie, Dorrie?"

Dorrie drew a long breath, her head sagging against Elsea, the teddy bear dropping out of her arms. Her eyes remained closed.

Then Elsea saw the dust on Dorrie's pajamas, and the round, little grimy spot in her bed where she had slept. Frowning, Elsea brushed at it without much success.

"Dorrie, where did you get your pajamas so dirty?"

The child didn't answer, nor did she open her eyes. She remained heavily asleep.

"Dorrie, baby, you have to wake up now. We're going to take Stephanie and Tommy to school. Dorrie?"

Elsea gave up and carried the child to the bathroom, sat her on the vanity stool and began to pull the pajamas off. The dust was no longer an issue. Waking Dorrie and getting her dressed for the day was the important part. Time was passing.

Dorrie wobbled on the stool and at last opened her eyes. She sat blinking heavily as she was washed and dressed in clean little overalls and a long-sleeved knit shirt. Elsea collected the pajamas along with other items that would have to go into the washing machine today. With her mind now on locating the school, or schools, where she would leave Stephanie and Tommy, she urged Dorrie down the twisting stairs to the kitchen.

Hours later Elsea sat at the kitchen table with a

cup of coffee and thought back over the hectic morning. There had been only one school, thank God, a modern, small, glass-and-brick affair with a parking lot filled with several long, yellow buses. The kids were enrolled and would ride to and from school on the bus. That was an advantage she hadn't considered. The mail would come and—

The knock on the door startled her. But then with a rush of pleasure she saw beyond the glass the bearded face of Corey Stapleton.

"Hey, come in," she told him as she opened the door. "It's great to see an adult. Want some coffee? I was just relaxing for the first time since I started the day."

"You wouldn't rather relax alone?"

"Definitely not. How are you today?" She gave him a quick once-over glance as she poured his coffee. "Outside of being slightly damp, that is."

He smiled. "Up here, you get used to being slightly damp. But this weather is a little unusual for this time of year, so it should be clearing up. What did you do with your kids?"

"Stephanie and Tommy are back in school. I took them this morning, found the school without any trouble, enrolled them, and just left them there. They could have waited until tomorrow to start, but they both were interested in staying." She shrugged. "And Dorrie is back upstairs in her huge treasure house."

Corey looked puzzled, and Elsea explained.

"My grandmother's attic. It's filled with all kinds of goodies. Every toy that was ever owned by any child in the family is still up there, I'm sure. There are several toy boxes filled to overflowing. When I was a little girl I wanted to go up so badly and play, but Grandmother would never allow it. So now Dorrie wants to spend all her time up there, and so far as I'm concerned, she may. It's safe. She's happy. One of these days she'll have investigated it all to her heart's content and come down, maybe without being dragged. Until then, I thought I'd just leave her alone."

"She sounds like a loner."

"Yes, she is." Elsea looked down. "More so, I think, since her daddy died."

A long moment passed before Corey answered. "It takes time."

"Yes. And I'm afraid time is what I'm going to have now. A lot of it. Sitting here right now is great, but I have a feeling I'm going to be getting very tired of it before long." She looked around. "Of course there's the house to clean."

He watched her, saying nothing, and she became more aware of him and what he might be thinking.

"Sorry," she said. "Not a very interesting conversation."

"I think you're anticipating a not very interesting life."

"No, I guess not."

"Why did you come up here? So far away from old friends and all that was familiar to you?"

"Finances. It's going to be a tight squeeze even with free rent. Maybe too tight."

"Have you ever thought of doing any writing?"

"Writing!" Elsea almost laughed, but she saw that Corey was serious. A long-buried memory emerged.

Corey waited. "Doesn't everyone go through a phase of wanting to write stories? You love a book, or several books you've been assigned in English class, and your teacher gives you an A-plus on your composition, and so you have dreams of becoming a great novelist someday and writing books like *Jane Eyre*."

Corey smiled. "My favorite book was *Call of the Wild*. But if you like romances, you've already jumped the first hurdle. They're the most popular novels being written now. Why don't you try one?"

She stared at him.

"No, I'm serious," he said. "I'd be glad to teach you a few of the techniques I've learned. You supply the characters, the story, do the writing. You might find it much easier than you'd think. What do you have to lose? It can keep your mind occupied, and it might prove to be a bonanza for you. Certainly it could supplement your income. Do you have a typewriter?"

"A small portable."

"Good enough, if it works."

"Yes, it does."

"Then I'll help you set up an office. How about the library? It has a good desk, an even better atmosphere. You could write a regency in this house."

"Corey . . . I don't know if I could."

"The first words are always awkward. Always. You could try, though. I'll watch over you as faithfully as a guardian angel, considering you won't be trespassing on my territory." He smiled. "Or would you prefer writing wildlife features?"

Elsea returned his smile, but before she could reply, Dorrie came into the room and leaned against her knee. Elsea bent and kissed the child's cheek, and drew back to brush dirt from her lips and Dorrie's face.

"I have to drag the vacuum cleaner up those stairs and get rid of some of that dust. Dorrie, you're a mess."

"Hi, Dorrie."

"Hi," Dorrie said in soft bashfulness to the bearded man. She hadn't known he was there, and his presence almost made her forget why she had come to the kitchen.

Corey stood up. "I'll help you. Where do you keep it?"

"No!" Dorrie said.

Elsea looked at her little girl in surprise. Corey waited, watching them, his thumbs hooked in his hip pockets.

"Dorrie, what on earth are you so adamant about?"

"I don't want you to bring a vacuum cleaner up there."

"But why not? It would take up the dust and you wouldn't get your clothes so dirty."

"Because I don't want you to! A vacuum cleaner would scare my dolly and animals."

"Oh." Elsea smiled apologetically at Corey. "She was always afraid of the vacuum cleaner. She'd get on the highest perch she could find, usually on top of the couch, and stay there as long as the vacuum was on. I can do the cleaning later with a broom and dust pan. There's probably no place to plug in an electrical appliance anyway. But thanks for the offer."

"I've seen those attic steps. Getting anything up there would be a problem. Someone did a fair job of it, though. It looked like it was almost full."

Dorrie got a grasp on Elsea's blouse sleeve and tugged. "Mommy."

They looked over her head into each other's eyes. Corey was standing, and Elsea knew he would soon leave unless she somehow stopped him. Even with Dorrie there in the house with her, the house was too large, too quiet. She wasn't ready to be so alone yet. She didn't want him to leave. When he was there she forgot her loneliness. Now, standing here and facing him, she became aware of that. In some way he had alleviated more of that terrible deep-down loneliness than anyone else had. She thought of ways to keep him awhile longer. Just to talk. Just to be there. He had offered to help set up an office for writing. He had said he would watch over her efforts to put together a romance novel. Even if writing proved too difficult for her, it would keep him coming to the house regularly where otherwise he might soon drift away.

All she wanted was his companionship. Nothing more.

"You said you'd help me. Did you really mean it? It wouldn't be too much trouble? Take up too much of your time?"

"I meant it, and the answer to all the rest is no."

Dorrie tugged harder on her mother's sleeve. "Mommy!"

Elsea patted Dorrie on the head. "We're not going

to vacuum the attic, Dorrie, so you can stop worrying. Mr. Stapleton is going to help me with some things."

"Mommy, I want some food for my kitty!"

Dorrie looked up at them, at the adults so far above her, and saw at last that she had their attention. Both faces, the smooth, soft face of her mother, and the bearded face of the strange man, stared down at her.

"What kitty?" her mother asked.

"My kitty upstairs. And I want food for my horse, and my lion, and my funny monster with the horns and the long nose. My horse wants hay. Do you have any hay for my horse?"

The adults looked at each other again and laughed. It was a sound of relief and of indulgence. Dorrie couldn't put definite words to her feelings about being treated that way, but it made her draw back from her mother and stand to one side. They weren't listening to her. They weren't really hearing her because they didn't think she knew anything. And as she expected, her mother reached out again and touched her hair with the tips of her fingers, and Dorrie moved farther away and stared at them, one after the other, with a set and stony face.

"Honey, they can't eat. They're just—just toys."

The man said, "Aren't we forgetting something?"

"What?" Elsea asked.

"Didn't we use to feed our toys? I had a hobby horse that I loved, and I was always feeding him grass from the yard."

Grass from the yard.

Suddenly Dorrie didn't feel the bearded man was

an intruder. He had become a friend. She ran, shouting back at them, "I'll get it!"

She went out the back door and across the porch and down the steps to the wet grass. She clutched two handfuls and tugged, and bits of the grass, dead and brown from among the tougher green new sprigs, came away in her hands. She ran back across the porch and on through the kitchen. Later, she could get food for her kitty. Without asking anyone. But if the bearded man had fed grass to his horse, then she could feed grass to hers.

When she reached the attic steps, she paused long enough to close the door. They must not come up, her mother and the man. The toys would not like it. The dolly, she knew, would hate for anyone to come into the attic.

The little wood horse stood where she had left him, and she dropped to her knees and bent over. "Here, horsey, I brought you some hay." She pushed the grass against its carved mouth, but the horse stood braced on its four blunt little legs, and its mouth remained only half open.

Dorrie got down on her elbow and looked into its mouth.

"You don't have any teeth," she said. "You can't eat."

Her attention was drawn to the little celluloid doll. She had made it a bed of an old doll quilt that she had found, but the doll was moving, one arm and one leg wriggling slowly as though the other side was paralyzed. Its one eye glistened at her.

Dorrie looked back at the horse. Its eyes were made of wood, little round balls carved outward just as the mouth was carved inward. She began to stroke its back. She put her mouth to the mouth of the horse.

"Live, little horse, live."

Something was moving on the floor, scratching faintly. Dorrie sat up. The celluloid doll had gotten off its bed and was creeping slowly along the boards of the floor toward her.

"No," Dorrie said, and left the wood horse to pick up the doll. She put it back on the bed she had made. "You must take your nap. Now you lie down here and be a good dolly, and you'll be getting well faster. You must stay in bed." She stroked its dented limbs, straightening and repairing. She breathed again into its mouth.

"There. Now, you just rest."

She turned and stopped. Sitting still, she stared at the horse.

Where before it had been facing the stairway, it was now facing her. It had turned. Its head had risen and its eyes glowed deep in the wood of their being as if a fire had been lighted there.

Dorrie smiled.

In her attic there would be life. There would be no dying. But she knew now it was not food they needed, but her breath.

She would give them her breath, and they would live.

The horse's mouth was opening, slowly, and Dorrie saw that it had teeth. Square and broad and sharp in its upper jaw.

SIX

Elsea sat at her desk, staring out the window at the dark forest of trees. In the lower edge of her vision she could see the fresh sheet of white paper in the typewriter. It had been easier than she first thought, and had kept her mind occupied so that the days had slid by, numbered by pages written. Corey had coached her so that she was able to branch out on her own, creating characters that came alive in her mind, characters that began to interact and form their own storyline. It was the wording of that story that sometimes made her want to tear her hair and run screaming from the torture of not being able to transfer actions in her mind to words on paper.

71

But instead of screaming like a mad woman, she paused to stare out the window.

The deep green of the tall pines calmed her.

And then other things entered her mind as the story receded. School, almost to the end of spring semester now, and Stephanie and Tommy both excited about going with Corey into the mountains for a weekend. It was Corey who had decided that the outing would last only one day unless she and Dorrie went along. Dorrie wasn't interested in going, at least not that she had expressed, and Elsea couldn't see herself camping out in the wild the way she had with Vern. It somehow seemed disloyal. So she had declined, and after the roar of objections from Stephanie and Tommy, they had agreed that one day was better than none. Neither of them could understand why their mother had to be along in order to make the trip last a weekend, and for that matter, neither could Elsea. She trusted Corey Stapleton with her kids. Completely.

"Mommy?"

Elsea jumped, and then let out a long breath. She pressed one hand to her chest. "Dorrie, you surprised me."

Dorrie leaned heavily against her leg and laid her head in Elsea's lap. "Mommy, I'm tired."

Elsea brushed back the dark hair from the pale forehead. The southern California tan had faded away, leaving her youngest child with a whiter complexion than Elsea had known she possessed. Or was she ill?

Elsea gathered Dorrie up into her arms and

72

hugged her fiercely, to ward off any illness that might touch her. To think, as she sometimes did against her will, that one of her children might become weak and ill as Vern had done, was more than she could bear. The thought would edge into her mind, and she would push it away instantly, never quite letting it form. Writing the romance novel—trying to write it—had been good for her. Even with the frustrations it caused, she had begun to feel better, to feel freer and lighter in her mind. But now, with Dorrie pressed close in her arms, she found herself thinking that Dorrie was thinner. Dorrie was less energetic. Dorrie was pale.

"Are you not feeling well, Dorrie?"

The child sighed, her head now on her mother's shoulder. "I'm tired."

Elsea stood up. She hadn't carried her little girl in a long time. "Want Mama to put you to bed for a nap, baby?"

"Okay."

Elsea carried Dorrie up the stairs, the worry that tried to burst open in her heart held back with effort. In Dorrie's bedroom, Elsea sat the child on the side of the bed and knelt at her feet to pull off dusty white socks and sneakers. When Dorrie was stripped down to undershirt and panties, Elsea covered her and sat watching as the long lashes lay still on the white cheeks and Dorrie's face relaxed into the angelic sleep of innocent childhood.

The house was quiet, as only a house in the country could be. Elsea found herself listening. Something had moved somewhere, drawing her attention away from Dorrie. She heard the soft, almost soundless breathing of Dorrie. And movements, somewhere, that were so subtle they were only faint whispers between the deep breaths Dorrie drew.

Upstairs.

Elsea's neck began to ache, and she realized she was staring up at the ceiling. Something was moving across the floor of the attic.

Mice? Too large for mice. Heaven forbid—not rats!

Elsea got up, looked down at Dorrie again, and the small pile of dusty clothes that lay on the floor. Had she been letting her baby play in an attic that not only was dirty, but had rats also? She'd been intending to do some cleaning up there, and had been putting it off. Now, while Dorrie slept, was her chance. If there were rats in the attic she'd have to insist that Dorrie no longer play there.

From the closet in the hall she took a broom, dustpan and a paper bag. She found that Dorrie had closed the attic door, and she opened it cautiously. She wanted to catch a glimpse of whatever animal was roaming the attic. She knew nothing of rats except what she had read. But she knew they carried diseases.

She went up the attic steps as quietly as she could. The single bulb above gave out an almost sickening lack of real light. She saw the webs on the ceiling, and the dust on the bulb. She paused, listening. Nothing now. Whatever it was had heard her and had scurried to hide. Or maybe it really was mice, in the walls, in the open area between the ceiling of the bedroom and the floor of the attic.

She stood beneath the light in the attic and looked around. Footprints in the dust, everywhere it seemed, small footprints that belonged to Dorrie. An area near a large, open toy box was almost free from dust, as though Dorrie had swept it away herself. Or, more likely, she had played there so much that she had finally carried the dust away on her clothes. Lined up there against the box was an array of toy dolls and animals of all shapes and sizes, and as Elsea looked at them her skin tingled and froze.

She stared, frowning.

They stared back at her, the shadowed light creating on their faces hideous grins and malevolent leers. Within their eyes a steady flamelike hatred burned at her. It was as though they stood daring her to enter their world, to come closer. If she moved, they would move. They were ready to attack.

Elsea closed her eyes tightly.

That's crazy, she told herself in silence. *Crazy*.

The soundlessness in the lower part of the house had followed her, accompanied her, and now she heard nothing.

She didn't look at the toys again. She began to work, sweeping, dumping dust from pan to bag. The broom didn't take up all the dust, but a major part of it. She swept out only the open center of the attic, a small area no more than twenty feet square. Beyond that the light hardly reached, and piles of furniture and boxes took up most of the space. She would tell

Dorrie not to go beyond the cleaned area.

She stood at the top of the stairs looking around when the sounds of movement came again. A soft scraping, as of something being dragged. She turned. To one side of the lineup of toy animals was a small bed Dorrie had made, and an ugly little celluloid doll lay on the floor beside it. An arm moved, and a leg. Elsea stared. Her forehead ached with the intensity of her stare. The doll lay still, its bent and twisted body face down on the floor beside the small bed.

Of course it hadn't moved, Elsea told herself. It had fallen. Rolled. It was made of such light-weight material, a draft of air could have caused it to fall.

There was no draft of air.

Elsea turned away, shuddering, and said aloud, "How can she stand it up here?" And suddenly she knew what was wrong with her. It was psychological, dating from her own childhood when it had been wrong and disobedient of her to come into the attic. She could almost hear her grandmother saying, "Now don't go into the attic and bother things. You might break them."

She started to turn out the light, and then remembered that Dorrie wouldn't be able to reach the string. And she decided, suddenly, definitely, that she would not keep Dorrie from going into the attic. She would talk to Corey about the possibility of rats there, and what to do about it. But Dorrie would have free reign of the attic and all the toys that had been denied to her own childish curiosities.

Dorrie was still asleep when Corey came over in the afternoon. Elsea saw him beyond her window, and left her desk with gratitude. The past hour of trying to write had been worse than the hours before that. Into her attempt at concentration kept coming thoughts of Dorrie, and she had gone upstairs four times to check on her. She was relieved to have a real excuse to leave her desk.

She met Corey at the back door.

"How's it going today?" he asked.

"Terrible. I'm so glad to see you I could get down on my knees and thank you for rescuing me."

He laughed. "I know the feeling. I think you're hooked."

"I think I hate the whole thing. I also think I might have rats in the attic, and I want to know what people usually do about controlling rats."

He took his place at the table where a cup of steaming coffee was already poured for him. His amusement at Elsea's attitude toward writing was replaced by seriousness.

"Rats? I've never seen any around here. What makes you think you've got rats?"

"I heard something moving around up there, and it sounded too big for mice. I'm just guessing about rats."

"My guess would be squirrels."

"Squirrels! In the attic?"

"Sure. They're harmless, though. You didn't see any sign of rats, did you? Or mice?"

77

"I'm not sure I'd know what to look for."

"Pills."

"Pills?"

Corey grinned. "Wastes. Feces. Commonly called pills."

"Oh. Of course. Mouse pills." Elsea laughed.

"Apartment dweller comes to country," Corey said.

"Yes, it's been awhile since I've had a mouse in the house."

"Maybe you don't know then that wherever there are mice, or rats, there are also trails of pills. They seem to drop them everywhere. It won't take long to find out if you have mice in your attic."

He started to rise, but Elsea motioned him to sit still.

"I've been there already," she said. "I swept up half a sack of dust, and there were no mouse pills. Not one. Nor, I guess, rat ones, either, although I wouldn't know one of those if I saw it."

"They seem to have more control than mice, but I still would make a bet that you have a curious little squirrel in your attic. If so, he'll go out again. I'll be glad to go up and check it out."

"I don't think it's that serious. If I keep hearing things—actually, today is the first day I've heard anything up there, and we've lived here almost a month now, haven't we? Since I got involved with that terrible business of trying to write a novel, I've lost all sense of time. But anyway, I haven't heard anything before. And I would hate to admit that I couldn't handle a small animal or two in the attic. I

78

won't bother you with everything, every noise, every problem."

"That's what I'm here for."

"That's not what you're here for."

After a hesitation he said in a low voice, "That's what I want to be here for. To be needed by you."

Elsea had no answer for him. She got up quickly from her chair and busied herself with arranging sweet rolls and doughnuts on a plate. The intimacy in his voice, the near-pleading in some way made her very uncomfortable. Embarrassed? Their relationship had been so casual, so easy. He had given her companionship and a sense of security she hadn't had in many long months, perhaps in years. But she wanted to keep it at that level. She wasn't ready to handle anything more.

When she returned to the table she didn't look at him directly, but she saw him lean back in his chair and raise one ankle to rest on the other knee. He cleared his throat.

"Otherwise," he said in the voice that was more familiar to her, "how's the writing life going? Got your characters straightened out and busy on their own?"

She sighed with relief. It was easy to sit down and start discussing the problems and frustrations that he remembered from his early days at the typewriter. It was even easy to admit that perhaps she didn't have the personality to become a writer, even though she knew she didn't have the personality of a quitter. She would write that novel or die trying simply because when she started something she liked to finish it.

Corey stayed only a short while longer, and when he was gone Elsea sat at the table looking into her coffee cup. Emotions had taken over thought. She wasn't sure of what she was feeling, but she needed to get away from it.

She went upstairs to check on Dorrie, and found her yawning and rubbing her eyes.

"Time to get up?" Elsea said, kissing Dorrie's forehead.

Dorrie nodded.

Elsea brought clean clothes from the dresser drawer, and paused to listen for noises in the attic. Nothing now but the sound of Dorrie sliding off her bed and coming barefoot across the floor.

Elsea drew a long breath of relief. Maybe it had been a squirrel. And the squirrel had gone back to its tree, or wherever it stayed when it wasn't in the attic.

"Just one more week of school," Tommy whispered to himself as he pulled on his pajamas. He hopped around on one foot in a sudden frenzy of excitement. School would be out for the summer, and Corey would take him and Steph into the mountains for a day of hiking and animal photography. A great day. He could hardly wait. When he thought of it he got so excited he could hardly manage to get to sleep. But then, the next thing he knew he'd be awake and it would be morning again and Mom would be calling him to come on and get ready for school again.

Except lately it hadn't been happening that way. Sometimes he woke during the night, and lay listening to strange, soft sounds above his room in the attic. How could something so soft, so nearly soundless wake him?

He found himself listening, holding his breath.

But there was nothing.

He climbed into bed and turned out his bedside lamp. The darkness was total and surrounding for a few minutes until his eyes adjusted and the windows began showing up in the dark room as lighter rectangles. Beyond those windows lay the mountains, and the meadow Corey said he would take them to see, where the deer grazed and the—

Thump.

Tommy caught his breath and stared upward as if he would be able to see through the ceiling. There came a series of more thumps, softer, as though something had jumped to the floor and hopped along. Yet there was something about the movement that made Tommy immediately reject living animals. Maybe something had fallen and rolled, bouncing. Maybe Dorrie had laid a ball on something. . . .

That soft movement again, the one that woke him at night lately. Sliding, sliding. Pausing. He didn't like it. Suddenly he was feeling as though the ceiling above were made of glass and whatever it was that lived and moved in the attic was staring down at him.

He reached a stiff arm out and felt for the lamp. He found the switch and turned it. The ceiling above was still there, solid, and nothing was looking through, yet he still felt as if he were helpless in a cage.

He left his room, and the light from his lamp spilled out into the narrow and twisting hallway and touched upon the attic door. He shied away from it toward Stephanie's room. Her door stood open, her light out. In the shadows of the room he could make out the shape of her bed and the lump in the center that was Stephanie.

Tommy slapped the highest portion of the lump with his hand. "Hey, Steph," he whispered, running the words out into a low whistle between his teeth. "Steph!"

The lump moved and Stephanie's voice growled out loud at him, "What do you want? You woke me up, Tommy!"

"I meant to. Listen, Stephanie, do you hear anything? And don't talk out loud! It might hear you."

Stephanie sat up, her face an oval blur in the shadows of the room. She whispered cautiously. *"Who* might hear me?"

"I don't know. Not a who, but a what. Something's in the attic."

"Oh that," Stephanie said, aloud again, her voice loaded with disgust. Her face turned away from him as she arranged her bed for settling down again. "It's only squirrels."

"How do you know that?" demanded Tommy.

"Mama said so."

Stephanie lay down, her back toward Tommy. He

stared at her blond hair above the blanket that she had pulled up to her chin.

"Go away, Tommy. Go to sleep."

"I don't believe it," he said. "When did Mom tell you that?"

"A couple of days ago." Stephanie yawned, slurring her words. "I kept hearing this noise up there, so I asked, and she said Corey said it was squirrels. They won't hurt you. Go back to bed."

"I know they won't hurt me! I never said—" Tommy felt his face turning red. Even in the darkness. It was times like these that made him think he hated his older sister. To even suggest that he might be afraid of squirrels in the attic!

He left her room, deliberately not replying to her goodnight. In the hallway he stood in the edge of light from his room and stared at the attic door. It seemed to stare back at him, daring him to approach, to enter. Beneath the door was a sliver of light. So the attic light was still burning.

And suddenly he knew something.

Squirrels would not come into the attic at night. They were not nocturnal animals.

He tiptoed hurriedly back to Stephanie's room and pecked her on the hip again. "Steph."

"You again? I thought you went to bed."

"Listen, Stephanie, that's not squirrels up there."

"How do you know that?"

"Ssh. Because they're daytime animals. They wouldn't be roaming around at night, would they?"

Stephanie sat up, slowly, and her pale face took shape in the shadows. She sat very still, looking at him. When she spoke her voice was so low he could hardly make out the words.

"Then maybe it's some other kind of animal. Something that does roam around at·night."

"Like what?"

"Mice?"

"No mouse ever made sounds like I heard."

"What did you hear?"

"Something fell, or jumped, and then went thudding along, like it was hopping, or bouncing."

Stephanie giggled, and Tommy knew she was getting ready to make fun of him again.

"Maybe it's a kangaroo," she said.

He wanted to hit her, but restrained himself. He'd been in trouble too many times for giving in to his instincts and letting her have it. He could just hear her screaming, "Mama!" and waking the whole house just to have their mother come and bawl him out, and maybe even take away the privilege of going on that hiking trip with Corey.

As he was thinking it over, the ceiling above creaked softly, as though someone, or something, had stepped on a loose board.

He forgot Stephanie. He stared up, waiting for the sound to come again. Nothing now but silence in the attic, but a waiting kind of silence, as if whatever was there was staring down at them in a challenge, it too waiting, waiting to see what they would do next.

Tommy began backing toward the doorway, one step, two.

Stephanie reached out and grabbed him.

"It's a burglar!" she whispered shrilly.

Tommy swallowed. Fears generated in the city, fears he thought he had left behind clogged his throat. What was worse, fear of man, or fear of the unknown?

Stephanie scrambled out of bed and dug her fingernails into his arm. "We'd better get Mama," she whispered in her shrill voice, stinging Tommy's ear. It was the kind of whisper that would carry through walls.

"Shut up!" He tried to listen, but all he heard was Stephanie's intake of breath.

"Maybe we ought to get Corey."

Courage came back to Tommy in the face of his sister's cowardice. She wasn't making fun of him now. She had turned to him for protection.

"Maybe it's just Dorrie," Tommy said. "Maybe she went up there to play."

"She's asleep! We should call Mama."

"No. Leave Mom alone. What would a burglar be doing in the attic?"

"I don't know."

"There's nothing up there but junk."

"Then what is it? Something is there."

"I know. That's what I told you earlier, and you had to get smart."

They looked at each other through the gloom of near-darkness.

"Well, what're we going to do?" Stephanie demanded.

"I know what we're *not* going to do, we're not going to call Mom, not yet anyway. And we're not going to go over to Corey's. Maybe we ought to take

85

a look ourselves. What would a burglar be doing up there? That's crazy. And if we run to Corey, he'll think we're such babies we can't go on a hiking trip. Let's go up and see what it is."

Stephanie looked toward the ceiling, and Tommy watched her, his ears alert for any continued sound of movement above.

"Maybe it was just the house creaking, the way they do," Stephanie whispered. "Old houses do."

"Yeah, maybe. But not what I heard awhile ago. That wasn't. I'm going up. You going along, or are you going to hide like a sissy girl?"

He felt the strength of her glare. She moved away from him, leading the way. In the hall, though, she waited. Side by side they went toward the attic door.

Tommy turned the knob of the attic door slowly, making no sound. He edged the door open, facing into the spill of light that came weakly down from the naked bulb far above.

An attic step squeaked when he stepped on it, and he stopped, Stephanie close behind him, and stood listening, his body cold and taut with tension. There was no sound from above. But like before, it seemed to be a deliberate silence, a listening silence, in which something waited.

He didn't want to go on up, but he couldn't back down with Stephanie behind him. He wanted to see what was there, and yet he didn't. It would have been so easy to go back and hide in his bed.

He whispered, "Maybe there's nothing there." Stephanie didn't answer, but he hadn't spoken for her benefit anyway and scarcely noticed. In his heart a battle raged, and some fierce instinct told him to go on, so that then, having conquered the enemy, fear, he could return to a safer territory feeling better about himself.

He took another step, and another, and at last his head was above the attic floor and he could see from one end of the long, dark room to the other, where tiny attic windows reflected the light of the bulb. Huge shadows were cast by pieces of furniture and piles of boxes. He hadn't realized there were so many hiding places up here.

Stephanie hissed from behind his shoulder, "Do you see anything?"

He had almost forgotten her. She was holding on to his pajama shirt, and he reached back and loosened her fingers.

"No," he said. "But—"

"But what?"

"There's so many places to hide. Listen."

They stood still, listening, hearing their own heartbeats. Stephanie touched Tommy's back, pushing him. "Let me see," she said, and Tommy carefully took the remaining steps into the attic with Stephanie close behind.

They stood under the light.

There was nothing in the center of the attic but the opening of the stairwell and a cleared spot that was edged by toy boxes and toys. Tommy glanced over them quickly. He could see where Dorrie had been playing, but Dorrie wasn't here now. Nobody was here unless they were hiding in the dark shadows behind something. And now that he was here too, he sensed the emptiness, the lack of humans other than himself and his sister. Yet at the same time a coldness enveloped him, a warning chill that made his skin come alive and the material of his pajamas feel thin and stinging. He edged to the right, away from the top of the stairway, toward a pile of boxes that was stacked almost to the ceiling. He peered around them, and even in the shadowed recesses of the aisle that it formed he could see that nothing was there.

He moved around it, going through the dark, narrow aisle, and coming into the light again.

From the corner of his eye he glimpsed a movement on top of the boxes, and suddenly something the size of a small cat was flying through the air directly toward his head. He saw flat, mindless eyes that, in the instant of their meeting his, held something far removed from life as he knew it, and a terrible, primitive fear held him staring. He saw a mouth, open, with a snarl that was beyond animal warning. He saw protruding teeth in the upper jaw. He ducked instinctively, throwing his arms up for protection, and felt a sharp, needlelike ripping across his arm, and a sudden weight from the thing that was hanging there, its teeth fastened into the material of his pajama sleeve.

He heard a small scream, and felt his own choked cry as he struggled to fling the thing away from him.

It hit the floor with a *thunk,* and lay on its side staring with its carved, blank eyes straight ahead, its mouth open, a row of square teeth sharp-edged in the upper jaw. He saw now it was a horse, hand-whittled roughly from a solid piece of wood.

Stephanie was whimpering softly, her hands over her mouth. Each backward step was taking her closer and closer to the open stairwell.

"A horse!" Tommy cried. "A goddamned little wooden horse!"

Stephanie stopped, her eyes large over the edge of her hand.

"It bit me! It jumped at me!"

He was sobbing without tears. The horse lay still on its side, and he started to kick it away with his bare foot, but drew back and ran around it to the top of the stairs. Stephanie took her hands from her mouth and grasped Tommy's arm.

Tommy looked, and saw his pajamas had been torn, and his arm scratched. Beads of blood had popped up along the scratch. But logic was forming beneath his first crazy thought.

"It fell," he said. "Dorrie must have put it up on the top of the boxes right against the edge, and it fell off. And its teeth got hooked in my sleeve."

He looked at the toy horse on the floor. It lay dead still on its side, its four blunt little legs sticking straight out. He looked too at the top of the boxes from which the horse had fallen, and he wondered, *How did Dorrie get the horse up there?*

"Let's go," Tommy said, pushing Stephanie lightly. "There's nothing up here. Just the squirrels, like Corey said."

Stephanie didn't remind Tommy that he had said squirrels weren't nocturnal animals, and he was glad she didn't. All he wanted was to get out of the attic. As he went down the steps behind Stephanie,

89

he felt the hair on the back of his neck rise, and it took all the control he could muster not to push Stephanie even faster down the steps.

When they reached the hall and had shut the door they stood huddled close for a moment, and Stephanie whispered, "We didn't turn out the light."

"It's on for Dorrie. She plays up there and she can't reach the string." He was telling her something she already knew, but his mind was on something else. If Dorrie could play up there all day long and not be afraid, then what was the matter with him? He was a bigger coward than his little sister, and he couldn't bear for anyone to know. Even Stephanie. He wished fervently he could erase the past hour.

"Listen, Stephanie, don't tell anyone, okay? We might worry Mom if we told her we thought a burglar was in the attic."

"Yeah, okay. But what about your pajama sleeve? She'll see that."

"I'll take care of it. You just keep your mouth shut."

He realized they were still whispering, but at the same time he became uncomfortably aware of how close they were standing to the attic door. He moved.

"Listen, I'm going to bed."

"Okay, me too."

In his room Tommy removed his pajamas and pulled on another pair, then he stuffed the ones with the torn sleeve under the mattress.

He climbed into bed and pulled his covers up to his face, over his chin and mouth. He stared at the ceiling and wondered again, how did Dorrie manage to get the toy horse to the top of a pile of boxes? And suddenly he knew. Dorrie hadn't done it at all. The horse had been there all the time, put up there years ago by someone tall.

Or it had climbed there by itself, like a mountain goat, going from narrow cliff to narrow cliff.

SEVEN

Dorrie went up the attic stairs, counting as she took each step. "One, two, three, four . . . one, two button your shoes, three, four, open the door. . . ." Tommy and Stephanie had run down the driveway to catch the long, yellow bus while she stood on the front porch watching. She had seen a lot of kids looking out the windows of the bus. Some of them were moving around, changing seats, waving books, papers, yelling. The big man at the wheel of the bus had looked around and shouted at them and they sat down. Someday, she too was going to ride on that school bus and go to school. Except she wasn't sure she wanted to. It would probably be like the nursery school she could remember going to where there were so many other kids. Sometimes, she didn't like being with other little kids. They made her feel . . .

alone. They made her feel like she wanted to go home where she didn't feel alone anymore. She chanted, "Five, six, seven, eight, someday I'll go to school, real school, and carry books and pencils and notebooks, nine, ten . . ."

Her mother had gone into the library after the school bus left, and it became quiet in the house for a while. In the library was a desk in front of the bay windows, and on the desk was a typewriter, and if Dorrie listened carefully now she could hear the pecking of the typewriter. Mama was writing a book. But it didn't look like a book yet. It was just a pile of papers on the desk that no one was supposed to touch.

"Eleven." Eleven steps into the attic.

With the door of the attic shut Dorrie couldn't hear the pecking of the typewriter, though she listened intently.

She stood on the attic floor at the top of the steps. And suddenly she saw the little wooden horse. It lay far away from where she had left it, on its side, helpless, as though it had died again. She ran to it and picked it up.

"Oh, poor horsey, did you fall down and couldn't get up again?"

She pressed it against her face and felt that its body had lost the warmth that her hands had rubbed into it, and its eyes were flat and wooden and staring at nothing, the bits of blue paint that still clung looking like foreign objects that would sting and hurt. She tried to pick them away, but only one tiny piece loosened and came off. A terrible lump of sadness came into her throat.

"Oh, don't be to dying, horsey, please."

She sat down on the floor and cuddled the little wood animal in her arms. Lifting it to her face, she began blowing her breath into its mouth. When she felt the inner glow return to its body, when again its eyes looked at her and recognized her, she took it back to the row of toys beside her favorite toy box and set it in place.

"Now don't you run away again, horsey. You have to rest and take care of yourself, and I'll help you. I won't let you be to dying, I promise."

She picked up the cat that was made of straw and a material that was coming apart at the seams. She poked the straw back and tried to pull the material in place. She held the cat close to her breast and began to caress its back, crooning softly. "Live, kitty cat, live, live. Don't be to dying, kitty cat." She put her mouth over its small muzzle and breathed out until she felt weakened from the effort.

"Live, kitty, live," she whispered, and the cat moved, its head turning on its neck, feebly, jerkily, until the bead eyes were looking into Dorrie's.

Dorrie smiled, caressing the body of the cat. A leg moved, and a paw touched her arm, and Dorrie gasped. For, in the paw, lengthening as she watched, were needle-sharp claws, and one of them pierced her skin. She put the cat away from her, among the other toys and animals on the floor. She watched it a moment. It lay on its side, and its legs moved awkwardly and slowly, but the claws kept growing until they curved out of each foot like fish hooks.

Dorrie turned her back and picked up the little celluloid doll. It was no longer stiff and cold in her hands. It no longer felt the way it had when she had first found it. It was warm and soft and pliable, and she loved it.

She kissed it on the top of its head.

"And now you go back to bed, dolly, and rest, and regain all your strength. I'll cover you. Here, now, rest, dolly."

She stretched out on the floor and began to play with all the toys she had been bringing back to life, and they grew animated and began to swarm over her, and she giggled and rolled with them, and when the claws of the cat hurt her, she didn't cry. Even when the teeth of the horse raked her skin and made it raw and hurting she didn't cry. She gently pushed them away, and then reached out to caress them, to show them she loved them even though they hurt her.

Elsea tore the sheet of paper out of her typewriter and stared at it in disgust. Why couldn't she say what she wanted to say? Why couldn't her characters act like people instead of stick horses? She had chosen as her background a historical setting in old New Orleans because she had found a fascinating history book in her grandmother's collection. Reading it, she could almost see the city when it was only a town. She could hear the roll of the carriage wheels over the stones of the streets. But when she tried to describe it on paper she was helpless, and nearly frantic. Did the iron rim of the wheels crack, clank, strike bits of fire from the stones? Damned if she knew! What she saw in her mind she could not transfer to paper.

She put her head in her hands, her elbows resting on the typewriter. Corey had said, "It gets easier with experience." And she could see herself, years gone, hair gray, still sitting with her head in her hands and her elbows on the typewriter, still lacking the experience to make writing easier.

She wished for a diversion.

Why didn't the phone ring?

There was no phone.

Why did writers want to go into the quiet of the country where they could work without interruption?

She wanted interruption, rescue from the torture of trying to write a scene she saw but could not describe. Therefore, she must not be a writer. She would never be a writer. She would rather go mop the kitchen floor. But the kitchen floor didn't need mopping. She had done that yesterday, when the words became too hard to drag out.

"Mama?"

Elsea turned and grabbed Dorrie up into her arms. "Hey, baby, great to see you. What have you been doing?"

Dorrie pushed back from Elsea's hug and frowned faintly, staring at her mother.

"I've been playing with my dolls and animals," she said solemnly.

"Is it lunch time?" Elsea looked at her watch. Only two hours had gone by since the school bus took the older kids to school, since she had forced herself into the library to write. "No, it isn't lunch time. But if you're hungry, we could have a snack."

"I'm not hungry," Dorrie said. She had pushed Elsea's arms away, but she remained on her lap. She looked at the silent typewriter and poked gently at the keys, "Mama, could we go find Daddy?"

"What?"

"I want to go back home where we used to live and find my daddy."

Stunned, Elsea looked over Dorrie's head at the dark forest of pines. Late spring sun fell on the grass between the house and the stand of trees like yellow icing on a cake. But no sunshine penetrated the forest. It was a perpetually dark, quiet place. And now, with Dorrie's words still repeating themselves in her mind like a strengthening echo, the forest looked darker than it ever had, and the sunshine a farce that would fade in a moment, leaving the whole world gray and gloomy and dangerously silent.

"Darling," Elsea said, "your daddy is dead. We left him in—in a graveyard, a cemetery. It's a place of rest. He—" Elsea breathed deeply. What could she say? How could she explain without terrifying a little girl only five? This was the first time Dorrie had mentioned a word about her daddy. The first time that she knew of. And so much time had passed now. The weeks had slipped by into months. Even her own grief had become numbed. Her own adjustment was coming along better than she had thought it would. And both Tommy and Stephanie had stopped saying "daddy" every other word, including him in everything they did or thought, as they had at first.

They were dropping him out of their lives.

Elsea's heart felt as though it had been freshly torn

98

and was dripping her life's blood away. Even though she knew it was better that they go on, she felt as though she, Tommy and Stephanie had abandoned him. But here was Dorrie, who hadn't spoken of him at all, now wanting to see him.

What could she say?

Dorrie was the one who spoke. "But we can go get him, Mama, and bring him to live with us here in Great-grandmother's house. I want to go get him."

"Dorrie, we can't. When you're older you'll understand. Daddy has been buried, because he—he stopped living with us, in our world."

Dorrie twisted on Elsea's lap and put her hands on Elsea's face, her small warm palms pressing her cheeks. Dorrie's dark eyes stared unblinking into Elsea's.

"I can make Daddy not to dying anymore. I can make him live again, with us, the way I made my dollies to live again. And my horse. And my kitty cat, and the monster with the horns. The funny horns. I can make my daddy to live too!"

Elsea stared at her child, speechless, a slow horror creeping into her, and she realized what must be happening, what had happened to Dorrie. In all the months in which Dorrie had been pushed aside, during Vern's illness, and cautioned not to disturb her daddy, in all the months since his death when nothing had really been explained to the little girl, strange morbid thoughts had been going through her mind. Now Elsea saw she had handled it all wrong. Dorrie's grandmother had been right. Or nearer right. How was one to know with a child that was still more baby than most five-year-olds? Or so

99

Elsea had thought. Yet in the child's imagination strange things were happening. An obsession with life and death had occurred. Now she was imagining that her toys were living creatures.

Elsea felt a helplessness far beyond that which she had been feeling with her insignificant little story. It was a helplessness beyond even seeing her husband slip away in a slow death. Then, at least, she knew what she was facing. Now, with Dorrie on her lap, her serious little face so close to her own, she didn't know what to do.

Talk. Explain. Try to explain.

"Dorrie, when someone dies, you can't bring them to life again. In our religion we're taught there is a heaven to which our dead ones go, where it's always beautiful and lovely, and there's never any cold, nor too much heat, nor hunger, nor pain. It's a beautiful place, and because we think it's there, and our loved daddy is there, we can stop hurting so much and accept that he's gone on, and that he'll be waiting for us so someday we'll all be together again. But you can't bring things back to life, Dorrie."

"I can! My dolly, and all my dollies, and my toys!"

"Dorrie, no! Now listen, you imagine your toys live. Look, see this story here on these pages that your mama is trying to write? In a way I'm bringing them to life. It's in my imagination. In my mind. And if I'm fortunate, and my story gets made into a book, then whoever reads it will use their imagination to bring my characters to a kind of life. And that's probably what you're doing with your toys. In your imagination they are coming to life, but that's not real life, Dorrie. That's only in your mind."

Dorrie sat back, her hands dropping into her lap. But her dark eyes remained fixed on Elsea's.

Elsea touched Dorrie's forehead with two fingers. "Here," she said. "Your mind is in here. Your imagination is like your dreams. You know how real your dreams seem to you?"

Dorrie nodded.

"That's how your imagination works to make lots of things seem real. When you're playing with your toys, you imagine they're doing all kinds of things. And that's very good, because your mind needs that exercise."

"Does my 'magination make my toys come to life?"

"Yes, in a way. But only in a way."

Dorrie frowned.

Elsea felt the restriction of helplessness return. For a few minutes, as she talked, it had faded away, and she had felt more in control. But now she wished she had a glimpse into her daughter's thoughts. She wondered if she had helped, or hindered, with her explanation of the powers of imagination.

"Oh God," she said softly aloud, but to herself, She looked at the still, dark forest and wished Corey would emerge from it and help her figure this out. Or was she making too much of it? The complexities of adulthood against the simplicities of childhood?

"Listen," she said, sliding Dorrie off her lap as she stood up. "Why don't we drive down to Redding and see Grandma and Grandpa? Would you like that?"

"I want to go get my daddy," Dorrie said, yet her voice was not as confident. She was not as sure of herself as she had been when first she insisted on

101

going after her daddy. "My 'magination will make him live again, and talk to me again. I want him to come back from heaven and be here with me."

"Dorrie, I'm sorry, but I'm going to have to insist that you get that out of your mind. You're making Mama very unhappy when you talk that way."

Dorrie looked up, her eyes now warm with concern. Her hand slipped into Elsea's.

"Don't cry, Mama."

"No, I won't cry. But you must promise me that you'll try to separate what's real from what's not real. Can you do that?"

Dorrie looked for a long while into Elsea's eyes before she answered. She didn't understand, yet she couldn't tell her mother that. She had left her toys moving about in the attic, but she was confused. Faintly, hesitantly, she murmured, "I promise."

Suddenly her mother looked happy. There was a smile and the little nod of her head and sideways glance of her eyes that used to mean she had thought of something especially fun to do.

"Let's hurry," she said, "and maybe we can get to Grandma's in time for lunch. We'll write a note to Stephanie and Tommy in case they get home before we do."

She took a small notepad and a pen and wrote a few words on it. Dorrie looked over her hand as she wrote, and recognized a few letters. *A, r, i.* And even a word—*be.*

Elsea noticed with relief the attention Dorrie was giving to the note. "Do you know what it says?"

Dorrie pointed. "That's *be.* And that's part of the alphabet. *A.* And there's a *b,* and another *b,* and

102

some *o*'s. But I can't read it, Mama, you know I can't read."

"You can read more than I thought you could. It says, 'Be back soon. Gone to Grandma and Grandpa's for a while.' Is there anything else you'd like to say?"

Dorrie shook her head.

"Then sign your name."

"I can't write either."

"I'll help you."

Elsea put the pen in Dorrie's small fist, and closed her own hand around it and carefully printed Dorrie's name. When they had finished, Dorrie wore a satisfied little smile on her face and Elsea felt a leaded weight lift from her heart. Getting away for the day, going down the mountain to the old familiar home, was the best idea she'd had since the last time they went down there, all four of them, one week ago last Sunday.

Dorrie was quiet as they drove, looking out her window at the scenery. Occasionally Elsea pointed out something that was especially beautiful or interesting. When they reached the outskirts of Redding she began pointing out to Dorrie places she had gone when she was a girl—the drive-in for Cokes, hamburgers and french fries; the park with the swings where she had sometimes played; the school. Privately she relived times she had spent with Vern in some of the places they passed, but she decided against mentioning his name. Dorrie seemed to have her mind on other things for the time being. Or did she? Elsea was no longer sure.

She drew a long sigh when the white frame house

of her childhood and youth came into view. Her dad was in the large yard, spading among flowers that were colorful and glowing in the soft warmth of the sun. He looked at the car and pleasure lighted his face. He lay aside the gardening tool and came toward them, opening the door on Dorrie's side, taking the little girl into his arms.

"What a surprise! How are my girls today?"

Dorrie hugged her grandpa's neck. She had gotten to know him well enough to like being with him, to recognize him as someone special, whereas before, when they lived in the apartment in the city, he had mostly been a voice on the telephone. He had a chuckly voice that fit him. A round, warm voice, like his round face, and body. He was like Santa Claus without the funny red-and-white suit and the white beard. In the weeks that Dorrie had lived with him and Grandma, after they first came to Redding, she had grown to like her grandpa more than any man except her daddy. As he carried her into the house, she relaxed against him, and she was glad they had come down the mountain to visit Grandma and Grandpa.

They went into the house through the back door and the smell of baking cookies came with the woman who hurried to meet them. Dorrie turned from her grandpa to wrap her arms around her grandma's neck for a big hug, and then freed, she climbed uninvited onto a chair by the table.

"You haven't had lunch, I'll bet," Grandma said, bending over Dorrie. "But would you do Gram a favor and eat a bowl of stew before the cookies come out of the oven? Then you can have all you want of

104

nice, warm chocolate chip cookies."

"We came on impulse," Elsea said, peeking through the glass door of the oven. Each time she came home she was reminded pleasantly that she had not been one of those children who was in any way deprived. There had been no abuse of any kind, neither physical nor mental. As an only child she had been carefully protected, totally loved, sometimes spoiled. But not until she was an adult and knew a lot more about the world was she able to appreciate her childhood fully, to realize that maybe her parents had spoiled her a bit. But with love and concern, only with her welfare in mind. She hadn't been given all she had wished, she had learned she must earn it at least to a degree. So now, many years out of her childhood home, when she read of blaming all of one's troubles on some past imaginary failure on the part of the parents, she fumed. Most of the parents she had known, parents of her friends, had done the best they could. In her opinion, an adult had to take responsibility for himself, or herself, and accept the blame for his own actions, regardless of the kind of parents he had. But, with her childhood, could she judge? Now, trying to be both mother and father to her children, she was feeling unsure of herself. Would Dorrie one day blame her for not understanding her problems?

After lunch, when Dorrie had gone outside to play on the swing that still hung in the old play yard, Elsea sat across the table from her mother.

"I wouldn't have come down without Stephanie and Tommy," she said, looking out the wide kitchen window beside the table, watching her dad push

105

Dorrie on the swing, "but I think Dorrie has developed a problem. The other kids don't even know we're here, and we can't stay long. I'd like to get home before they do. I left a note in case we don't, and I'm really not afraid to leave them alone for a while. It's so quiet up there, and Corey isn't far away. Do you know there's hardly a car on that road? Only the people who live farther up, and hunters and a few tourists."

Her mother was smiling patiently. "I lived there until I was married," she said. "Haven't I told you?"

"Oh. Sure."

"You always rattled when you were worried, unless you were extremely worried. Then you wouldn't talk at all. So what is the problem Dorrie has developed?"

"Now that I'm here, it doesn't seem like such a serious problem. It's just that she mentioned her daddy to me for the first time today. He's been dead almost three months, and not once before has she spoken of him, or said his name, or anything. Not until today."

"Of course she wouldn't have forgotten him this soon, Elsea," Grace said gently. "Dorrie is a quiet little girl most of the time. You know the old saying, still waters run deep. And she's very young. Too young, maybe, to understand what happened, why he isn't with you. Is she asking about him now?"

"It was more than that, Mother. Dorrie wanted to go get him and bring him back to life. Because, she said, she had brought her toys to life."

The bright, warm kitchen seemed suddenly to have been permeated by the coldness of permanent death. Both women looked out the window at Dorrie on the swing, at the cheerful and rotund man who was laughing as he pushed her. Dorrie was laughing as well, her long, dark curls swaying back and forth behind her as she swept upward into the air and swung back again. The lovely little face held no morbidity, no confusion now. It was a creation of happiness, however momentary.

"She's only a little girl," Grace said, as though that explained it.

"Yes. I tried to explain, but I don't feel I did a very good job."

"Of course you did the best you could," Grace said. "In time, she will understand."

"I wish now I had done what you wanted me to do when Vern was buried."

Grace looked at her daughter, at the sad, dark eyes, so much like Dorrie's. The eyes that could now, and always had, make her heart feel as though it were breaking when the unhappiness showed.

"I wish," Elsea said, "that I had let you bring Dorrie to the cemetery so that she could see the coffin closed and lowered into the ground. Maybe then she would understand more than she does."

"And maybe not. I wasn't sure I was suggesting the right thing. How can a person ever know for sure? What is right for one child isn't necessarily right for another. Dorrie looks like you, Elsea, but her personality is entirely different. You know your child better than I ever could."

Elsea's eyes left the child on the swing and looked across the table at her mother. "I don't know Dorrie at all," she said. "I just realized that today. I don't know her at all."

Tommy jumped down from the door of the school bus and ran up the driveway ahead of Stephanie. Today he ran unfettered by his usual load of books because today had been the last serious day of school. From now on, there would be half-days, days of playing, and then the last day when they would all be turned loose on the countryside like a bunch of criminals paroled from the state prison. Those weren't his words, they were the words of a teacher he had overheard in the hallway. But he rather liked the sound of them. It fit, at least in part, the way he felt. A prisoner, aching for parole. Then, delirious with the freedom of parole. He jumped the first and second steps of the porch, hit the third and the fifth and then the floor of the porch itself. The whole house seemed to rattle, especially the front door with the stained glass.

"Hey, Mom!" He wanted to tell her about the prisoners released on parole before he forgot exactly how the teacher had said it. "Hey, Mom?"

The house threw back a weird echo at him, and then dropped a net of silence. He stood uncertainly in the narrow, twisting hall and peered back into the emptiness beyond the hall door. He heard Stephanie's steps, the squeaking of boards on the porch, and her entry behind him. He also heard her drop a load of things on the hall table. A pencil rolled to the floor, and she picked it up.

"Mom isn't here," she said.

"How do you know so much?"

"The car's gone."

"Oh."

Tommy stood still. He felt betrayed, deserted, and he knew he would forget all but the gist of what the teacher had said by the time his mother and little sister got back from wherever they had gone. "Where'd they go?"

"How should I know? To the store, probably."

Stephanie went past him, and on through the doors and hallways toward the kitchen. Then silence descended again, and Tommy felt as though even Stephanie had disappeared, leaving him all alone in the house.

He went in search of her, and found her at the kitchen table looking down at a sheet of notepaper.

"They went down to see Grandma and Grandpa," Stephanie said, with no emotion.

"Why'd they do that?" Tommy demanded, filled with emotion that bordered on anger. "They've never done that before! Without us." Tommy visualized his mom coming to school to pick him and Stephanie up for the trip down to Grandpa's, and he felt more cheated than ever.

Stephanie shrugged. Without answering, she went through the door toward the library, and a few moments later, when Tommy peeked in at her, he saw that she had settled into the cushioned seats of the bay window with a book. He glared at her a moment. He hated it when Stephanie stuck her nose in a book. It was like she had become unconscious. You had to yell to be heard by her, and even then sometimes it didn't work. When Stephanie had her nose in a book she was no fun at all.

And it was no fun coming home to an empty house, either.

He felt cranky, and he had to take it out on someone. "You'd better change your clothes, Steph," he yelled at her. "You know Mom doesn't want you to get your school clothes dirty."

She raised her head and gave him a piercing stare. Then she went back to reading her book.

"I'll bet that's a silly romance," Tommy said. He'd lost the point on the clothes. It was just too obvious that she wasn't doing anything to get them dirty, not now, and not later. She wasn't planning on roaming through the junk in the old carriage house with him today. She looked up again.

"You're the one who'd better get his clothes changed. You're the one that can't stay out of grimy places."

"I'll bet you're not even supposed to be reading that book! I'll bet it's on the taboo list!"

"There is no taboo list here in Great-grandmother's library, idiot. Now go away."

Tommy gave up. He had lost interest in trying to get Stephanie to move. He had lost his anger, too, and only felt lonesome.

He went to the front door and peered through the stained glass. He could only barely make out the white gravel of the driveway. If Mom had driven in, she had gone on back behind the house. He listened. There was no slam of doors, no voices. Tommy sighed. He went back down the hallway to the crooked, steep stairs that led up to the second floor. At the base of the stairs he flicked the switch that turned on the light far above and helped dissipate the perpetual gloom that hung over the stairway.

The second floor was lighter, with windows at the front end of the hall. But the first thing he saw when he rounded the corner leading toward his room was the door to the attic. It was closed, as usual, and he was glad.

He began to whistle.

In his room he changed from school clothes to tattered runabouts, old jeans and a knit shirt that had gone through the washing machine a thousand times and could stand anything from creek water to motor oil. The only thing they hadn't been able to take, to which a peppering of tiny holes testified, was battery acid. He and a couple of buddies had found an old junk pile down in L.A. that had a battery in it, and he had gotten some of its acid on his jeans. All his mom had said about that was, "Now you've got them air-conditioned."

He was pulling his old shirt down over his head when the sound came from the attic above his room. *Peck, peck, peck, peck.* Tommy jerked his shirt down and listened. There was a pause, and then another series of pecking sounds, as though something with tiny hooves was running around the floor of the attic.

Silence then, inside the house. Total silence. Outside the walls, in another world, some birds sang, but in here, Tommy's chest began to hurt, and he realized he was holding his breath. He let it out slowly, quietly, his ears straining for more sound. In a moment it came, but this time it was soft and dragging, as though something lame was taking a step, pausing, dragging forward the lame leg, taking

111

another step . . .

Then again, silence.

The silence was broken by sound that did not come from the movements of any creature. This time it was murmurs, so soft they were nearly inaudible, but murmurs that caused Tommy to begin moving slowly and cautiously toward the door, for whatever he was hearing did not come from any of God's living creatures.

Of that, he was sure.

They were tiny voices, like make-believe demon elves in a dark forest. Voices without words. Voices that growled deep in unreal bodies.

Tommy reached his door and opened it and looked toward the attic door. It hadn't opened. And yet something was there. He felt it. Something was staring through the wood at him, or it sensed him in some other way.

He stepped back into his room and closed his door softly.

Now again, it was quiet.

The footsteps were gone. The murmurs were gone.

He began visualizing the attic above, and he saw the top of the steps that led up to it, and all the boxes and piles of furniture pushed back from the cleared spot, and he saw the cleared spot with its toy boxes.

The place where Dorrie played.

And it was directly over his room.

EIGHT

"Here," Grace said as she bent over Dorrie, putting a paper sack into her hands, kissing her on the cheek. "Take this bag of cookies to Stephanie and Tommy for me, will you?"

They stood in the driveway near Elsea's car. It was past time to go home, and Elsea was feeling the nervousness of a sudden need to get started. She opened her door, climbed in and slammed the door shut, leaving her parents to help Dorrie into the passenger seat.

"We have to hurry or they'll be home from school before we get there. Come on, Dorrie, up."

Dorrie's grandpa helped her into the seat, closed the door, reached in and locked it. "Fasten your seat belt, Dorrie," he said. "Drive carefully."

"Sure, Dad." Elsea started the car and began

backing slowly down the drive as Dorrie pulled down the seat belt and fastened it. Elsea's parents stood together beside the drive, and Elsea had a twinge of the old feeling. They looked so alone. Yet they were so perfect for each other. Like cupid dolls, a matching set. She had been driving off and leaving them for many years now, and always their faces had that look of sadness around the smiles they affected, and always Elsea felt the guilty twinge of desertion. Yet it wasn't that, she told herself. She always came back. They knew she would. And if they got lonesome they knew where she lived. Probably, it wasn't as upsetting to them to see her take her brood of kids and leave as she imagined it was.

She laughed as she turned from the street onto the highway leading up the mountain. "They're probably glad to be rid of us so they can relax in peace."

There was no answer from Dorrie. There had been no word out of Dorrie at all since she had said goodbye to her grandparents. Elsea looked at her, and saw the little girl was sagging sideways in her arrangements of belts, fast asleep. Her hands had dropped away from the bag of cookies on her lap.

Elsea smiled and turned her attention to driving the curving mountain road home.

Tommy stood rooted in his room. For several minutes now there had been no sound from the attic, but he was afraid to move, as though to start moving around would agitate the *things* up there to move too.

Squirrels, he told himself, *squirrels*. Who's afraid

of squirrels?

Cute little furry animals with long tails that they could sweep up over their heads like umbrellas. Little animals who used their paws like real hands and held nuts to their mouths for eating. Little guys who sat on tree limbs and looked unafraid at people as they passed by.

Oh yeah, Tommy knew all about squirrels.

They jumped from tree limbs onto the roofs of houses, and went into attics if they could find an entry, and they played like kittens. They played tag. They ran. They flitted their tails at each other and chirped almost like birds.

But they couldn't jump long distances. The tree limb had to be twenty feet or closer to the house.

Almost unwillingly, Tommy turned his head and looked out his windows. There was no tree at all within the yard on his side of the house.

He heard a noise then that released him from his inability to move. A car on the road, tires crunching gravel as it came into the driveway. Without another thought of the attic, or of trees or squirrels, he ran. His bedroom door was thrown open with such exuberance that it bounced against the wall and came close to shutting itself again, but Tommy didn't notice. He was already on his way down the stairs.

When he reached the driveway, Elsea was on the passenger side of the car, bending in and unfastening the seat belts that tied Dorrie in. She glanced over her shoulder at Tommy, smiled and said, "Hi," then handed him a brown sack.

"What is it?" he asked as he peeked and saw the

bag was almost full of homebaked cookies. "Grandma made these, huh."

"Sure. They missed seeing you and Stephanie."

"Yeah, me too. How come you went without us?"

"Just took a wild hair. We'll go again soon. As
soon as school is out."

Dorrie made a whimpering sound as Elsea pulled
her from the car, but she didn't wake up. Elsea
carried her, with Dorrie looking long-legged, drooping as she was with her head on Elsea's shoulder.

Stephanie met them at the door and held it open.
Tommy followed as his mother carried Dorrie up
the back stairs and into her bedroom. He was telling
Elsea everything he could think of about school, and
she was answering in monosyllables and exclamations as required to show interest even as she
undressed Dorrie down to her underclothes, removed her shoes and socks and put her into bed with
a blanket covering her. Tommy, standing close
behind, even remembered the crazy thing the teacher
had said about paroled convicts. He giggled as Elsea
rewarded him with a hearty laugh. It made him feel
good. It was the first time he had heard her laugh in a
long, long time.

When she straightened, she put her hand on his
shoulder, and together, they left the room.

Tommy looked at the attic door. It was so close to
Dorrie's room, even closer to hers than it was to his.
But of course there was nothing to be afraid of.
Didn't she go up there and play all the time she was
awake?

When they reached the kitchen they found
Stephanie peeling potatoes, but she had a mouthful

116

of something that crunched, and it reminded Tommy of the bag of cookies. He had left it on the table, where it now stood open. He reached in, but Elsea caught his wrist before he could grab a cookie.

"Not before supper," she said.

"Steph is! She's eating one right now."

Stephanie looked over her shoulder at him and made a face, her eyes and nose wrinkled and her mouth stretched into a caricature of a smile. Just as quickly, before he could threaten her with his fist, she turned back to peeling potatoes, and Elsea saw none of it.

"You creep," Tommy said.

"Is that any way to talk to your sister?" Elsea asked.

Tommy felt betrayed again. The good feeling between him and his mother had been ruined by Stephanie and her mouthful of cookies.

"She's eating cookies. That's not fair."

"She's being very adult and getting our dinner started. Why don't you help her?"

"Naw. I got some things to do outside."

He went out the back door, but then he ambled around the house with his hands in his pockets and his eyes examining the ground. There was something he had intended to do outside, but what was it?

Suddenly he remembered. He was going to check for trees in which squirrels might play, from which they could jump onto the roof of the house. He looked up, and it took no more than the single glance to show him that nowhere near the house stood such a tree. There was a tall spruce, or pine, back toward the old building that was a carriage house, a kind of barn where a harness still hung on the walls. But near the house was nothing except short shrubbery.

He went slowly around the house, looking at porches, at porch posts, at angles of the roof. And high above, in the sharp peaks of the attic, were only two tiny windows. The west one was reflecting the setting sun with a fiery brilliance. It was like a square ruby set into the old green shingles of the house.

As he watched, the colors changed, part of the window pane darkening, like the face on a full moon.

A face.

Staring at him from the lower edge of the window. A small face that had eyes, and ears, and four horns, and a snout with the nose pressed against the pane. Even as Tommy stared back at it his reason told him there was no such creature. Not in all existence. It was only a trick of the light, the changing rays of the sun as it sank lower over the trees in the west. Perhaps it was even a shadow thrown by the tips of the tall pines beyond the boundary of the yard. A shadow that looked like an evil little face that stared at him with a hatred that was worse than anything he had ever seen.

Tommy closed his eyes, and when he opened them a second later the image was gone, and the window pane was turning black all over as the sun disappeared beyond the forest.

He crossed the driveway and walked down the blacktopped road that wound past the house, past Corey's trailer, and on toward the mountain peaks that were still covered with a heavy layer of snow.

He looked toward the spot where Corey's driveway led through an open space in the trees, and thought about going over there. Immediately, he changed his mind. Mom had told him not to bother Corey, not to go uninvited. Of course Corey had said come on over anytime, but that wouldn't wash with Mom. She didn't believe he could really mean it. What grown man wanted to be bothered with a kid? That was what she thought, Tommy knew, even though she hadn't said it exactly that way. So, instead of going to Corey's, Tommy crossed the highway and went down the hillside toward the creek.

He could hear it long before he could see it. Water splashed like white froth over the boulders, sounding like it was rushing over a dam. He stopped at the creek's edge and stood looking at the swiftly running water. In places he could see the bottom clearly, and knew the creek wasn't as deep as it sounded. Corey had said the waters would slow down as the snow on the mountain tops melted away, and the creek would become a gentle stream that could be waded. Tommy wondered when that would be. August? Although it already seemed like summertime now in June, the waters of the creek roared with a fury greater than when they first came, almost two months ago.

Had it been that long?

In many ways it didn't seem like two months. Only when he looked back on all the draggy days of school did it seem like two months.

Tommy turned back toward the house. Long shadows were reaching out from the trees beside the yard when he went up the driveway, and the area beneath the trees was already filled with the darkness of night.

With effort Tommy did not look up at the attic window.

The moment he entered the kitchen his mother said, "Tommy, go up and bring Dorrie down, will you, please?"

Although he knew better, because he had been told many times that it was rude, he said, "Make Stephanie."

Stephanie was putting flatware on the table, and she stopped and looked at him.

Elsea said, "Fine. Stephanie can go get Dorrie and you can finish setting the table." She didn't look around at her two eldest children. She was busy at the sink preparing lettuce leaves for salad. Experience had taught her a few things too. The situation would take care of itself, and there would be no argument as to who did what. Tommy did not surprise her.

"Never mind," Tommy said. "I'll go get Dorrie."

He went on through the kitchen, and took the rear stairs up to the second floor. They twisted and turned in much the same way the front set of steps did, and enclosed as they were, needed artificial light even in the brightest hour of day. But the bulb overhead barely managed to light them. Sometimes, Tommy felt, the house was not a pleasant place to live in. At least not lately, not since whatever it was moved around in the attic. At first, when they moved into the house, he had thought it would be a fantastic place. Now, he wished they had a trailer house like

120

Corey's. It was cozy and comfortable, and in it he felt almost like he thought a chipmunk would feel in its little burrow.

He looked at the attic door as he passed it, expecting to see it open. But then he remembered something that did not make him feel any better. When Dorrie went up into the attic to play she always closed the door behind her. Maybe she was up there, instead of in her bed asleep.

Her bedroom door was open. But her room was dark. He walked softly to the door and looked in, saw her bed and a pale arm thrown across the covers. With considerable relief he felt for the switch beside the door and turned on the light. She stirred, turning her face away from the bright glare of the light in the center of the ceiling.

"Wake up, Dorrie, time for dinner."

He pulled her into a sitting position and she blinked at him. He looked around. "Where are your clothes? Oh, here. Okay, put your arms in here."

"We went to Grandma and Grandpa's today," Dorrie said. "And she gave us some cookies to bring home. For you and Stephanie."

"For you too," Tommy said, reaching for her shorts and guiding one of her feet into the right leg. He wondered if he hadn't been able to dress himself when he was her age. "You sure are a baby, Dorrie. Why can't you put on your own clothes?"

"I can put 'em on!"

"Oh yeah?"

"Yes, I can too. And I can make my dollies live."

"What do you mean you can make your dollies live?"

121

"My 'magination makes my dollies live. And all my other toys too, that used to be my great-grandmother's toys. I can make them all live."

"Well, you might *think* . . ." Tommy paused. His fingers, lacing her shoe, slowed. "But that's your imagination, I guess. Who told you that?"

"Mama."

Tommy finished tying the one shoe and picked up the other. Her foot was uncooperative and her toes doubled under. He straightened them. "Don't double up your toes, Dorrie. How can I get this shoe on your foot if you double up your toes?"

She wasn't listening to him. She was staring dreamily over his shoulder. "I brought my toys back from dying, and made them to living again. And now they can walk, and some of them can run, and they can climb. Hear them, Tommy? I hear them walking upstairs. Can you hear them?"

Tommy stared at her face, at her attitude of listening. And he heard tiny footfalls above, as something ran in a circle on the attic floor. And with the terrible fear that gripped him came an anger that was born of fear and made worse by the look on his little sister's face. For there was no fear in her face, but a strange adoration, a worship, an acceptance of something that was not natural.

He jerked her off the side of the bed and then found himself over her, his hands hard on her shoulders. Her head bobbed back and forth as he shook her. His voice sobbed out in fear and anger against her.

"Stop it! Stop that! Don't you ever in all your life say anything like that again, or something terrible will happen to you! Don't you do that! *Don't! Don't! Don't!*"

He saw she was crying, crying as hard as he was shaking her. Small hands had come up to circle his wrists and try to push his terrible grip away. She was looking at him in a fear as terrible as the one he felt. And suddenly he was torn with sorrow and shame. He dropped to the floor and gathered her into his arms, and for a while they cried together, with his arms tight around her, and her arms just as tight around his neck.

"Don't," he was saying softly now between sobs.

"I won't," she replied, "I promise."

After a long while they grew still together, and Tommy tried not to hear the soft sounds in the attic. Then, blessedly, there was no sound at all except for the sweet familiarity of his mother's voice calling.

"Hey, up there! Come on down, you two."

Tommy got up and with his shirt tail wiped the tears from Dorrie's cheeks and his own. He looked at her critically, and saw that she would probably pass inspection from his mother. She wouldn't notice that Dorrie had been crying unless she was told.

"Dorrie, I'm sorry I made you cry. I didn't mean to scare you, or hurt you. Don't tell Mom. Don't tell anyone."

She whispered, "I won't. I promise."

Tommy led her down to the kitchen, her hand in his, and as she let him pull her along she thought of him, and her mother, and her toys upstairs. And she made a vow to herself, a decision. Never again would she mention making her dolly to living, nor all her

123

other toys. There was something about it that her mother and her brother did not like.

The really bad time for Tommy came that night when he woke and had to go to the bathroom. He held himself, reluctant to get out of bed, and tried to go back to sleep. But the need to relieve himself became more and more urgent.

Fully awake now, he listened. The house was as silent as it ever had been, and, it seemed, darker. The only light came in his windows, a faint gray that was really no light at all.

Had he forgotten to go to the bathroom before he went to bed? He never woke up at night needing to go unless he forgot.

He reached into the darkness for the lamp on the table. With a subdued light now filling his room he put his feet out of bed and sat for a moment, listening. The whole world, it seemed, was sound asleep. Tommy felt as if he were the only living thing within miles around that was awake. It was not a bad feeling. Instead, he felt as though a cloak of protection had been wrapped around him.

He opened his bedroom door and peeked out into the hall. All the lights had been turned out. It was the new policy, only one way of saving money.

Yet there was one light that had been forgotten, that was still burning, and showed itself only as a thread of yellow beneath the attic door.

Tommy looked at it for a long moment, and then started across the hall to the door of the bathroom. His feet made barely a sound on the wood floor, a whisper of movement that reached his alert ears. Then, coming too as he moved, was the other sound, at the bend in the hall, at the door with the thread of light beneath.

Scratchings.

Clawings against wood.

Not frantic, hurried, or loud, but slow and deliberate and deadly determined.

Tommy stopped, halfway across the hall to the bathroom door, and stared unbreathing at the slim streak of light beneath the attic door. The scrapings on the wood stopped, waited and then started again.

And a portion of the light at the bottom of the door was suddenly blocked out.

Tommy stared at the narrow shadow.

It was no wider than his finger. Whatever stood there, stood on a leg that was smaller than his finger, or, standing on the first step up, it reached out to the door with a body that threw a shadow as thin as a pencil.

The shadow moved, blending in with the shadows at the edge of the door, and the sliver of light was unbroken. For a minute, too, the silence in the house descended and there was no sound at all. But the protective cloak was gone, and Tommy stood chilled to the bone in the dim light that spilled from his room.

The scratchings on the door began again, and moved from the sound of claws against wood to claws against metal. The doorknob rattled faintly. It was a white knob, old porcelain, and stood out against the dark wood of the door like a pale eye. It moved, it seemed to Tommy as he stared, not

125

around, but loosely up and down, just slightly, as though whatever it was that tried to open it knew only that it held the magic of freedom, neither knowing nor understanding fully in just what way it held that freedom.

It moved, Tommy thought, as if the nearly mindless thing that was trying to open the door, did not yet know that it had to turn the knob.

Could Dorrie have been telling the truth about the toys?

Tommy backed up, and turned and ran into his room and closed his door. He stood against it for several long minutes, his ear pressed to the cool wood. But now he heard nothing.

Finally, he went back to bed. But he left his light on.

That night, for the first time in his memory, Tommy wet his bed.

NINE

Corey was thinking of the family next door. He thought of them too much. When he went to bed, when he got up, when he was trying to work. Sitting there with his typewriter buzzing in front of him, he'd find himself with a drifting mind, and into it would come Elsea's face, and behind her, surrounding her, the faces of her children. He had grown fond of all of them with the youngest, Dorrie, the hardest to reach. She was almost mouselike in the way she kept to herself, and came and went quietly when she did appear. Tommy, loaded with exuberance, was a kid after his own heart. Corey had a feeling he was looking forward to summer vacation just as much as Tommy was.

On Saturday morning he woke early. Too early to traipse through the strip of forest to the old green-shingled house with this idea that had popped into his mind when he realized that school had ended on Friday. As the sun came up with its colorful shades of red and gold, Corey was busy preparing a picnic lunch. He had baked a ham, and now he sliced it. He would leave the bone in the wilds for a raccoon to find and enjoy. Into the picnic basket went a pile of paper plates, plastic spoons, forks, knives, cups. He made a Thermos of coffee and a larger Thermos of Kool-Aid. "I hope these kids like orange flavor," he said aloud to the dog he wished he had. Like most kids, he'd had his pet dog when he was still at his parents' home, but since he had left for school and then become a wildlife writer and photographer, he hadn't gotten another because he had to be away from his house too much, and also because when he went after the wild animals he had to go without a dog. To leave one behind struck him as a cruel way to treat a loved pet. So he compensated by being slightly eccentric and pretending old Buster was still there with him. Buster, a blue merle Australian shepherd, was born when he was two years old, and lived to be fifteen. They had left the same year. Buster had gone on to the other side of life, wherever that was, and Corey had gone away to college. Someday, Corey thought, when he married again and had a yard with about three kids in it, he would get a pup. A blue merle Australian shepherd. Smart dogs. If treated with love and plenty of attention they could almost talk to you.

He could almost see Tommy running with a shepherd puppy.

He could see Dorrie sitting in her quiet way with her arms around that puppy.

And Stephanie—she would be the one who would brush the silky fur.

And what would Elsea do? Stand at the kitchen door and demand that the dog wipe his feet before he entered?

Corey smiled, and then admonished himself. He was dreaming. For the first time it occurred to him just how much he had been dreaming. Thoughts of Elsea had taken the place of thoughts of his dead wife. Life was moving on, just as it was supposed to.

He closed the picnic basket, then remembered that he had forgotten all the little junk the kids would like. Olives, pickles, chips. They sat on the table in plain sight. He checked more thoroughly and saw he hadn't even put in the bread.

"Some cook I am," he said to Buster the Second. His dreams were getting ahead of him, leaping at least a year ahead. He'd had no indication that Elsea even liked him, beyond simple friendship.

He waited until the sun was above the treeline in the east, then he tossed the picnic hamper and the Thermoses into the back of his Blazer and drove out his driveway and up the graveled drive beside the tall, green house.

He went to the kitchen door.

Stephanie answered his knock. He saw beyond her that they were having breakfast. At least part of them. Tommy was the only one missing.

Elsea got up and took a cup down from the cupboard. "Come and drink a cup of coffee with us."

"Thanks. How's everybody this morning?"

"Fine, except Tommy."

Corey sat down, a lot of the happiness and excitement going out of him. "What's the trouble? Not sick, I hope."

Stephanie said, "He must be. He even did a load of laundry without being asked, and when Tommy does something like that, he must be sick." Her tone of voice didn't agree with her statement. It was filled with sisterly derision.

Elsea said, "He's not sick. At least he doesn't have fever or any pain. I can't figure it out. He's just . . . not himself the last couple of days."

"Where is he?"

"I don't know." Elsea looked at Stephanie.

"He went outside. Want me to call him?"

Corey said, "I thought he'd be feeling great on his first day of no school. I was hoping you'd all honor me with your company today."

They stared at him, except for Dorrie, who was busy finishing whatever was in her dish, waiting to hear what he had in mind.

He said, "I've packed a picnic lunch. I thought we'd drive up to a meadow I know of that will be in full bloom right now and spend the day there."

Stephanie's face brightened. "Really?"

"Full bloom?" Elsea urged, her voice dreamy soft, the look on her face making Corey's heart beat faster than he could remember.

"California poppies, in all their glory. A beautiful sight."

Dorrie looked up, and her eyes took in the faces of

130

all of them, but she said nothing. Stephanie gave a hop and a skip toward the kitchen door.

"Let me go call Tom!" She had barely gotten to the door before her voice rose in an ear-splitting screech, *"Tom-my!"*

Elsea cringed, smiling, and as Stephanie went out into the back yard yelling she said, "This is very thoughtful of you, Corey."

"I wasn't sure you would want to go, so I think the right word is presumptuous, not thoughtful."

"No, I prefer my own. Thoughtful. Of course we want to go. Tommy, and Stephanie too, have been looking forward to this since the first day they saw you."

"Well, we could have gone any weekend except for the snows. It's still too early to go high into the mountains, but I've been to that meadow every spring for many years, so I know the time is right. Still, I wasn't sure you and Dorrie would want to go."

Dorrie said, "I like picnics."

"Just for one day, yes, we'd love it." Elsea reached out and caressed Dorrie's long, dark hair. "But I would hesitate to take her out for an entire weekend, camping, roughing it too much, although we used to go, when we were a full family. Vern liked to camp out."

Corey didn't answer. He knew it was selfish of him, but something inside him did not obey what his mind thought was proper and doubled up and hurt like hell every time Elsea mentioned her dead husband's name.

Stephanie and Tommy came into the kitchen, and Tommy grinned, but Corey saw he wasn't quite the same. Tommy's exuberance seemed in some way destroyed, or at least temporarily subdued. But Corey could remember how sensitive he had been when he was Tommy's age, and under no circumstances would he embarrass Tommy by questioning him.

"Hi, Tom. How do you feel about a one-day trip up to a meadow of California poppies that should be in full bloom? I've got a spare camera or two along, and I thought you and Stephanie might like to help me get some good shots of flowers and maybe a chipmunk or two. Even a deer might show up."

"Sure," Tommy said, and his lips smiled, a wider, more enthusiastic smile. But that strange look was still in his eyes.

It was almost thirty miles up to the meadow, a place that was sunk between rising mountains that were covered with western fir and topped by several feet of white snow that glistened with such brilliance in the sun that it hurt the eye to look at them. The four-wheel-drive Blazer bounced over the nearly hidden little road that had been made by a few adventurers like Corey to the edge of the blossom-covered field. Corey heard cries of appreciation and exclamations of pleasure, and he felt good. The mountain air was cool and fresh. A soft, balmy breeze moved the meadow of yellow poppies so that they appeared to ripple rhythmically, like a pond of molten gold. Corey made a point of looking at Tommy, and was gratified to see that the dullness was gone. His eyes glowed with excitement as he jumped out of the Blazer.

Whatever it was that had made Tommy unhappy was now forgotten.

Elsea lay on her back in the warm sun, her head pillowed on one arm. The tender, spring grass grew tall around her. Near her, within easy reach, was Corey. The last time she had looked at him he was sitting up, knees bent, arms resting on his knees. He was watching the kids, who had taken off by themselves across the meadow of flowers, toward the trees on the other side, with one of Corey's cameras. Their voices, high with excitement, were fading with distance. Elsea felt drowsy with food and contentment, but she didn't want to go to sleep. She didn't want to miss one moment of this lovely day.

"They sound so happy," she murmured. "It's as though we've left the real world behind and we're in heaven, or a particularly nice dream. I wish we could stay here."

"Maybe we could."

"How?"

"Well, we could buy it, and build a mountain cabin."

"Oh sure. So easy."

He didn't answer. She opened her eyes and peeked at him from underneath the arm that shielded her eyes from the sun. To her surprise he was looking down at her, and his face was serious and yearning. She quickly closed her eyes again. There was nothing to say now. Except, perhaps, something that would bring them back to reality.

"That was a great lunch you packed."

"Thanks. Glad the kids liked it."

"You've had a lot of experience packing lunches, haven't you?"

"Yes, sure. I've spent a lot of time backpacking, as well as going out for one day. The kind of food I take along when I'm headed for a week in the woods though is quite a lot different from the kind we had today. Can you see me hauling a ham and a jar of pickles around on my back?"

Elsea laughed. "Yes, and it's a funny sight."

"How's the book coming?"

"Now that's not funny. I hate it. I've never hated anything so much in my life. I take out all my furies on that damned pile of paper. Book? Are you kidding? Why did you have to remind me of that on such an otherwise unblemished day?"

Corey laughed, a deep chuckle that was easy and low and amused. "Sounds like you have become a full-fledged writer. You'll never quit now."

"How can you say that when I just got through telling you how much I hate it?"

"Have you thrown it away yet? Burned it?"

"Well . . . no. But I've thought about it."

"Still, you keep working on it. How many chapters do you have?"

"Twelve."

"Pretty good."

Elsea grunted.

Then she asked a serious question, one that she had been wondering about off and on since she had started the book. "Is there ever a point when the writer likes writing?"

"Of course."

"When?"

"When it's going well. And when it's finished."

They both laughed. Elsea turned over onto her stomach and supported herself on her elbows so that she could pick a flower and examine it.

"I guess it's been good therapy for me, hasn't it? I haven't been sitting around worrying the way I was. In fact, I haven't been able to get my mind on anything else but those hateful characters that just won't do what I want them to."

"Let them do what they want, and see how it goes."

"And forget my outline?"

Corey lay back. By turning his head toward her, their faces were separated by only a few inches.

"Sure, forget your outline." He paused, and Elsea found she could not look away from his eyes. He was drawing her into him in a way she had never experienced. "Forget everything. For a while, think of me. I . . ."

He stopped. He didn't know how much he dared say to her before she would pull away and run from him, emotionally if not physically. He wanted her more than he had ever wanted any woman, it seemed now, and he wanted her forever, not just for an hour or a night. And for that reason he was afraid of her, of himself.

When she didn't move away from him, or look away, he reached up slowly and put his hand on the back of her neck. The touch of her was electrifying, and he felt the tension sweep his body and harden it, muscle to muscle. Gently, he pulled her face to his, and for an instant her lips were warm and soft against his own. But then, as he had feared, she pulled abruptly away.

She got to her feet.

"Hey," she said. "The kids are out of sight. We'd better go after them."

He rose too, and with effort spoke as naturally as was possible. His own ears detected a huskiness that he hoped hers did not.

"They're all right. They've probably just gone into the edge of the forest."

"But what if they met a bear?"

He gave in. "I expect there would be three surprised kids and one surprised bear. If you're worried, we'll follow them."

"I'd rather," she said, her voice suddenly soft. She glanced up at him, and then she held out her hand. He took it, and was surprised at its smallness, its fragility. He realized he had never held her hand before.

"Feel like running?" she asked.

"Sure. Ready?"

They ran, jogging easily through the field of yellow poppies to the edge of the trees. They found the kids within minutes, and spent an hour or more wandering through the trees that bordered the meadow. When they came out again the sun was dropping low in the west. By mutual agreement, they decided to eat a picnic supper from the leftovers before they started home. As they had during lunch, they sat among the flowers, and the conversation was monopolized by Stephanie and Tommy talking at the same time. Corey tried to listen to both of them, and wound up with a jumble of words that conveyed some idea of pictures they had taken of trees, chipmunks, a couple of squirrels and something else that Tommy thought was a raccoon and Stephanie argued was nothing but a blackened stump. Tommy started yelling.

"Stumps don't move!"

"It didn't move! It was the light that made it look like it was moving."

"You're crazy!"

"You're imaginative."

Dorrie spoke up for the first time. "I got that too."

But that was all she said, and Corey noticed that the two older kids ignored her, and went on with an argument that dwindled away and became agreement on another subject. Corey looked at Elsea, who smiled at him before glancing away.

"Won't it be dark when we get home?" she asked.

"Yes. Does that matter?"

"No, I suppose not."

They started, at last, with the kids in the back of the Blazer, silent now. Corey suspected they had all gone to sleep, and when at last he drove into the driveway by the side of their house, he saw he was

137

right. Even Stephanie was sleeping soundly.

Elsea woke Stephanie and Tommy, and they climbed staggering from the auto and went up the walk toward the house still half asleep. Corey picked up the little girl and carried her cradled in his arms as though she were a baby. She didn't so much as draw a long sigh, she remained so soundly asleep.

When Dorrie was tucked into her bed, still wearing all her clothes except her jeans and shoes, Corey followed Elsea from the room. They stood in the hallway. He knew he should go, and yet he couldn't. The house was quiet. Stephanie was in her room, Tommy in his, Dorrie in hers. For the first time Corey felt completely alone with Elsea, alone in that they were not likely to be disturbed.

And he didn't want to leave her.

He whispered, "Where's your bed? I'll tuck you in."

She pointed toward the door to the front room, but she said, "Goodnight, Corey. It was really a great day."

He touched her, and felt her withdraw slightly, but before she could step away he pulled her into his arms. At first she stood unyielding, but her breath quickened, was indrawn and held, and her lips parted as he bent over her. He gathered her against him, felt the womanly curves of her body and the sexy sweetness of her mouth, and then he forgot everything else.

She was naked in a man's arms for the first time in

138

a long time, and it seemed that she was not herself at all but someone she had never known before. Her body throbbed, pulsed, ached, yearned, gave, took, yielded, and in turn ravished. Her bed was closed off from the world that she had known. It was a world in which nothing existed but herself and the man she was with. She heard the whispered words, "I love you," over and over as he made love to her, as she made love to him. And then she heard, felt, the words, "I love you," coming from her own mouth as her body released all the sexual buildup of months, years past. And the shock of it drew her back from the heaven in his arms, to a strange new hell on earth.

She pulled away from him.

The bedside lamp burned softly, and she saw him, the stranger, in her bed. "Oh God," she whispered, "Oh my God!"

He touched her, tried to pull her against him, but she drew back against the wall and covered her face with her hands. She was horribly aware of her naked body, and she pulled the sheet up. She had a terrible feeling that Vern was standing at the foot of the bed looking at her, his eyes hurt, hurt beyond help.

"Oh please, go away," she whispered. "Please."

"Elsea," he said, the hurt she could see in Vern's eyes expressed in Corey's voice. "What's wrong? I love you. I do. Don't . . ."

"I'm sorry," she said. "But please leave. I'm sorry. Oh God, I'm sorry."

He said no more. She didn't look at him. She couldn't look at him. He got out of bed and she heard him dressing. Then she heard him walk to the door and pause, and she knew he was looking at her.

"Elsea? What did I do wrong?"

"No, no, no. It's not you, Corey. It's just me." She sat up, pulling the sheet with her to cover her body, but she couldn't look into his eyes. "I can't . . . I shouldn't have . . . I'm sorry. That's all I can say. I have to be alone now, Corey."

He left her, left the house, and drove home. For hours he stared at the ceiling, until the sun began to rise again. He knew now what the problem was. He had known it for a long time. Perhaps all along.

Elsea had not yet buried her husband.

And in his sorrow, Corey realized that she might never bury him.

He waited almost a week before he went back to see Elsea and her children, and he went in as though nothing had happened between him and Elsea although it was difficult to look at her and not think of it. At first she seemed as uncomfortable as he, if not more so, but with the usual cup of coffee, and Stephanie serving him a piece of the cake she claimed proudly to have made all by herself, the tension left.

"How's it going?" he asked Elsea after he had taken a bite of cake and complimented Stephanie.

Elsea smiled. "You mean the book? I hope you don't, because I don't want to talk about it."

"You're still fighting with it, eh? No, I just meant generally."

"Not bad. I've had a time keeping Tommy from

going over to your place. Every day he wants to go see you."

"Why do you stop him? I'd like for him to come over. I'd like all of you to come over."

"I was afraid he'd pester you to death."

"No chance. Where is he now?"

"I don't know. He spends most of his time outside."

"Let him come over. You know he's welcome. If I see him when I leave I'll tell him, if it's all right with you."

"It's all right with me if you'll not let him stay very long. I know you have work to do, and Tommy can talk your ear off all day long." Elsea hesitated, adding, "At least he used to. He hasn't been talking much since school was out. After the, uh, picnic he was back to normal for a couple of days, then he . . ." She stopped, and drew a breath that Corey heard clearly. He knew what she was thinking of, and he could see on her face that she didn't want to think of it.

He didn't stay much longer. Stephanie was busy cooking something else, stirring vigorously in a bowl. Dorrie was nowhere around.

"Where's your little one?" Corey asked.

"Upstairs, I guess. She loves that old attic."

"No danger in that, is there? At least you know where she is."

Stephanie said with a wrinkling of her nose, "A couple of weirdos, that's what I've got for a brother and a sister. Dorrie stays up in that smelly, dark old attic, and Tommy rummages around in the old carriage house. Weirdos." She thought a moment.

"And Mama! My mother is almost as bad. Only she's off in the library most of the time banging on that typewriter."

"Just so she doesn't start banging her head against the wall," Corey said, hoping to see Elsea smile again. She made a scoffing sound instead.

"That's next," she said.

Corey sat for another minute, then he got up to leave. Elsea went with him to the back porch. But when he looked at her, she glanced down, unwilling to meet his eyes so directly.

"If you need me," he said, "you know where I am."

She nodded. "Thanks, Corey. You've been a real friend."

More than your friend, Elsea. But he couldn't say it. When she turned back toward the kitchen door, Corey went down the old brick walk toward the carriage house. Nearer the house was a modern garage, built to shelter the wider cars of more recent years. But the doors of the carriage house were no wider than would have allowed the passage of a buggy. At one side was a narrow door, standing part way open.

Corey looked in.

On the tongue of an old buggy Tommy sat. He was leaning forward, his chin in his hands, his elbows propped on his knees. He appeared to be staring at his feet. Corey watched him for a long moment, puzzled at this stillness of a boy who had seemed so full of life, sensing in him a disturbing problem that he apparently didn't want to discuss with his family.

"Tommy?"

142

Tommy shuddered convulsively and cried out as though in a nightmare. He jumped up. The terror that Corey's voice had caused was on his face, in its lack of color, in the blank stare of his eyes.

In that first instant there was no recognition at all in his face.

TEN

"Tommy?"

Tommy saw the huge, shadowed bulk of the man in the doorway, the bright sunlight outside surrounding him like a halo. His fear subsided slowly, like blood draining away in clots. It was not a man he was afraid of these days and nights, not a person, not anything large—but tiny things that moved around in his nightmares, unexpected things, the pencil from his school supplies, the small knife from his pocket. The nightmares carried over into the hours of day, making him feel on edge all the time.

Corey stepped into the shed, and Tommy felt like running into his arms and staying there where nothing could reach him, where the nightmares would go away. But he stood still.

"Hi." He couldn't think of another word to say. His mind buzzed with activity, but no sensible set of words formed. He felt he should talk kind of man-to-man with Corey, but he couldn't because he didn't know what to say.

Corey came close, and passed by to look into the buggy. "Funny old things, aren't they? Can you imagine two people sitting in that seat?"

"Skinny people," Tommy said. "Or squished close together."

Corey patted the cracked and peeled side of the buggy. "A lot of nostalgia connected with these. The quiet days of horses and buggies, and no television or radio with bad news all the time. If there was a war someplace it was over before the news came. How about that kind of life? For entertainment people had one another. They visited at the store, at church, at homes."

"I'd like that, I guess."

"Most of us *think* we would, at least."

Corey stepped back and sat down on a wood sawhorse that had once been used to hold a board as it was being sawed. He folded his arms across his chest and looked at Tommy.

"I've got this feeling, Tommy, that you're in some kind of trouble. Want to talk about it?"

Tommy shook his head vigorously. What would Corey think if he told him he was having little kid nightmares about things moving around him and coming after him? Dorrie was the baby in the family, not him. "No, I'm not. Really. What makes you

146

think so?"

"Just a feeling." Corey hesitated. "You were deep in thought when I spoke to you. I startled you."

Tommy shrugged. "I don't know."

"Do you spend a lot of time out here?"

"There's not much to do."

"Why don't you come over and talk to me?"

"Mom said not to bother you."

"I wouldn't consider it being bothered. I promised I'd send you out when I had to work. You come over and we'll make plans for that three-day trip to the mountains, OK?"

"OK." But Tommy felt no enthusiasm, and he could see by the look that Corey was giving him that Corey was not fooled. There wasn't anything else to say though, except for a question. "Would Mom and Dorrie be going along?" If they were, then everything would be all right.

"I don't think so."

Tommy sat down on the buggy tongue again and began making figures in the soft, fine dirt floor with his finger. "When are you—are we going?"

"We have to wait for the heavier snows to melt so we can get there. It depends on the weather, and how much sunshine the mountains get. Another three weeks or a month. Maybe July, maybe August. But we could make our plans, right?"

"Yeah, I guess so."

Corey got up and put his hand on Tommy's shoulder. "When you feel up to it, come on over. Tell your mother I said it's all right."

"Okay. Thanks."

147

"And Tommy? . . ."

Tommy looked up.

"When you decide you want to talk about anything, feel free. I can be an understanding guy."

Tommy had another strong urge to wrap his arms around Corey's waist and never let go, but as he stood up he doubled his fists and shoved them deep into his pocket. "Yes, sir."

Tommy followed Corey out into the sunshine. He had been in the old carriage house for so long the sun hurt his eyes. Still, he watched as Corey crossed the yard and went to the faint little path that led through the trees to his trailer house. Within yards, he was out of sight and there was nothing left but the numerous tall, dark trunks of pines and the deep and perpetual shadows among them.

Tommy went toward the house, up the back steps, across the porch and to the kitchen door. He could smell something good, like cookies baking, but it didn't make him hungry.

Stephanie spotted him. "You can't have any unless you wash up the dishes for me," she said.

Tommy crossed the kitchen floor, and went toward the hall. "I don't want any."

Stephanie stared at him, her lower lip hanging down in surprise and disappointment. "What's the matter with him, is he sick?"

Elsea watched him go on through the door to the hall. "I think he's bored. Since school was out he doesn't act himself. There isn't much to do here that's fun."

"I've noticed," Stephanie said. "I'm getting fat."

She listened, expecting Tommy to call back some insulting remark, but he didn't. His footsteps faded away, going slowly, wandering without purpose.

Tommy stopped at the base of the back stairs. He looked up. He had heard every word his mother and sister had said, but hadn't felt like saying anything. He thought of Dorrie, and called back to his mother, "Where's Dorrie?" He knew, and yet he hoped he was wrong.

"She's in the attic playing."

Tommy's throat tightened. Slowly he began to climb the stairs.

He felt mad at Dorrie. And at the same time he felt afraid for her. Why didn't she come downstairs and go outside with him? Together they could look at all the junk in the carriage house. She hadn't even seen the buggy that he knew of. Also, their mother would probably let him take her down to the creek if they were careful, and he would be. He'd watch her closely, and make sure she didn't fall in. Together there were a lot of things they could do. But instead, she hid herself in the attic, and then told him things that were not true, but made him have bad dreams. And at night, when he heard the movements in the attic he always thought of what she'd said. He couldn't separate his fear from his anger.

But he was going to have it out with her. Seeing Corey had in some way made up his mind. He wanted to go back to looking forward to a trip to the mountains. He wanted to do all the interesting things that he had planned to do with Corey.

He opened the attic door and called, "Dorrie!"

149

A long moment passed before she answered. And her answer was as short and curt as his call had been. "What?"

"Come down here."

"Why?"

"I just want you to."

Silence again now, as she didn't answer. He listened for her footsteps to come running across the floor, but they didn't.

After a long silence she said, "Come up here, Tommy, and see my dolly."

Tommy slowly began to climb the steps. When he looked out over the top he saw his little sister sitting near a toy box with her back to him. Aligned between her and the box were only a few of the stuffed and carved animals and toys that he had seen before. Instead, she had found an assortment of dolls, terrible, ugly old dolls that should have been thrown in a junk pile long ago. Some of them stood tall, taller than Dorrie in her sitting position, with heads of hair half gone, faces scratched and peeling, false eyelashes hanging askew, dresses that had once been very elegant now tattered and torn and faded to ugly pinkish gray.

"Golly, Dorrie, what do you want with those old dolls? They're the ugliest things I ever saw."

She glanced over her shoulder. "Sssh. You'll hurt their feelings."

"Stop that, Dorrie! They don't have any ears or feelings. They can't hear me."

"They can too!"

He had moved closer, and now he saw that in her

150

lap a pink, naked thing was moving and wriggling in her hands. Tiny hands with fingers missing twisted and turned and writhed. The body too writhed, like some repulsive slug from out of the ground, and to Tommy's horror he saw it had a head, and in that head was one eye, and it fastened on him and gleamed with an evil, mindless power.

Somebody made a gurgling cry in his throat. It might have been him, but he wasn't sure. As soon as he recognized what Dorrie held, as soon as he saw it was the celluloid doll moving about in her hands like his nightmares come to life, he reached down for it and snatched it away from her.

It felt slippery and rubbery in his hands, and before he could throw it to the floor it had wrapped its arms and legs around his wrist, and he had to use his other hand to wrench it away, to try to wrench it away, for it clung as though it had adhered itself to him permanently, the one eye gleaming at him as though the devil had personally infused it with life.

Tommy was half screaming, and so was Dorrie, on her feet, reaching up for her doll as Tommy tore it free from his wrist.

He shoved away from Dorrie and threw the doll to the floor, and then he stomped on it, and stomped and stomped, until the doll was nothing but a flattened mass of celluloid. The bead eye rolled across the floor and stopped, its blue glass reflecting the light in the ceiling.

Dorrie was crying in a horrible, wounded way. She rushed past Tommy to the broken doll and gathered it up into her hands. She hovered over it,

151

holding it against her stomach. Her voice at last began to vocalize definite sounds, words. "Oh. Oh! *Oh!*"

Tommy turned and fled. He was shaking so hard, and the tears were falling so fast, that he was almost helpless in finding his way out of the attic. He stumbled going down the steps and almost fell. With his hands out against the walls, he finally made it to the lower hall, and at last to his bedroom. He fell across the bed and wiped his face on his arms.

The tears were gone, but his body was still shaking. He felt as though he had been wrapped in ice since the day he was born. It permeated his bones and made them feel brittle, and it had gone into his brain and numbed it against all reason. He couldn't think, he could only feel.

And he felt as though he were in one of his nightmares, for what he had just seen did not happen in real life.

Dorrie's tears dropped onto the broken celluloid doll.

It was only a pink blur in her eyes as she cradled it tenderly in her hands. In a sobbing whisper she encouraged, "Please, dolly, live. Please, don't be to dying. Don't be killed. Oh, ohhh."

She kissed it, and her lips were scratched by its broken body. She wiped the tears from her eyes and began to work with it, straightening the ripped edges, pressing them together again. Pressing the legs back to a semblance of curves instead of the terrible flat celluloid sheets Tommy had made of them. The head, with no eye at all now, was mashed as flat as the legs, and across the top, on the molded hair, was a slit long enough that Dorrie could insert her finger. Working slowly and carefully, her finger inside the doll's head, she pushed the face round again, and the back of the head, and the sides. The torn part of the skull came together on her finger and began to cut, and she withdrew it, and looked with sorrow at her doll. It would never be fixed again, never.

Dorrie crawled across the floor and retrieved the eye. She dampened the back of it with saliva from her tongue, and tried to make it adhere to the hole where it once had been. It fell away in her hands.

She began to weep again, silently, her mouth quivering.

The doll moved. Feebly. One tiny hand clutched her finger. With a lurch in her heart, Dorrie brought the doll to her face and began kissing it, and comforting it in whispers, for never, never again would she let Tommy, or anyone else, know about her dolls and her toys.

"It's all right, my dolly. You're not to dying after all. You're going to be all right. It won't matter if your eyes are all gone. I'll lead you."

She set the doll on the floor, and watched as it began scrambling away, dragging itself on its side with the leg she had put back together, and the one arm that had missed being destroyed. Over by the toy box one of her new creations, a tall china doll with bits of hair sticking to a cloth scalp, began to

153

take steps toward the celluloid doll, walking in stiff-legged animation, and far back in the attic, behind the rows of boxes and piles of furniture, came the running steps of scores of little feet. Dorrie recognized the clop, clop of the horse, and the soft padding of the lion, and the sliding movements of her monster, the one with four horns, a long snout, and odd little ears set low on the sides of its head. She began to hear something new, too, as she listened, something that made her heart leap with joy, that made her forget what Tommy had done to her celluloid doll.

Voices.

Tiny, soft, high, low, murmuring voices. They were talking to her. Soon, if she didn't stop them, they would be talking to everyone, and then they would be destroyed, they would be killed again, and all her work and her wishing would be killed too.

She jumped up and ran, her fingers to her lips, looking at all of them, the kitty on the top of the pile of boxes, the horse that was climbing up to the top of another pile, the monster, the dolls that had wandered into the darkened areas of the attic, all of them that she could find.

"Ssh! Be very quiet. You must not talk to anyone but me. You must not!"

The cat jumped just as she passed beneath the box on which it stood, and the sound it made as it came toward her face was a soft *sssst*. Its lips were drawn back, showing teeth Dorrie hadn't known were there, claws stretched out, curved and long and sharp. Dorrie stood unmoving, staring as it came

154

full length against her face. The claws on its front feet caught her on the scalp, in her hair, and the claws on its hind feet pierced the neckline of her shirt.

She grasped it around the body, instinctively, and pulled. But the claws hung fast, stinging, sinking into her head, tearing at her shirt collar.

"You're hurting me, kitty cat." She wasn't quite crying again, but tears were close beneath the surface of her surprise, her confusion. "Don't kitty!"

At last she pulled it away, and it twisted in her hands and reached its claws for her arm. She dropped it quickly to the floor, then stood back and watched as it spat at her once more before it ran into a dark, small tunnel made by the pile of boxes.

She hurried back to the area of light, and put her hand to the tiny stinging wounds of her head.

When she drew her hand away there were flecks of blood on her fingers.

Elsea sat at her desk trying to think. Sometimes she wrote a few words, and sometimes she back-tracked and X'd them out. But she had a scene in mind that she felt would work, if only she could keep her mind on her work. During the day she tried hard not to think about Corey and what they had done together, but at night it nearly drove her crazy. Lying in her lonely bed she was torn between wanting him and feeling that there was nothing wrong with wanting him, and feeling it was worse than adultery. Worse, much worse, because she was being disloyal to someone she had loved very much, someone who wasn't with her through no action of his own. He stood in spirit beside her, and guilt was eating her alive.

It was so much better during the day when she could keep her mind occupied with other things. Her characters were becoming her saviors.

She heard footsteps behind her just as a clear-cut sentence entered her mind and was ready for transference onto paper. Not Dorrie this time, or Stephanie.

She leaned back in the chair and asked with a disgusted sigh, "All right, Tommy, what is it?" She immediately was sorry she had been so short with him, and turned away from the desk and gave him a smile. "Sorry, hon. Got something on your mind?" She frowned, her thoughts now totally on Tommy, for he looked unhappy, lost, sad. He looked much like he had during the week of his daddy's funeral.

"Mom, you busy?"

"Not too busy, Tommy. Is something wrong?"

He wandered to her desk, went around the other side and began riffling papers. But she could see that he was not reading. His handling of the paper, the paperweight, the picking up and putting down of anything his hands touched, was almost unconscious in its action. Yet he didn't answer her.

She asked, "Can't you find anything interesting to do since school let out?"

He shrugged.

"Maybe you could mow the yard more often, then the job wouldn't be so hard. The shorter the grass is, the easier it is to mow."

Still he said nothing. He kept picking up and putting down, his long-lashed eyes avoiding direct contact with hers. She began to wonder if his problem was like her own lately—comprised of guilt for having done something against his own morals.

"Are you in some kind of trouble, Tommy?"

"No."

"Then what is it? You didn't come in here just to rearrange the stuff on my desk, did you?"

He put down the pen he had picked up and stuck his hands into his pockets. "Mom," he said, "I want you to make Dorrie come down out of the attic."

"What?" She couldn't believe it. Was this all? "Why?"

"Because—"

She waited, but he said no more.

"Because why, Tommy?"

"Because she doesn't need to stay up there all the time, Mom!" He was suddenly, surprisingly adamant, his voice stringent, his eyes screwed up into a scowl. "That's no place for a little kid like her to play! There's no sunshine, or fresh air, or anything. Just that dusty, dirty old junky attic! It's not even a fit place for mice or rats. Or squirrels either for that matter! It's no place for her to play. I even found her asleep up there one day right after we moved here. And I never see her playing anywhere else. I want you to make her come down!"

"Tommy! You're giving me orders! Like a drill sergeant or something."

Tommy's shoulders slumped. He looked away.

157

Elsea asked, "Why on earth does it bother you that she likes to play up there? And she isn't there all the time, as you seem to think. She does come down."

"When? Just to eat or sleep!"

"Tommy, there's more behind this than—well, you act as though you're jealous or envious that Dorrie has something that entertains her."

"I am not! I wouldn't touch those ugly old toys she plays with. Mom, have you seen what she plays with? She's got a crazy little doll that's only got one eye, and stubby little hands that someone chewed the fingers off of, and it's made out of some kind of material they haven't used in a hundred years!"

"Celluloid."

Tommy's face was contorted again, and his eyes were narrowed as if he were having trouble keeping tears back. "What?" he demanded.

"Celluloid," Elsea said. "And of course I've seen the doll, and it's made of celluloid and what difference does it make how old it is?"

"Well, why doesn't she stay in her own room and play with her own toys?"

"I suppose because the old ones upstairs are more fascinating. If you'd take a look at them yourself, all of them, you might find something interesting too."

"No!" he shouted. "No! I want you to make Dorrie come down!"

Elsea stood up. It hurt to get angry with him, but never in his life had he talked to her as he now was. And she couldn't, wouldn't allow it.

"Tommy, I'll have no more of that talk from you.

158

Understand? I am still your mother, and I still expect you to have some respect for me. I don't understand your reasons for insisting that I make Dorrie come down from the attic, and if you have a sensible reason I'll listen to it, but you've got to talk to me in a civil tone. Do you understand that?"

Tommy had dropped his chin to his chest, and Elsea was looking down on the top of his head. When he answered her it was with contrition in his voice, but also hesitations as though he were sobbing softly somewhere deep within himself.

"I—I didn't mean to yell at you, Mom. I just worry about her." He made a small lunge at Elsea and wrapped his arms around her waist and held his head on her chest. He had grown so tall that his hair was against Elsea's cheek as she put her head against his.

"Mom," he whispered, "I'm afraid she'll get hurt up there."

Elsea patted his shoulder, held him close in her arms, and felt an odd, twisting hurt in her stomach.

"But Tommy, it's really a very safe place. She's been playing up there since the first day we came, and she hasn't been hurt yet. It's far safer than having her outside wandering around."

"I'd watch her, Mom, if you'd make her come outside with me."

"Tommy, when Dorrie gets bored with all the things in the attic, she'll come down on her own."

"I want her to come down now."

That tone of voice was coming back. Tommy drew away and looked up at his mother. Elsea looked perplexed into the shadows of his eyes, trying to understand.

"Tommy, you have never been like this before. I know you must feel lost here, with not much to do, no friends close. If you want Dorrie to come down and play with you, why don't you ask her?"

"She wouldn't for me. You ask her, Mom."

Elsea's patience ran out suddenly. If it weren't Stephanie asking about the recipe for something, now that she was in a phase of cooking everything that struck her fancy, it was Tommy with his sudden demands.

"I will not ask her. I will not tell her to stop playing in the attic. Dorrie is the only one of you three who doesn't make silly demands on me. Now when you can come to me with a reasonable excuse for making Dorrie change her method of play, you say so, and until then go find something to entertain yourself with. And if you can't entertain yourself, try doing some work. The porches need sweeping, the grass could stand a mowing. Just try to keep yourself busy, and leave me alone!"

She put her hand to her mouth, too late, for Tommy was running from the room. She called out, "Tommy! Come here, please."

But he was gone, and a few moments later she heard the front door slam.

That night she stared into the darkness in which her bedroom ceiling was lost and let her thoughts drift. Tommy had stayed out all afternoon, and

160

when she saw him again at dinner, he had nothing much to say. That was typical of him lately. Although she hadn't told him again that she was sorry, mainly because she didn't want to have to explain anything to Stephanie, she had kissed him. So in a way she had let him know that of all things she didn't want to fight with him. His demands that she make Dorrie play elsewhere than the attic had turned her attention to the little girl more strongly than ever, and she saw that Dorrie was practically nodding over her plate, she was so tired and sleepy. Right after dinner Elsea carried Dorrie upstairs, bathed her and put her to bed. Dorrie had never been a talkative, energetic child. Was she even less so now? Whatever she did in the attic certainly took all of her attention, was it taking her energy too? Maybe it would be better for both her and Tommy if she were made to spend at least an hour a day out of doors.

Corey . . . as she drifted into a relaxed state, her thoughts went to him against her will. Her body betrayed her, and went liquid with longing. She turned over, changed positions, and for a few minutes it helped, but as she drifted toward sleep the needs of her body took over again, and she knew she would dream of him again tonight, taking in her dreams what she couldn't allow herself to take in reality. She had forgotten what a thrill it was—or perhaps she had never really felt the kind of thrill that Corey's touch gave her, or even the nearness of him, a look from his eyes meant only for her . . . and so the guilt came back. Vern was her husband, and

161

as though his feelings had now become hers, she was hurt for him to think that she could turn away so quickly after his death into another man's arms.

It was something she would not do again. *Would not.*

A sudden rush of almost inaudible movements began above her ceiling. Like a soft rush of air moving leaves across a lawn, or paper across a floor, something came from deeper in the attic and crossed into the area above her room. Her attention focused, seeing the attic, the stacks of furniture and boxes that were pushed to the front of the house, which was the section above her room. It had been quite awhile since she had heard noises up there, and now as she listened, she thought she heard murmurs, voices, tiny and pixieish. Not mice, not squirrels. Not chirping of any kind, or squeaking. But in some way humanized, fine, tiny, like the characters in a cartoon.

What on earth? . . .

She was sitting up, straining to hear. But all her ears detected now was the wind. It had come up sometime in the past few minutes and now whistled faintly under the eaves, a musical sound that she might have misinterpreted as coming from the attic.

She lay down again, stretching onto her side with one leg pulled up in her most comfortable position. And just before she fell asleep a thought entered her mind. Was it really the wind she had heard? For again, the night was still.

Completely still.

Later, when her door closed softly, she did not

hear it.

Tommy had not slept any. He stayed awake at night as long as he could, with his light on and his door open. He watched the hallway, and at times he went to his door and checked to make sure the attic door was still shut. The time would come, he knew, when he would find that door open. For every night, sometimes at midnight, sometimes nearer three or four in the morning, he would hear them come down the attic steps to the door, and the fumbling at the knob would begin.

So he had decided there was one thing he could do. Only tonight he had decided that. After his mother and sisters were asleep he would close their doors, to keep them safe, and only then, only when the pink light of dawn came into the far eastern sky, would he allow himself to sleep.

He went first that night to his mother's door, and he stood in the dark listening to her soft, even breathing. As quietly as he could then, he shut her door. He went back down the hall to Dorrie's door, and after a hesitation he went into her room and leaned over her. He could see she had something in bed with her, but he couldn't make it out well in the darkness in her room. He snapped on her bedside light, and saw with immense relief that it was only her old teddy bear with the dented nose. There was nothing weird about this toy, or any of the toys in the pink and blue toy box against the wall. Tommy started to turn out the light, but stood instead looking at her face. She was almost as pale as the pillow beneath her head, her almost-black hair making the contrast scary, because it occurred to Tommy that something was wrong with Dorrie. She was getting sick. The toys in the attic were doing something terrible to her.

Couldn't anyone else see that?

Couldn't their mother see? Or Stephanie?

He had tried to talk to their mother, and couldn't. Even as he tried to tell her, he knew she would think he was crazy and might even send him away to a hospital, thinking it was for his own good. And there, no one would believe him. He had thought about making Dorrie tell, but no one would believe her, either. He hadn't, when she had told him.

He had to try one more time. He had to talk to someone who might believe. Who hadn't grown so old yet that she would scoff at him. After all, hadn't she been with him the night they went into the attic and the horse attacked him?

He would make Stephanie believe.

As he left Dorrie's room he closed the door, and he wished he had a way of locking it. But there were no locks on any of the inside doors that he knew.

Locks.

He looked at the attic door, with its little thread of light at the bottom. And he knew what he was going to do tomorrow. He would find an old lock in the carriage house and he would put it on that door.

But, for now, he had to talk to Stephanie.

She was snoring. He could hear her even before he crossed her threshold. For a minute he almost forgot

164

his mission. She would hate knowing she snored, and if he didn't want her cooperation he'd tease her about it. He couldn't resist saying something as he shook her awake.

"Hey, you're snoring!"

"What?" She almost jumped out of bed, and then when she saw who it was she slapped him on the chest and shoved him back. "Tommy, what are you doing here? How come you woke me up?"

"You were snoring so loud I couldn't sleep." He knew he shouldn't be saying this, but the temptation was too great. Now, in her room, with the strength of her company, he was less afraid than he had been for hours.

"I don't snore! Now go away, Tommy." She snuggled down into her bed. The light from his room made a faint track from her door to her bed, fading almost to nothing. With his back against the light, she could not see the expression on his face. But she had a feeling that it was something else that had brought him to her room, not her snoring. Knowing him, she had never snored much in all her life or he would have said something before now. So she asked, when he didn't move to leave, "What's the matter?"

"I've got to tell you something, if you'll promise you'll believe me."

"Sure, I promise."

"Promise, really promise."

"Yeah, I do," she said, losing patience. She yawned. "Hurry up. It must be at least midnight."

"No, not yet. It's eleven-thirty. Listen, Steph, do

you remember how that horse fell off the top of the boxes and bit my arm when we went up into the attic that night?"

"*Bit* your arm!" she said with derision. "How could it bite your arm? It scratched it, dope."

"You promised to believe me, and already you're making fun."

Stephanie stared at him, tried to see him, and finally sat up and turned on her light. His face was serious.

"Okay, Tommy, it bit you. Then what?"

"You've got to believe me. You promised."

Stephanie frowned, puzzled, almost afraid, beginning to be oddly afraid. She drew back away from Tommy. What was wrong with him? He'd been strange lately, going around with his head down, not talking much, staying out by himself somewhere, not even eating all the cookies and brownies she had been baking. Something crazy was going on, and she wasn't sure she was going to believe anything.

"What?" she asked cautiously.

"You know the sounds in the attic?"

"I haven't heard anything lately."

"That's because most of the part they play in is over my room, not yours or Mom's. Mine. The place where Dorrie plays is over my bedroom, and I hear things all night long. I even hear them come down the attic stairs and try to open the door."

Stephanie half-laughed, and said with obvious doubts, "Squirrels?"

"No," Tommy said, slowly and with special

166

enunciation of his words, "the toys, Stephanie. The toys up there are *alive*."

"*You're crazy!*"

It was almost a shout. An abrupt, spontaneous objection that burst from her without planning or thought. Tommy sank down, sitting on the side of her bed, slumping, his head lowered. Not angry, but something else. A kind of hopelessness in him that stirred pity in Stephanie even as she wanted to pull away from him in dread. Was he really going crazy or something?

"I knew you'd say that," he whispered. "I just knew it. I don't know why I bothered. I wish I hadn't. But I didn't know what else to do. Nobody's going to believe me."

He got up and Stephanie made no effort to stop him as he left her room. She didn't object when he pulled her door shut behind him.

For several minutes she sat in her bed staring at the opposite wall, wondering about Tommy. She was beginning to wish they could move somewhere else, for things weren't right here in this house, in the country so far from anyone. The only good part was Corey.

She looked up, and thought of the attic, pictured it in her mind. The top of the stairs came out just about the edge of Tommy's room, and, as he had said, the portion of the attic that was cleared of junk, the area in which Dorrie played, was probably right over his room, at least in part. And she hadn't told him the truth when she said she hadn't heard any sounds lately, for she had. But she had tried not to hear, and she thought that at last she was getting used to the occasional little padding sounds that might be a small, running rodent. If you let your imagination go, strange things could happen to you.

See what had happened to Tommy.

He was going crazy, and that scared her more than anything else.

ELEVEN

Tommy slept better just knowing that all the bedroom doors were closed, and if the toys did manage to get the attic door open, they would be blocked by the other doors. Once they got out of the attic, what would they do? Maybe they wouldn't hurt anything at all. Dorrie played with them every day, and they didn't hurt her. But on the other hand, maybe it was like a master with a horde of vicious animals . . . no, not animals. He couldn't think of them as animals even though a lot of them were in animal form. They were something else. Something that struck dumb fear in him because he didn't know what they were.

He slept heavily when he slept, with an occasional nightmare that was no worse than waking up to realize that his real world had become worse. When morning came he was up and out of the house earlier than anyone else. The doors were still closed when he hurried quietly along the hall and down the stairs.

In the carriage shed he searched through piles of rusted hardware for a lock, any kind of lock, and found none. He went on to another shed, and still found nothing. The sun was well up, shining brightly when he heard sounds in the kitchen and knew he had to go eat, and he had to act like nothing had happened last night so that Stephanie would forget she had called him crazy. Sometimes, when he stopped to think about it, he wondered if he had actually become crazy, like one boy he had known in school back home, with terrible hallucinations in which he couldn't tell what was real from what was not real.

It was something to think about.

It was better than the other.

Maybe he should go to a hospital somewhere, like the other boy had, and let the doctors make it all go away. Maybe he would find that he was really back in Los Angeles in the apartment, and that his daddy hadn't died, that none of this had happened.

But then he thought of Corey. And he knew he couldn't imagine someone as great as Corey, for next to his very own dad, Corey was the greatest.

Would Corey help him, or would Corey start thinking he was crazy too?

After he ate his breakfast, which he had to force down so that Stephanie would stop looking at him with those funny, sideways glances, he went back outside. And suddenly he saw something he hadn't noticed before. The carriage shed had a kind of lock

170

on the small door, on the outside of the building, a very simple little block of wood that was nailed to the wall loosely so that it could be turned to hold the door.

It would do. It was better than none. He could transfer it without much trouble or noise to the attic door.

He took a claw hammer from the shed and pried the block of wood off the wall. Then with the button lock and a long, sturdy nail in his pocket, he went into the house through the front door so that no one would see him and ask him questions.

But when he reached the attic door he looked at it helplessly. If he began hammering now, all of them would come and ask him questions. Also, he would be locking Dorrie upstairs with those things.

So at last he turned away and hid the button lock, the nail, and the hammer underneath his bed. He would wait until they went shopping. Then he would stay home alone, and he would nail the button on the attic door, and he would lock it at night and open it early each morning and no one but him would ever even notice it was there.

Dorrie cried out softly in pain, and turned to see what had bitten her on the back. It was the horse, turning now to scurry away as though it wanted her to chase it. She rubbed her back, and the pain eased, and then she began searching for the horse in the game of hide and seek.

"One, two, three, here I come, ready or not."

She peeked into little dark tunnels beneath

furniture, among piles of boxes, and in one she saw two eyes gleaming in the dark. "I found you," she cried joyously and reached in. The bite on her hand was unexpected and cutting, the pain stinging as though the teeth of the little horse contained a poison, and she drew back swiftly, perplexed, bewildered at this turn her playmates were taking against her. She left the little wooden horse and went back to the dolls by the toy box. Most of the dolls she had brought out from other boxes had bodies of fabric stuffed with straw, and heads made either of china or another kind of hard material from which the outer layer, the skin, peeled in hideous strips. But she didn't mind that they were ugly. They were hers, and they were very old, and she had brought them back from dying to living, and they walked, and now they were beginning to talk, with little voices that were soft and musical, but they talked with words and sounds she didn't understand, and sometimes when they talked among themselves and looked at her as they talked, she felt isolated from them, and she felt they were in some way aligning themselves against her, and the reason they talked in a language she couldn't understand was because they didn't want her to know what they were saying. Sometimes she felt as though she was no longer wanted, or needed, except when they came to her and put their mouths to hers in a kind of long kiss, in which they drew from her the breath she had first given them to make them live.

Sometimes she felt she should leave the attic now. That they didn't want her there anymore.

That was why the kitty cat scratched her and

172

hissed at her. That was why the horse bit her and bruised her skin with his hooves and ran to hide from her. Sometimes they all hid, so that when she came into the attic none of them were there to play with her, and she would have to search and search before she found them.

At other times they rolled on the floor with her, and gave her long, long kisses, until she was so tired she fell asleep. And as she lay with her eyes closed she could hear them whispering, whispering among themselves, as though they were talking about her.

She didn't like the little wood horse very much anymore. Nor the kitty with the straw coming out the seams and the fish hook claws. Nor the monster with the horns and the long snout. She didn't like the way they were hurting her with their bites, their scratches, their mean little ways.

She sat down beneath the light and looked around. Not even her little celluloid doll, her favorite of all, was really hers anymore. It never stayed on the bed she had made for it. Now, again, it was gone, like most of the others. Listening, she could hear them moving about, in all directions. A whisper here, a little clump, clump there as something ran in the darker parts of the room.

She remembered something she had heard another child say in nursery school one day.

"I'm not going to play with you anymore if you don't be nice," she said aloud, just as that other child had. She waited, looking around. For a while the room was very quiet. Then the celluloid doll came out from behind a box in its odd little crawl, and made its way to her using one arm and one leg.

Though it no longer had any eye at all, it knew where she was. She rushed to meet it and gathered it up to her face with a loving kiss.

"I'm not mad to you, dolly, really I'm not."

She heard soft footsteps, and looked around, and the dolls with the straw bodies, their little feet wearing soleless shoes that were faded with age, came walking out, their eyes gleaming in the shadows like the eyes of an animal in car lights at night.

They came to her with their arms out, soft arms with cloth hands and a separate little thumb on each clubby hand. Their faces, peeling skin, scraggly hair falling in all directions, came to her for her kisses, and sucked at her mouth, smothering her so that she hardly had breath left for herself. Their arms, so soft, had a strength beyond her own, so that as they tightened around her neck, like the bodies of snakes, she began to feel strangled. She tried to talk to them, to tell them they were hurting her, but her voice was closed off only to a deep, soft cry.

She began to struggle against them, rolling on the floor to dislodge them, pulling at their arms with her hands. But still they held on, though their bodies were flattened beneath hers, and though her fingers dug into their arms and pulled at their hair.

She was gasping for breath, and at last she began to cry, to sob. And as though they had been playing a kind of game with her, suddenly they released her, and murmuring amongst themselves they ran away from her again, back into the darkness from which they had come.

Dorrie scooted closer to the top of the stairs

174

leading down from the attic, and sat up directly beneath the light. She wiped tears from her cheeks and looked around. She was alone again. Even her little celluloid dolly was gone.

She had never felt so alone.

After a few minutes she got up and went down from the attic, slowly, unhappily, wondering, why didn't her toys, her dollies, like her anymore?

For the first time she forgot to shut the attic door.

Elsea ran the vacuum cleaner over the carpet in the hall, and moved on into the corner front room that had been called a parlor by her grandmother. It was a rather pretty room, very fussy by today's standards, with lots of bric-a-brac, too much furniture, and quaint little doilies on the tops and backs of chairs and sofas, and even on tables beneath lamps. Some of them had been crocheted, and some tatted. All of them, Elsea suspected, had been made by Grandmother, or maybe some, the more fragile ones, by her grandmother's mother or aunts. It was a room well-preserved, rather dark with few windows, and hanging on its walls were old photographs of people who looked as though their faces would break if ever they smiled. Why, she wondered, were all old photographs and paintings of such somber quality? As though it had been a sin to look happy.

Elsea bent to vacuum beneath a chair. The sofa, a few feet away, angled from the chair but with its back to a wall, had legs at least six inches high. From the corner of her eye she saw something dart back into the dark beneath the sofa. At first she drew back, slightly startled, with a revolting feeling that she was going to come face to face with a mouse. And yet she knew it couldn't have been a mouse, for it was much too large for that. With that realization a chill went over her. What was living here in her grandmother's house? Not rats, heaven forbid.

She shut off the vacuum cleaner and lay the hose down. In the sudden silence nothing moved. Whatever it was was hiding from her.

Elsea got down on her knees and looked under the sofa, and at first she thought that whatever she had glimpsed had gone on elsewhere, for nothing moved there now. In fact, there was nothing at all under the sofa except a doll, pushed tightly back against the wall, lying on its side.

Elsea stared at it, then went on looking beneath other furniture in the room. There was no rat, no other living creature in the old parlor.

The whole thing had been her imagination.

She went back to the sofa and reached under and dragged the doll out. It was one of the ugliest things she had ever seen. Its large body was made of straw, even to its feet, and held together by a grayed material that had tiny holes here and there from which bits of the straw stuck out like pins. Its head was made of some kind of molded material from which the outer layer had peeled in long strips. Strands of coarse, artificial hair still were glued to the scalp in places, but it looked as though some child, long years ago, had combed it nearly to nothing, leaving huge bald spots revolting in their ugliness.

There was no dust on the doll.

Its nose, the only part of its face that was not peeling, was pink, as though it had been rubbed recently. Its blue glass eyes gazed at her with a jeweled depth that she found unnerving for a moment, before she began to laugh at herself.

She knew where the doll had come from, and how it had gotten there. Dorrie, of course. But why had she pushed it so far beneath the sofa?

Elsea took the doll back upstairs, opened the attic door and laid it on the step. She called out, "Dorrie? Here's a doll you left downstairs."

There was no answer, although sounds of movement reached Elsea's ears as she waited.

Louder, she called, "Dorrie?"

And from her bedroom, behind Elsea, Dorrie's voice answered sleepily, "What, Mama?"

Elsea turned away from the attic door in surprise and went quickly to Dorrie's bedroom. The little girl was on her bed, huddled tightly around her old brown teddy bear.

"Why, baby, I thought you were upstairs. What are you doing here?" She sat on the bed beside Dorrie and smoothed back the soft and silky hair from her perfect, beautiful little face.

"I got tired," Dorrie said. Her lower lip trembled. "And my toys don't like me anymore."

"Of course they do. They love you, we all love you."

"No. Even my celluloid dolly doesn't like me anymore."

"Why, Dorrie, what a thing to say. You must be feeling very sorry for yourself today, right? When we

177

think nobody likes us that means we're feeling misunderstood by them, and so we compensate and sympathize with ourselves, and if we brood about it, it becomes self-pity. And that's not very good, is it?"

"I don't know."

Elsea pulled the child into her arms and cuddled her a few moments. "Want to come downstairs with Mama?"

"Okay."

"Want to go to the store and help pick out the groceries?"

"Yes, all right."

They left the second floor, going down the twisting back stairs that were so steep they had to walk slowly and carefully. Elsea kept Dorrie's hand tight in her own to keep her from falling. And not once did she think of the doll, the attic, or the attic door.

She too had left it standing open.

Stephanie was in the kitchen, but Tommy was nowhere in sight.

"Do you have your grocery list, Stephanie?" Elsea asked. "I think we'll take a trip to the market."

"Today? I thought we usually go on Friday."

"I just feel like going today. Wouldn't you like to? We could have a special treat at the drive-in, maybe eat our lunch there. I know Dorrie would love to have a hot fudge sundae after she eats her sandwich." She looked down at Dorrie, but didn't get the response she expected. A faint worry rose. Wasn't Dorrie thinner? Paler? More listless? And wasn't she, herself, borrowing trouble? She had known after Vern's illness that she would have to guard against the fear of seeing those symptoms in her children.

"Where's Tommy?" she asked, even though she knew what Stephanie's answer would be.

"Grief, Mom, I don't know. He hides out so he doesn't have to help with the dishes, I think."

"Well, maybe he'll be happier if he can fill his belly with all that nice junkfood he likes."

"Can we afford it? He eats like a horse when he gets to a drive-in."

Elsea smiled. "I think we might be able to splurge once a month. It's been a long time since we've been out."

"I have to change," Stephanie said, looking critically down at her shorts.

"What on earth for? We're only going to the grocery store and the drive-in, and the shorts you'd change into would probably be exactly like those. Come on. We don't even have to lock up the house. Just get in the car and go. Isn't that great? Such freedom!" She was trying to instill some enthusiasm in her two daughters, but not succeeding too much. Dorrie still clung to her hand, looking as though she would start sleeping the moment she got into the car. And Stephanie was making up her mind about her shorts.

Elsea took her purse from the table by the kitchen door and led the way out. On the back porch she began to call for Tommy. After the third shout he came from around the corner of the house and stood looking at them, his hands in his pockets, the sun turning his hair almost white, silver-blond where it fell forward over one side of his forehead. Elsea's breath caught. All her children were beautiful. How fortunate she was to have this legacy from Vern.

How terrible she was for feeling the presence of Corey, not far beyond the cool, dark trees, and for wanting to run to him, leaving her children behind, out of her hours with Corey, innocent of her experiences with him.

She made herself think of the afternoon, and how carefree she and her children would be, shopping together, sight-seeing perhaps, having a meal out if only at a fast food place.

"Tommy," she said with forced, bright enthusiasm, "we're going to eat out, and then go to the market, and maybe find us a shopping center somewhere. I think we can afford a few dollars for fun. How do you feel about a Big Mac and a ton of fries?"

Tommy's lack of expression changed only slightly. He glanced sideways, toward the house, and hastily looked at his mother again.

"I'll stay here," he said.

"What?" This, she couldn't believe. Tommy refusing a trip to McDonald's?

"I got some things to do," he said.

Stephanie was staring at him open-mouthed. Elsea felt almost as astonished as Stephanie looked.

Tommy could see that he had created a minor upheaval in everyone but Dorrie. Dorrie didn't look as though she gave a damn about anything. He saw she had something hugged in one arm, and with great relief he saw it was her old brown teddy bear. He slumped a little, some of the tension going out of him.

180

"I've been mowing," he said. "It would be easier and faster if we had a power mower. You don't have to push them. It's going to take me all day to finish mowing." And the button on the attic door—that would take awhile too. But at last he had his chance.

"No," Elsea said. "You can finish the mowing a couple of hours at a time the rest of the week. Today, you're going with us."

She sounded as if she meant it.

"But why? If I'd rather stay here, why can't I?"

"Because, Tommy, I want us all to go out and have a good time for a change. We'll forget everything else for the rest of the day, even good nutrition. We'll eat what we want, and drive around a little, and just get away."

Tommy relaxed. He didn't have to make a decision because his mom was laying down orders, relieving him of something he didn't want to do anyway. He had never been left here alone before, and now the thought of staying all by himself made him feel like running.

"OK!" he said, and headed for the car. He was the first in. Settled back and ready to go, he looked up at the roofline of the house, with the peaks and gables that had been built for no good reason at all beyond what the builder had thought was decoration, and he was more than glad to leave it behind for a few hours.

He wished they could leave it forever.

The house was silent. Not even a bird lighted on the roof. There were no sounds from downstairs, no clack, clack from the typewriter, no music from the radio or voices from the television. There were no footsteps. The humans were gone.

The doll on the bottom step of the attic stairs raised its head. The door stood open. Freedom lay beyond. It rose to its feet and leaped down from the step into the hallway.

Above, in the attic, the murmurs began, softly, whispering like faint night breezes. The toy animals, the dolls, began moving, gathering beneath the light at the head of the stairs. The murmurs became chatters, and as they sensed more fully that the humans had gone and given them access to a wider world by opening the door that had enclosed them in the attic, the chatters grew to squeals and chirps and deep-throated grunts of approval. The stronger among them began going down the steps. The weaker lingered behind, waiting, watching, measuring with their sensibilities the depth of each step down, the height of each step back up when the need would come to return. The sounds of their success rose, as their voices reached out from one to the other.

TWELVE

Corey followed the winding path through the trees. He had stayed away from Elsea and her kids as long as he could, and today he finally had thought of a good excuse to go over. For one thing, he was going to help Tommy mow the yard. For another, he had some material on romance writing for Elsea. Any excuse at all that he could come up with lately would do. But no longer could he just drop by as a matter of course, the way he had in the beginning. He was too self-conscious about it, too self-conscious when he was around Elsea. He had to keep his eyes away from her to avoid seeing her in his mind the way she had been that night on her bed, her lovely body naked and pushing against his.

The yard, when he came out from the cool shadows of the forest, was hot and bright with sunshine. No one was in sight. He could see, though, where Tommy had abandoned the old-fashioned push mower at the end of a neatly cut swath of grass.

He went on toward the kitchen door, coming up onto the screened porch.

He stopped abruptly, listening.

The house seemed to be filled with a strange kind of sound, voices that were not human or animal, but an unsettling mixture of the two. It was a soft sound, drifting, waning, rising to distinct chatters, falling away again as though created by a kind of wind that moved through all the chambers and cracks of the shingled house. He took a step across the porch floor, and abruptly all sound was gone. He stood still, listening.

What the hell?

The television, he decided. A child's cartoon show, with crazy background sounds. And someone had turned it off.

The kitchen door stood open and he stopped at the threshold and looked in, knocking as he waited. Stephanie had obviously been cooking again. The counter by the sink had pots and mixing bowls on it. But the kitchen was otherwise neat and empty. There was a pleasant smell of chocolate.

"Hello!"

There was no answer. The silence, in contrast to the sounds he had heard as he came up onto the porch, was almost too silent. He felt conspicuous in his bulky presence, as if he were the only one there.

He walked into the kitchen. "Anybody home?" his shout echoed from somewhere in the house and was magnified by the high ceiling.

There was no answer.

He stood awhile longer, then laid the magazine and dope sheet he had brought for Elsea on the kitchen table. At last he thought to look in the garage for their car. He hadn't thought of it during his approach to the house, but now he was sure it hadn't been parked in the driveway as it usually was.

He went out, saw the garage doors were closed. But a brief peek through the crack in the doors showed him the car was gone.

Disappointment enveloped him. He turned his back on the garage and looked at the old green house. It stood tall and rather ugly, and at this moment, very desolate. But of course he was transferring feelings from within himself. Not once while he thought of excuses to come over had it occurred to him they would be gone.

He went to the lawn mower and began to push, working off his disappointment as the grass went down. If he worked long enough, hung around long enough, they might come home before good sense drove him back to his own digs.

The mower made no noise beyond a faint squeak of one wheel and the snip of sharpened blades against the grass, and once he thought he heard that strange sound in the house again, a drifting of grunts and chatters that reached him above the squeak of the rusty lawn mower wheel, but when he paused to listen, and to wipe the sweat from his forehead, there was no other sound at all beyond a truck climbing a hill somewhere far away.

Corey spent the afternoon mowing and raking, and when at last he put the lawn mower away, the sun was lowering behind the spike tips of the trees to the west. And still Elsea and her children had not come home.

Corey walked slowly around the yard, looking at shrubs, at flowers that grew in protected places. Some of them he recognized as being from perennial bulbs, but others were wild flowers, sowed no doubt by birds that perched on the eaves and dropped the seeds in the soft dirt below. He found a few wayward weeds snuggled in among the roots of the flowers, and pulled them. All the while he watched the road, knowing he should just go on home now and come back another time.

As the sun lowered an uneasiness entered him. What if they had had an accident? A flat tire, engine trouble, or any of the numerous things that could happen and delay their return home?

He considered going after his own automobile and starting in search of them, and wondered if Elsea would appreciate too much concern on his part.

After a few minutes he decided to wait awhile longer and then make up his mind whether to search for them, or back off and mind his own business.

He went around to the porch at the front of the house and sat down. Shadows from the trees across the driveway to the west fell long and unbroken across the yard. The windows in the house reflected the dying light. A gusting wind was rising, tearing at times around the corners of the house, and once again he heard beyond the walls low murmurs, almost-voices, rising, falling. They had a gleeful sound, like wildwood sprites in a child's show. But now he knew it was only the wind.

The car came unexpectedly from behind the trees to the east, and turned into the driveway, its headlights sweeping the trees and angling out directly down the driveway. Corey stood up. They were home, thank God. He'd say hello to them and be on his way.

It was then he heard a sudden rush of quick, little footsteps in the house behind him, going away from the front door that contained the stained glass, down the hall toward the back of the house, toward the stairways, out of the rooms on each side of the hall as though an army of tiny people were gathering toward one goal.

He looked around, staring at the windows of the house. But all they gave him was the reflection of the outdoor light. All within was darkness. And now the sounds were gone, the house was still. And Corey had to face the truth. He had heard no footsteps at all, for there was no one in the house.

The only occupants, Elsea, Stephanie, Tommy and Dorrie, were getting out of the station wagon in the driveway and coming onto the lawn to greet him.

Tommy felt better than he had in a long time. It was good being in town, getting a Big Mac and fries and a shake and going with his sisters and mother to a little park with benches and trees and swings. All of them had been happy, for the first time in a long time. Even Dorrie had laughed and played. And he had swung her and taken her round and round on the merry-go-round until he was dizzier than she was.

Getting home hadn't even been too bad, for Corey was there. The only trouble was Corey didn't stay. Only long enough to help them carry in the groceries as he always did when he happened around on shopping days. He wished his mom would think of something else for Corey to do so they could keep him longer, because otherwise he left too soon. Not that he hadn't done a lot already. Corey had even mowed the whole yard for him. It was just that he wanted Corey to stay. And stay, and stay. When Corey was around, Tommy forgot, almost, the attic and the toys, and his terrible growing fear.

As he watched Corey disappear into the darkness of the forest where the little path led to the trailer house, Tommy said, "Mom, why don't you and Corey get married?"

Elsea gave a sound that was a mixture of many things. Surprise, embarrassment, disbelief that Tommy could have thought of such a thing so soon after his daddy's death. Soon? In some ways, she suddenly realized uncomfortably, it seemed years. A long, long time.

Stephanie said, "I think that's a good idea, Mom. He likes you. And we wouldn't be alone anymore."

"We're not alone," Elsea said, "we have one another. Let's watch a show now and rest awhile before we go to bed. We're all tired."

She led the way into the small room where they had set up their portable television. The reception was not the greatest, and the choice of programs was limited, but at least it was diversion, and at this moment Elsea needed diversion more than ever. The thought of marrying Corey, of being with him always, made her feel breathless and oddly happy. But the thought that her kids were in favor of it, were in fact the first ones to think of it, was unsettling.

Tommy said, "I could talk to him about it."

Elsea at first thought Tommy must be kidding, but his face did not show any signs of amusement.

"If you ever say one word to him of anything even remotely resembling that subject, I'll wring your neck, Tommy! Of all the presumptuousness! And even you, Stephanie. What's the matter with you kids? Now, not one more word. What's on TV?"

Stephanie picked up the *TV Guide* that lay on top of the television, glanced at it and said, "Nothing."

"Fine," said Elsea, settling into a chair she had brought in from the library, one of the most comfortable chairs she had been able to find. There was a sofa for the kids, and a couple of beanbags they had brought from home. "We'll watch it until bedtime."

None of them noticed that Dorrie was not with them, that the beanbag chair she usually was hidden in during a television show was empty.

Dorrie went up the stairs to the second floor and saw the attic door was open. The light from the attic only partly lighted the attic steps, and she went up carefully, one hand on the wall for support. When she came out on the attic floor she saw that all her toys and dolls were gone. The toy boxes stood with lids up, as she had left them, with nothing within except a few old broken things that once had been little wagons, or parts of doll houses, or sometimes just a doll arm, or a doll head. Even the little bed she had made for her celluloid doll was empty, and she had gone to great pains to put the little broken dolly to bed and cover it warmly. But maybe with the summer sun on the roof now, the blanket had become too hot. Sometimes during the day now, it got very hot in the attic. So hot she could hardly breathe.

"Dolly?" she called softly, "where are you?"

Nothing moved, and a dread began in her. Had her toys gotten lost and, without her, gone back to dying? Even if they didn't like her anymore, she didn't want them to die.

"Horsey? Kitty cat? Dolly? Where are you? Come to Dorrie. Dorrie will help you."

She walked quietly to the edge of the light, to the beginning of dark shadows where the boxes made tunnels, and the piles of furniture formed great bulky mountains of darkness. She was hesitant to go into the dark.

"Dollies?" she called, squatting, her hands on her knees as she peered into the black tunnel beneath boxes. "Why don't you answer me?"

She listened, and heard nothing. She waited, and none of them came. At last she got up and went to one of the opened toy boxes that sat on the edge of the lighted area. From the box she took the head of a doll that had no body.

For several minutes she held it in her lap, looking down at it. This dolly had brown eyes, like her own. Almost all the others had blue eyes. This dolly's face was not peeled. And its hair was molded on its head.

It was a perfectly beautiful face. But where was its body?

She lay the head on the floor and began rummaging through the debris in the bottom of the toy box. When she found no headless body in that box, she moved on to the next, and the next. And there, beneath some faded old doll dresses, she found a ragged little body. It was a cloth body, stuffed with rags that were coming out the neck. She sat back and looked at the head on the floor.

"I found you a body, dolly, and I will make you a whole doll again. Just a minute."

She stuffed the rags back into the body. One foot was torn, and rags were stringing through. She stuffed them back also. It was a limp, wobbly body to have to hold up such a heavy head.

"Maybe that's why your head fell off, dolly," she said as she reached for the head. "Here now, Dorrie will make you to living again. Live, dolly, live. I will kiss you and make you live."

She put her mouth against the mouth of the doll, those tiny molded lips that felt so hard beneath her own, and she eased her breath upon it until she felt weak with breathlessness. She looked at the doll's face, and she saw it was different now, that its beauty had a softness it hadn't had before.

She whispered, "You may not have a body like all my other dollies, but you've got the most beautiful of faces, yes you do. And now I'll put your body on you. Just wait. Be patient, little dolly."

She worked, adjusting the doll's neck to the rag throat of the body, but it wouldn't stay. The head dropped off and rolled across the floor. She lay the body aside and reached for the head, and abruptly it moved away from her fingers, spinning, turning upright to stare at her with eyes that threw lights of defiance. The pouted lips were changing, lengthening into a smile that was threatening and ugly.

Dorrie drew back. The dolly head, like all her other toys she had brought to life, seemed not to like her either, and she didn't know why. Unless it was because she hadn't been able to put the body back on again.

"I'll fix it tomorrow," Dorrie said as she stood up and backed toward the stairway. "Tomorrow I'll make you all one piece again, dolly. Don't be mad."

Just before she left the attic she looked around once more for all the toys and dollies she had loved back to life, but none of them were there where she could see them. None except the one doll head on the floor, and Dorrie didn't look at it again, because she didn't want to see the mean look in its eyes.

Dorrie slipped into the television room and into her beanbag. Stephanie saw her, but said nothing. Dorrie lay back, and her eyes drooped. Almost immediately, she fell asleep. It seemed no time at all then that her mother was pulling her up, and taking her upstairs to her bed. She was too tired to cooperate in changing from daytime clothes to pajamas. The last she knew was the kiss from her mother, and then undisturbed sleep took her and held her for several long hours that for Dorrie were timeless.

Tommy closed the attic door before he went to his bedroom, and then sitting on his bed he waited until the sounds of his mother and Stephanie had drifted to silence as each finished with the bathroom and went into her room. He sat on his bed and listened, but the house was quiet. He grew sleepy, and still he listened. But tonight nothing ran across the floor above his bed. Tonight nothing dragged itself, nor whispered, nor moved. Still, before he allowed himself the luxury of sleep he went again to check the attic door. It was shut, but the light from the attic made its pale thread at the bottom. It was something alive like a thin snake made only of light.

He backed away to the safety of his room, closed his door, and went to bed.

At the deepest hour of night, in which life itself is most fragile, they began to move. Out from the boxes they came, from the crevices in the piles of furniture, from all the hiding places they had found. In soft murmurs they began to communicate. They were growing wiser now, and they went down the attic steps and by standing one atop another reached the doorknob that would open the door of their prison. In almost soundless chirps and grunts they discussed the turning of the knob. And the doll that had been blessed with fingers not torn away and lost in the long passage of time stood on the top of the horse's back and with both hands turned the knob.

The door fell open, and they toppled with it and came down into the hall. The sounds of their falling caused Elsea to turn in her bed, but she didn't waken. They huddled together, listening, waiting, sensing in their strange ways the movements of the humans, and at last the stillness of the humans as they slept.

In force then, they went to the door nearest the attic door, and entered the room. Through darkness, needing no light, they surrounded the bed.

Dorrie was smothering. In her dream a huge pillow was being pushed down upon her face, and the pillow became a black cloud that had reached down out of the sky and cut off her breath. She struggled. She tried to cry out. But in her dream she could make no sound.

She woke, and the nightmare fear was replaced by pleasure. They had come to her. All her dollies, her toys, the horsey, the kitty cat, had come to her. In the shadowed room she could see their outlines as they climbed onto her bed, and beside her on the pillow was the doll with the ragged hair and the body of cloth stuffed with straw. It was kissing her, putting its mouth to hers. Dorrie wrapped her arms around the doll and hugged it.

"You're not mad to me any longer? You're not mad!"

She was delighted to see them. She stroked the back of the kitten, and would have patted the horse's head had he not nipped at her hand with his sharp teeth. When the kitten sunk its claws into her neck as

194

it tried to reach her face, she simply pulled it away and then kissed it, for she knew it was her kisses they wanted.

"There," she said. "That'll be all right now, kitty. You'll be all right. Dorrie loves you."

Her daddy had talked to her that way long ago when she had fallen and hurt her knee. Her daddy had always talked with comforting words to her, and kissed her bruises and even her hurt feelings. Those, he found on the top of her head, and he kissed her hair and he said, "There, now my baby will be all right. All her sadness will be gone. It'll be all right now."

So when the dolls crowded upon her, and when the two teeth in their upper lips came down too hard as they searched for her mouth and she was forced to push them away, she then instantly comforted their feelings, in case they should be hurt, by kissing them on top the head.

"There, that'll be all right now, dolly."

She was so glad they had come that she turned on her light so they could play, but then she stopped and looked at them in bewilderment, for the light caused them to seek the shadows in the room, scurrying like rodents, and their faces were almost frightening in the changes she saw. Their eyes had become wild and gleaming, their teeth glinted and seemingly grown in length and sharpness, with bits of moisture dripping from them. Suddenly too they were making sounds. Soft, squeaking, grunting. Objecting sounds.

As Dorrie stared at them, as she drew back toward the safety of her bed, they ran from her. Out the door, into the hall, disappearing from sight.

She waited, but they didn't return. She turned out her light, and only the faint, far away light bulb in the attic kept her room from being totally dark. Still, the dolls and toys did not return.

Dorrie went back to bed, and gathered into her arms the comforting teddy bear that had lived with her all her life.

THIRTEEN

Elsea's alarm rang at seven a.m. She shut it off sleepily and put her feet out of bed. If she didn't put her feet out, she was lost. She had learned from experience that with her feet on the floor whatever little nap she then took was necessarily aborted by the fact that part of her was out of bed. Otherwise she tended to go back to sleep and stay that way until it was too late for whatever she had planned to do. Like getting the kids off to school.

The kids were out of school for the summer, she reminded herself as she sat with her eyes closed and her brain struggling against oblivion, so why did she have to get up at seven? Oh yes, the writing. It was easier, she had found, if she made herself get down to it at least an hour before the kids woke up. If she managed to write even one page she felt she hadn't completely wasted her day, for now she had decided to go ahead and actually finish the book, she would not rest until it was done.

So, down to writing. Yesterday she'd gotten some good scenes going. Whether anyone else liked them was now beside the point. She was beginning to enjoy living in another world for a while. In a way it was better than reading.

She went out into the hall and around the corner to the bathroom. She noticed immediately that the attic door stood open. It should be closed. She glanced into the bedrooms as she passed them, saw Stephanie and Dorrie still asleep. Tommy's door was closed, and she didn't open it. At the attic door she looked up at the dirty bulb that burned night and day and considered turning it off to save electricity, but decided to leave it on for Dorrie. She closed the attic door, and went on past to the stairway going down to the kitchen.

She made coffee, put it on the stove to perk. Then she went back upstairs, took a hasty shower and dressed. When she got back to the kitchen the fragrance of coffee finished waking her. With a cup of steaming coffee in her hand she went into the library and to the desk that held her typewriter.

She stopped abruptly, staring.

On the sheet of paper in the typewriter, in typed capital letters, were the words: "ONCE UPON A TIME THERE LIVED ONCE UPON A TIME THERE LIVED ONCE UPON A TIME THERE LIVED," on and on from the top of the page to the bottom, covering two paragraphs of story she had typed yesterday and continuing on through the section of the page on which she had not yet written.

She set her coffee down and ran for the stairs.

In the upstairs hall she stationed herself in a central section and shouted, "All right everybody, up! Do you hear me? UP!"

She waited, her hands on her hips, her heart pounding angrily at this bit of mischief that had no good reason behind it that she could see.

They came out, one by one, and she waited until they were all there, gazing at her, mouths drooping in surprise, eyes blinking sleepily or widening with astonishment. In all their lives this had never happened before.

Stephanie asked, "What's wrong?"

"I'll show you what's wrong," Elsea said. "Come with me."

They followed behind her down the stairs, her three young ones, coming in order of their birth, with Stephanie in front and Dorrie behind. They followed her from the narrow hall at the base of the stairs into the library and to the desk. Elsea pointed, and looked from Stephanie to Tommy, with her eyes remaining on Tommy.

"Who did this?"

They stared wordlessly at the sheet of paper. Dorrie, standing back, stared too, even though she didn't know what was wrong. She could see the big words all over the sheet of paper, and she recognized some of the letters, but she couldn't read what it said.

Elsea's shoulders slumped. "Tommy, what do you have to say?"

"Dorrie must have done it," he said absently, reading and rereading the words on the paper.

"She's always saying that. She says it a lot. I've heard her say it."

Elsea replied in short, chopped words, "Dorrie can't write, Tommy. She can't read, she can't write, and she can't use a typewriter to write words she can't read!"

"I didn't do it!" Tommy cried, looking at his mother. "Why would I do it?"

"That's what I'd like to know. One of you had to do it."

"I didn't." Tommy was shaking his head, and his voice sounded as though he might cry. No tears came, though. Just a brightening of his eyes and a look of hurt that Elsea couldn't stand. She relented and put her arm across his shoulders.

"I just don't understand why either one of my big kids would do this. And yet, what else am I to think? Dorrie can't write, Tommy. And what reason would Stephanie have for ruining part of my story?"

"But what reason would *I* have? I didn't do it!"

Stephanie said, "Mom, one night Tommy and I thought we heard a burglar upstairs. Maybe someone else came in and did it."

"A burglar? You didn't tell me."

"We didn't want to worry you."

"When you hear something that might be a burglar for gosh sakes I want you to tell me! When was this?"

Stephanie shrugged. "Oh, a long time ago. Before school was out. It wasn't anyone. But someone might have come in last night. I know I didn't do it."

Elsea pulled the sheet of paper out of her typewriter and laid it on the desk. She'd have to retype the paragraphs that had been destroyed.

"OK," she said, her anger gone and replaced by a feeling of tiredness that was more emotional than physical. She had a feeling that Tommy had done it, and yet she couldn't understand why he would. But he was the only one who was beginning to give her trouble. He was the one who wanted to move. He was the only one who might resent her time at the typewriter. Yet why would he take this childish, mischievous way of behaving? Why would he start lying now when he never had before? She sighed. "OK. Go on. Get dressed, and then make your own breakfasts. Eat cereal and grapefruit or something. I'm going to be busy for a while. If Dorrie needs help dressing and making her bed, will you help her, Stephanie? Or Tommy."

They went out of the library, and Elsea went toward the front of the house. There was a possibility that someone else had entered the house, but a very remote possibility. For one thing, a burglar wouldn't have done such a ridiculous thing, he'd have done what most burglars do and steal whatever he could and be gone. But, to make sure no one had entered, she made a point of checking the lower part of the house from the front door to the side doors that were never used, to the most frequently used kitchen door. All of them were still locked. So were the windows, just as she had left them last night.

Finally, she went back to the library and sat down at the desk. She ran a clean sheet of paper into the typewriter and retyped the words from the ruined page.

She was not aware that Tommy stood in the doorway watching her.

Tears filled his eyes, blurring shapes in the room. His mother's figure was blurred, as was the dark hair that hung down her back like the hair of a teenage girl. Sometimes she wore it up in a kind of coil, but this morning she hadn't put it up yet. His heart ached with love for her, with needing her approval. She had thought he was the one who had ruined her paper, and at first he had thought Dorrie must have done it, just for fun and without thinking the way a little kid would do, but then he'd been reminded: Dorrie couldn't read or write.

Then Tommy knew.

The toys had done it.

Somehow, they had gotten down from the attic.

And if they were smart enough now to write words on the typewriter, what else could they do?

A clutching, cold fear was in the middle of his stomach. He hadn't been able to eat any breakfast, and he had a feeling that he wouldn't be able to eat for a long time.

He stepped quietly back from the doorway and went out of the house through the front door, leaving it open, letting the growing warmth of the sunny day spread into the chill of the house.

He crossed the road and went down the hillside to the creek. There he sat on a boulder around which the clear water swirled, and stared at the gravel that was stirred and moved by the swiftness of the mountain stream. A large rainbow trout undulated toward him through the water and looked at him with fishy curiosity. He watched it without interest.

202

His thoughts were back at the house, and with the strange, animated toys that were smart enough now to know a language created by people. Aloud he murmured, "Once upon a time there lived." And again, in deep thought, "Once upon a time there lived!"

Dorrie!

After all, Dorrie had to be responsible. He had heard her say those words a lot, especially right after their daddy was buried, when she talked to her teddy bear. So then she must have talked that way to the toys in the attic, those old, old toys and dolls that were different because—because why? Because they were antique and had heard the voices of many children? And in some way thereby had been made wiser and ready to come alive? How had Dorrie made them live?

He didn't know. But he knew she had. And he wondered, did she have any idea of what she had done?

He got up and started running back toward the house. Breathless, he burst into the kitchen, and he almost collapsed with relief when he saw that Dorrie was still at the kitchen table eating slowly as she always did, when she ate at all. And for once he was glad she was so slow.

"Are you about through, Dorrie?" he asked, glancing sideways at Stephanie. He didn't want to talk in front of Stephanie. She would boo-hoo him out of the house. He had tried to tell her, and she wouldn't believe. If he could just talk to Dorrie now, maybe everything could be reversed, or at least stopped. Something had to be done about what she was doing to the toys, and he was the only one who knew.

Dorrie was nodding her head and pushing back from the table.

He took a washcloth from the towel bar by the sink and wiped her face and hands, talking in low gentle tones, hoping that Stephanie wouldn't hear and get her curiosity aroused. "I want you to come out to the back yard with me, OK? There's something *very important.*" The last two words he whispered close to her ear, and she smiled conspiratorially, ready to play their old game of secrets. It had been a long, long time since they had played that silly game, where Tommy would whisper instructions to Dorrie and she would run and do whatever he suggested, and then their mother or dad or Stephanie was supposed to try to guess what it was. Tommy had almost forgotten the game, but he was reminded now, and glad that Dorrie remembered. That might make it easier to make her understand.

With her hand in his they went out the back door. Stephanie paid them little attention. She went in the opposite direction, toward the room where the television was. There was a morning show she had started watching when school was out, but Tommy didn't even know what it was.

When Tommy and Dorrie reached the back steps they sat down. Tommy continued to hold her hand in his, playing with her fingers unconsciously, feeling their soft, tender tips.

"Dorrie, your celluloid doll that I broke, that I mashed. Did you get it fixed again?"

She looked up at him. This wasn't what she was expecting, and immediately she was suspicious. Why did he want to know? She'd never tell him again, nor show him her dollies and toys again, because she didn't trust him.

"Dorrie." The pressure on her hand became suddenly fierce. "You've got to tell me! Did you get it fixed?"

She jerked her hand away from him. "You hurt my hand, Tommy."

He motioned helplessly with his. They seemed like useless things to him at this moment, appendages that needed something to hold onto, or something to twist and bend and break. He finally clasped them between his knees. Then he tried to think of each word before he spoke it, and tried to make sure his tone of voice wouldn't scare Dorrie away.

"Listen, Dorrie. Remember you told me you made your toys live? The old toys upstairs in the attic?" She stared solemnly and suspiciously up at him, and after a glance down at her he proceeded carefully. "Well, now I believe you." He glanced down at her again, and he saw her lips part and the expression in her eyes change.

She whispered, "You do?"

"Yes."

He looked across the back yard, at the green grass that was beginning in places now to turn brown from lack of water. He looked at the garage, at the old carriage house and the other sheds and barns that were no longer used. He looked at the trees and the sky and he really saw none of it. He waited.

Dorrie whispered again, leaning closer, her

forehead near his chin. "Do you want to go to the attic and see them?"

A terrible chill ran over Tommy. He shivered. The sun, warm on his back, felt as though it had turned to a covering of ice. "No! I don't want to see them."

Dorrie leaned away.

"But I believe you," Tommy said hastily lest he lose her confidence. "And Dorrie, I think you—you shouldn't do it."

"Shouldn't do what?"

"Make them live."

"Why?"

"Because—because you know how mad Mom got because someone wrote on her paper?" Tommy looked sideways down at Dorrie, and saw she was looking puzzled. "They did it, Dorrie. They got down out of the attic and they played with Mom's typewriter and wrote those words all over the page."

Dorrie got to her feet, her fists doubled at her sides, her small body fiercely tense and protective. "They did not! They wouldn't do that."

Tommy felt like yelling at her. He felt like fighting with her, somehow, but he didn't know in what way he could. *"Did you do it?"*

"No! I can't write!" She stalked around in front of him, holding her body stiff. "And neither can my dollies and toys!"

"I think they can, Dorrie, and if you don't stop playing with them I'm going to tell Mom!"

"She said I could play with them." Dorrie's lower lip was beginning to stick out, the preliminary to tears. Her body yielded from its stiffness. "Mama said I could."

Tommy got up and bent over Dorrie. "But she doesn't know what you've done! And I do! And it's wrong, Dorrie, wrong! Don't you know that?"

"It's not!" The tears burst forth, a dam of emotion that overwhelmed Tommy. Dorrie was gasping and sobbing, and Tommy put his arms around her and looked over his shoulder in dismay. He wasn't sure if it would be a good idea for either their mother or sister to get in on this.

"I want my daddy," Dorrie was crying. "I want my daddy. I would make my daddy to living again, too. And he would tell you. He would tell you it's all right to make my dollies to living, too."

Tommy listened to her in horror. He backed away from her. Suddenly he was afraid of his own little sister. What kind of powers did she have? He didn't want to know.

He watched her weep softly, her voice stilled. He watched her hands form into little fists that looked boneless and soft and reach up to rub her eyes. He knew he should reach out and comfort her, but he couldn't. He only kept inching backward away from her, more afraid now of Dorrie than either the attic or the toys in the attic. Suddenly in his mind they were all connected, as though invisible threads ran from one to the other.

Dorrie looked up and stared down the driveway behind Tommy. Tears now in her eyes were mere drops of dewlike moisture clinging to her long, dark lower lashes. Her pink lower lip drooped, and Tommy could see the little white teeth. She was like a doll herself, with the parted lips, the pearly teeth showing, the glistening sparkling eyes.

"Tommy," she said, "there's a car coming in. Who is it?"

Tommy whirled. He hadn't heard a car drive in, but there it was, a small two-tone brown compact. And from it were coming two men he had never seen before. One of them was smiling and looking at him and Dorrie. The other man, the one from the passenger seat, was looking up at the roof of the house, then down at the walls and windows, at the porches, and around the yard. He was an elderly man, with white hair and a white moustache, older than Grandpa, and a lot skinnier than Grandpa. The man who had been driving the car was coming toward them now. A younger man, but still old in Tommy's eyes. He couldn't imagine who they were or what they wanted.

"Hello there, is your mother home?"

"Yes, sir."

"I'm Adolph McGraw from the McGraw real estate company. I've brought Mister Holland to look at the house. He's interested in buying."

Tommy felt as though the man had just handed him a precious gift. "He's going to buy this house?" That meant—that meant—*oh boy!*

"He'll have to look it over, first," McGraw said, still smiling confidently. "Could you run and ask your mother if we have her permission to look through her house?"

"Oh sure! Come on in, she won't care!" Tommy was running backwards, sideways, and any which way he had to in order to get to the screen door and be polite to the visitors at the same time. He burst into the house with a shout. "Mom!" He ran through the kitchen and into the hall and on toward the library. "Mom! A man has come to buy the house!"

Elsea met him at the door. She had seen the car from her windows, and guessed what was happening. If the house sold, where would they live? They couldn't afford to rent a house in town. They couldn't afford an apartment that would take kids. Or even one that wouldn't. But the look on Tommy's face was ecstatic. He whirled to a stop near her.

"This means we can move, huh, Mom!"

"Tommy, settle down, please. I have to go talk to Mr. McGraw and whoever he brought. The house isn't sold yet."

"His name is Holland, and he likes it. He'll buy it."

"How do you know?"

"I can tell! The way he looks at it."

Tommy followed closely at Elsea's heels to the back door. The men were coming in, and pausing to stand in the kitchen and talk to Elsea. Dorrie had followed them into the house and stood there too, and a moment later Stephanie silently joined the group. Tommy stood nervously on one foot then the other, listening to the kind of adult conversation that could drive him away in boredom, ordinarily. Talk that really said nothing specific. But this time he stayed, waiting, hoping to hear the man say he'd take the house.

Elsea looked at her kids, "You stay here while I show Mr. Holland the house."

But the smiling Mr. McGraw said, "It's not necessary that you come along at all. I can show him the house. We don't want to disturb you."

"Oh, fine," Elsea said. "I'll make a fresh pot of

coffee while you look the house over."

The men left the kitchen, and the questions began. From both Stephanie and Tommy, buzzing against Elsea's ears like gnats. "Are they going to make us move? When do we get to move? Are we going down to Grandma and Grandpa's? Will we ever get to see Corey again?"

"Oh keep quiet!" Elsea finally said. "Look, go watch television, or something. Or go outside. Whatever you do keep away from that poor man. He's not used to kids."

"How do you know he's not used to kids?"

"At his age, people seldom are. That's probably why he wants to move out to the country," Elsea said with a smile at Tommy, "to get away from mouthy little creatures like you."

She poured herself a cup of coffee, just as the real estate agent came back into the kitchen.

"Mr. Holland likes the house very much, but he'd like to get a feel of it alone. So I thought I'd join you here for a while if you don't mind."

"Of course I don't mind," Elsea said. "Do you like coffee? Plain? Sweet? Creamed?"

They sat at the table, and Elsea put out a plate of raisin toast. Tommy found himself hollow with hunger, and happier than he'd been in a long time. While his mother and the real estate agent drank coffee, Tommy ate toast and drank milk and listened to the story that was being told about Mr. Holland. He was a man alone, now retired, and he wanted to move back to the kind of home he had lived in when he was a boy. So here he was, looking through Great-grandmother's house. He was going to buy it.

And that meant they would have to move. Tommy didn't care where. A tent in Grandpa's back yard would make him feel good.

John Holland walked through the bedrooms on the second floor and thought of himself with amusement. He was seventy-four years old, and must be entering his second childhood. Why else would he decide to leave the apartment in the complex where he had lived for thirty years and come into the northern mountains of California and buy a house that didn't have another house within a mile? But buy it he would. Furnished. The moment he saw it he felt he had come home. Even the doilies on the chairs downstairs took him back, made him feel as though he had merely been passing time while waiting for this day to return to his life.

He wondered what he would do with all the bedrooms. Never would he close them off, for he couldn't stand a section of a house that was never heated, never enjoyed. He had no family anymore, and so few friends, he could count them on one hand. None of them would ever bother to make a trip three hundred miles to see him. Probably they wouldn't even know where he'd be, for he was leaving nothing behind that really mattered and would do no more than tell them goodbye.

A kind of peace entered him as he stopped by an open window and listened. Somewhere down the hill, beyond the thick growth of trees, water poured downstream. Perhaps over a small dam, or steeply down a canyon made by its own progress in times gone by. He breathed in deeply of the fresh air and his new-found contentment.

The hall turned and twisted, and he passed two open bedroom doors. On one of the beds he saw a teddy bear. The little girl's room. Pretty little girl, resembled her mother a lot whereas the two older ones didn't look an iota like her. They, he thought idly, must look like their father. Good-looking kids, all of them. Now . . . if he had grandchildren, wouldn't it be great to have them spend the summer in this house, in the safety of the country? But he and his wife had lived their long, pleasant marriage alone, without the added happiness of the children they both had wanted.

At a turn in the hall he came face to face with a closed door. He didn't like closed doors, unless they belonged to a closet. This door was not as large as the bedroom doors and he knew before he opened it what it was.

"An attic, be damned," he said aloud with pleasure. Of course a house as tall as this one would have a full attic. The thought had just slipped his mind.

He looked up long, narrow, steep steps that were closely walled on both sides. The risers were exceptionally high, making it a long stairway even though the number of steps were limited to twelve or thirteen. There were no handrails. Far above, hanging on a rope cord from the peaked ceiling, was a light bulb, burning. Its light barely reached down the length of the walled staircase.

He started up, slowly and carefully, as excited as a kid. What would he find? He wondered. Since the

212

house was being sold furnished if desired, then would the attic have some old leftovers? Broken furniture he could repair. Knickknacks he could bring out and dust off. Broken china he could glue back together again. Items saved from earlier generations that had been important to them but worthless aesthetically.

He was not disappointed. As his head cleared the attic floor, and he looked at the small clearing that was surrounded on all other sides by piles of boxes and discarded furniture, he stopped, gazing.

"Be damned!" he said aloud with pure delight. "Of course the owner will probably want to take a bunch of these boxes and crates out. Surely."

He climbed the rest of the way and stood on the attic floor. It was built of narrow hardwood boards that had never been varnished. Someone had cleaned a roundish area, so there was no dust to speak of, while at the edges the dust furred, although even there it looked well tracked up by someone. Dust motes drifted in the air beneath the light, and he felt a little choked, but it didn't dampen his enthusiasm. He wondered how much more it would cost him to buy the contents of this attic, as it was, so that in later months and years he could go through it at his heart's content. Antiques had always interested him. Maybe he could find some old treasures here. The glass-fronted cabinet, for example, looked as though it held real treasures.

He crossed the cleared area to stand in front of the cabinet and with his hands clasped behind him peered through the glass at fragile china dishes lovingly and delicately hand painted, at little figurines in the shapes of birds, cupids, angels, flowers. He had no idea the worth of these things, but he was prepared to bargain. Perhaps they were worthless except for their age. He didn't know, didn't truly care. He wanted them. He wanted it all.

The boxes, stacked in places almost to the slanting ceiling, intrigued him. Some were wood crates, and probably held old dishes wrapped in old newspapers. Some undoubtedly held clothes and simple trifles. Fascinating. *Fascinating*.

Would there be labels on the boxes? He peered to see. And something down in the dark between the boxes scurried deeper into the dark.

Rats?

Well, one could hardly expect rodents not to take advantage of a place like this. Were he a rodent, he'd live here too. And hope the new owner didn't bring traps along.

He walked on, deeper into the end of the attic, where the ceiling sloped downward, and the light from the single bulb became almost nonexistent. He saw chairs with broken legs stacked atop tables that leaned precariously against whatever support they could find. He saw boxes and crates stacked one atop the other, with pathways between the stacks. The pathways were steeped in shadow, but he followed them, hearing ahead of him, behind him, on both sides of him the scurrying sounds that were increasing in numbers.

He spoke aloud, as he had been doing since the death of his wife two years ago, "Lord a'mercy me. One rat, two, fine, but a hundred? Mice by the score?

I'm surprised these folks don't have their own traps out. Me, now, I'd have to bring traps for you fellows or you'd eventually gnaw the house down."

He squinted through the shadows for the droppings mice and rats always left behind, but could see nothing. Too dark, anyway, back here. But something else bothered him, and he walked more slowly along, his hands still clasped behind his back, trying to figure it out. Oh yes! The smell, the odor. There was none. Rodents left odors when their numbers multiplied. And there was no smell other than a musty, dusty odor of a long-closed room.

He glimpsed a movement on top of a stack of boxes in front of him and looked up to see a small animal crouched to leap. He stopped, staring through the darkness. Its body was outlined faintly by light from the far-away bulb, and it was not the body of a rodent. It stared at him with eyes that gleamed a cold, blue light. Small horns reached up from the center of its head. Tiny ears stuck out at the sides. It remained in its crouched position as he stood stock still, returning the stare of those strange eyes. A sound began emanating from it, so soft at first it was barely audible. A growl that was not an animal sound, but something else, something that made the old man feel as though he had entered the gates of a hell that was colder than outer space. Instinct told him not to move, for if he moved the thing up there would move also.

He became aware of the silence as he stood there. All the scurrying had stopped. It was as if they waited. Waited for it to begin.

God a'mercy.

His voice was gone. Only in his mind had he spoken.

He took a step backward.

It leaped, sailing through the air like a bat, the cold blue eyes coming at him with lightning speed, claws reaching out, small body arching. He threw up his arms and struck it full in the face and knocked it out of sight. He stood only a moment, breathing hard, before he turned and hurried back toward the light. Suddenly the sounds were there again, the pecking of something sharp and hard like long toenails or curved claws, the padding of dozens of feet, the soft sliding sound of something, many things, that pulled themselves along the floor, or glided like snakes. All around him they came, closing in. Above their sounds he heard his own, the gasping of his breath as he hurried. The pounding of his heart as his mind barely touched the edge of this horror he sensed and had not yet fully seen.

Oh God! Oh God! Oh God!

His voice was soundless, buried beneath his desperation. He did not call for help. He had never called for help in his life, and it did not occur to him now. He sought the light and the steps that would lead him down, away from this horror, from these non-creatures that pursued him.

Who were they?

What were they?

When he reached the cleared area he turned his head one time for a glimpse of them, and what he saw fought their battle for them, because he was struck helpless with shock. Dolls, all sizes from tiny to large, toy horses, cats with stuffing coming out the seams of their bodies, the fantasy animal with horns that had leaped at him, they all were forming a circle around him, and on their faces was evil, in all its terribleness, eyes that glittered malevolently, mouths that were pulled into grinning hideousness, fangs that dripped venom. Some of the dolls were two and three feet tall. Old dolls, with hair mostly gone, with the outer layer of their faces peeling away, hanging in strips. But dolls that walked, on soft cloth feet, with arms that reached out toward him, soft also, hands made of the same material, yet they would not be soft and harmless. That he knew.

They were beginning to whisper among themselves now and close in. His own choked grunts punctuated their non-human, non-animal sounds, and he merely stumbled backwards, instinctively, clumsily, holding out his shaking hands against them in a gesture of pleading that he knew would do him no good.

At last, mercifully, he stepped backward into nothing. He had reached the top of the steps that led down to freedom, and he began falling into that blessed darkness.

FOURTEEN

From the kitchen where they waited, they heard the sound. A crashing, far above, a falling of something that went on and on and seemed as though it would never end. But at last there was silence. And for a moment longer they all stood like statues, listening, their faces reflecting one another's dread.

Together they began to run. McGraw led the way, with Elsea close behind, followed by Stephanie and Tommy. Dorrie, hurrying the best she could, fell behind, so that as she was climbing the stairs she heard the cries from the bigger people who had already reached the upper hall. There were shouts, words cried out, a short scream.

"Telephone!" Mr. McGraw shouted. "Go call an ambulance!"

"We don't have a telephone!"

"Oh my God. That's right. I'd forgotten. Then I've got to drive back to town and get someone out here. An ambulance. A doctor. My God!"

Dorrie came at last upon the scene in the hallway. Sprawled like a broken doll into the hall, with his feet still on the bottom attic step, was the old man who was going to buy the house. But his head was twisted strangely to one side, and his eyes stared without seeing upward. Around him stood Stephanie, Tommy, Elsea, Mr. McGraw. Elsea had bent down, but was now straightening. Her face was almost as white as her shirt.

"I think he's dead."

There was silence again. Mr. McGraw stopped his agitated movements and stood still, staring openmouthed down at the twisted body on the floor. Tommy's eyes moved past Mr. Holland's body, up the stairway, and stared. Dorrie saw him, and she too looked into the narrow space of the attic that was visible. But all she saw was the disturbance in the air. It was filled with dust that made the light seem dimmer than ever.

Finally McGraw moved. "Well, I've got to go get help, anyway. The ambulance, a doctor, police." He appeared then to think of Elsea and her children and he looked at them, one after the other. "Will you be all right here?"

"Yes, of course," Elsea said. She put her hand over her mouth for a moment, and the hand was shaking visibly. "You kids—you go on downstairs with Mr. McGraw, and stay there. I'll stay here with Mr. Holland."

Mr. McGraw said, "I don't think that's necessary. You should go down too."

"No. I'll stay."

Dorrie didn't want to go. She looked up at her mother and felt a deep need to be held by her, noticed by her, to drive away that look on her mother's face and turn it to the softness and tenderness she was used to seeing when she was in her mother's arms. She pushed close against Elsea's side and clutched her skirt. She stepped nearer the man on the floor. She bent down to touch him, to breathe into his mouth and make him live again. Someone jerked her back, so she clutched her mother's skirt again. When Tommy pulled at her, she began to cry and to cling hard with both hands. But Elsea didn't notice her at all, and in dead silence Tommy pried her fingers one by one from Elsea's skirt and shoved her toward Stephanie.

Stephanie picked Dorrie up, grunted from her weight, bowed slightly backwards, but held Dorrie securely. "Shut up," she hissed in her ear.

Dorrie stopped crying. Sobs grabbed in her throat, and she looked back up the stairs at her mother until they turned the bend and Elsea was no longer in sight. Dorrie struggled. Stephanie put her down, but bent and whispered again into her ear.

"If you go back up there I'll spank you myself, and I mean it too. Mama said for all of us to come down here, and that's what we're going to do."

"I want my mama." But she kept her voice down, so that the strange man wouldn't hear.

Stephanie didn't answer. She squished Dorrie's small hand painfully in her own and hurried her on down to the kitchen.

Mr. McGraw glanced back at them with a frightened look on his face. He was glad to be getting away, but he felt guilty about leaving them. It was all there, on his face, in the red and white blotched skin, the widened eyes, the slack mouth. They stared at him, and moved closer together so that they huddled as though seeking warmth from one another. The man hesitated in the open door.

"I'll be back," he said. "I won't be gone long. I'll call for a doctor and an ambulance, and the police will have to come too. There'll be people—lots of people—around for a while. Not long, maybe. It was an accident."

Dorrie was reminded of when her daddy died, except the people that came were different. The only ones who belonged to their family was Grandma and Grandpa, and all the rest were men who hurried in and hurried out, and some who came back again and asked a few questions. Some of them wore uniforms, and Dorrie was afraid and pushed close to whoever would hold her: Mama, Grandma, Grandpa, even her brother and sister. But then, just as it had been after her daddy died, all the people went away and they were alone. This time even Grandma and Grandpa went away, even though it was dark now, and Mama asked them to stay the night. They all stood in the night air at the side of the car, and the only light came from the porch light at the back of the house, and from the dome light on the car when Grandpa opened the door.

"You're not worried, are you?" Grandma said to Dorrie's mama. "I mean, does it make you nervous to be here alone with the children?"

"Oh no. I have to get used to that again, anyway. It was only an accident. A terrible accident. I wish I had stopped him from climbing those stairs, but I never thought he'd fall."

"No, of course not. How could you know? You're not responsible for the poor old fellow's death."

They kept talking, Grandpa in the car, Grandma standing beside her door. Dorrie stopped listening to them. She saw Tommy draw away, slowly, very slowly, as if he didn't want anyone to notice what he was doing. He took a step backward, and another. And finally he stopped in the shadows between the lights from house and car and turned and looked up at the attic window, that tiny rectangle bit of glass that was set in the highest peak of the western side of the house.

No accident. No accident. It was the dolls, the animals, the toys. Somehow.

Tommy was certain of that. But he had kept his mouth shut all day long, from the moment they had first seen the poor old man lying at the foot of the stairs, to now, and he would keep on keeping his mouth shut except for one thing. He was waiting for his grandparents to leave, and then he would nail the lock on the attic door. Now, maybe, his mother would agree the stairs, at least, were dangerous. He had an excuse now, to lock the door. To keep Dorrie out of the attic. He had been waiting all day, with a terrible sense of urgency, for everyone to leave so he could take his hammer, the long nail, and the board that would hold the door from the outside. The urgency was growing, as the night grew. It was like having to urinate so bad he could hardly hold it in. It was like waiting for everyone to turn their backs so he could go relieve himself.

At last Grandpa started the car, and they were leaving. Tommy whirled and ran into the house, turning on lights as he went, everywhere, flipping switches while he kept running. He didn't want to be in the dark.

In the upstairs he slowed, and he began walking with extreme caution, looking into all the little crevices behind furniture, in corners, around doorways. Anywhere one of them could be hiding. He remembered, and started watching too the tops of the tall pieces of furniture that littered the upstairs. Old chests that seemed to have little purpose except to take up space. He couldn't remember what his mother had called them, but he knew the toys might be there, on top, hiding behind the fancy, carved, false fronts that reached up in a triangle. If the attic door had been left open, they might be all over the house, watching him, watching for everyone, all of them. They might be gathering to attack. To kill them all.

But when he turned the corner he saw the attic door had been closed. And at first he felt weak with relief. Then he remembered it didn't matter anymore if the door were closed. They could open it now.

He went into his bedroom and got down on his belly and slid in under the bed. It was darker there than he liked, and he looked up at the bedsprings from one end of the bed to the other, but there was nothing but the coils, and the cotton mattress above. He clutched the hammer hard in one hand, and held it as he put the nail in his pocket and then reached for the small wood plank. It was about three by six inches, and at least an inch thick. With the long, strong nail, it would hold against almost anyone.

He scrambled out from under the bed backwards, got to his feet and hurried out of his room. He stopped, staring at the door. It was still shut. The hall light, though, was slightly around the corner, and the shadows thrown on the door made it seem threatening. Tommy swallowed fear, and something as bitter as gall. His mouth turned dry. He was afraid to go closer to the door, and yet he had to.

He shifted the hammer in his hand and got a harder grip on the handle. Stiff-legged, he walked boldly on, into the shadows at the turn in the hall where the door seemed to stare defiantly down at him.

He reached high, so high that Dorrie would never be able to turn the lock on her own, held the wood lock against the door frame, placed the nail in the hole in the center of the lock, and began to hammer.

The sound rang and echoed through the upstairs, and the wall felt unfirm under the force of the hammering. But the nail scarcely budged; the hammer missed now and then and struck his hand instead. He gritted his teeth and kept hammering.

Elsea was watching the car lights disappear down

225

the highway when the banging began. After all that had happened, there was something about the hollow, staccato noise from inside the house that caused her heart to lurch in terror. What was happening? It seemed as though the house itself had suddenly turned against them all, against all humans, all life. That even as it killed, it pulled back again.

Dorrie's hand grabbed hers.

Stephanie cried, "What's that?"

It was then that Elsea noticed that Tommy was not with them. She looked around, but saw nothing beyond the lighted windows that threw streaks across the lawn and deepened the strips of blackness between. She hadn't turned so many lights on. So now she knew. In some way, Tommy was involved.

With Dorrie's hand in hers she began to run. Stephanie reached the back door before she did, and to keep up she finally bent and lifted Dorrie. They went through the kitchen and up the back stairs, the racket growing as they climbed higher into the house. All the walls, it seemed, vibrated with the noise.

Tommy stood at the attic door on his tiptoes and was driving a nail furiously through a small piece of wood. When he saw them he stopped, and a long smile slid almost ear to ear.

"I did it," he said breathlessly. "I drove that nail in."

Elsea stood beside Stephanie and stared speechlessly, comprehending nothing except that Tommy was delighted about having driven a large nail through a small hole in an ugly block of wood that looked as though it belonged on a shed.

Tommy turned the wood strip horizontally across the edge of the attic door. "See," he said. "It's a lock."

Elsea set Dorrie down. She felt weak now, unsteady on her own legs. "A lock," she said. Her mind began working. The lock Tommy had put on the door was obviously too high for Dorrie to reach. Someone would have to let her in and out of the attic to play, or it would have to come down, or . . . "Why have you put a lock there, Tommy? Without permission."

"The attic stairs aren't safe, Mom. Dorrie might fall."

Elsea had no answer for him. The vision of the old man lying dead with a broken neck at the foot of those steps, his body sprawled across the threshold of that door, was still too strong. At the moment she didn't care if Tommy nailed locks from the top to the bottom.

"All right," she said, turning away, "let's get out of here now. I've seen just about all I want to see of that door."

Dorrie's hand jerked out of hers and the little girl was suddenly, desperately banging with both fists on the attic door. "I won't fall! Take it off! Take it off my door! I can't reach it! I can't reach that old thing! How can I get up to my dollies and my toys?"

Elsea stared at Dorrie. Were there never any end to surprises about her kids? For the first time in Dorrie's life she was throwing a real temper tantrum. Words were beginning to fail her. Instead she now screamed, and she began jumping up and down and stretching as far as she could to reach the impossibly high button lock. Elsea sagged. She felt like just sitting down on the floor, putting her head in her hands and bawling as hard as Dorrie was.

Stephanie gave Dorrie a tap on the head. "Hey! What's the matter with you?" Her voice raised to a shout. "Shut up, Dorrie! If you want to go upstairs I'll unlock the door, or Mama will, or Tommy, or . . . for cripe's sake shut up! Mama, make her shut up!"

Tommy shouted, "Not me! I'll not unlock that door for her, and not for anybody, not anymore!"

Elsea said loudly, but barely over Dorrie's screams, "Tommy, we've all gone up and down that stairwell dozens of times without falling. Dorrie! Stop it!"

Elsea put her arms around Dorrie's waist and carried her, still kicking and screaming, to her bedroom. She had never spanked Dorrie in her life, and didn't want to now, but when the little girl immediately rolled off the bed and started in a run out of her room, Elsea grabbed her and swatted her across the rear.

"Enough," she said under the change in Dorrie's screams, and louder, as she spanked her again, "I said that's enough! You're going to bed, young lady, and if you ever behave that way again I'll not allow you in the attic at all. Do you understand?"

She stripped Dorrie down to her underclothes, and sorrow swelled to a painful throbbing in her heart as the child settled down to a gasping sob, yielding now as only a child, or a beaten animal, could. Elsea didn't like controlling her children in this way. But she had never experienced this kind of behavior before from any three of her kids, and didn't know how to handle it in any other way.

Finally, she pulled Dorrie into her arms, and pressed the child's head against her breasts. Tears burned her own eyes as Dorrie sobbed against her. When finally the little girl was still, Elsea picked her up and laid her between the sheets. Dorrie turned her face to the wall and hugged the teddy bear to her. Small jerks of her body remained of the tears, the screams, the sobs, but now her eyes were closed, and Elsea saw she was already sleeping.

She turned and saw Stephanie and Tommy standing in the doorway, and put her fingers to her lips. Without talking, they went quietly downstairs. When they entered the kitchen Corey was just coming across the porch, his face without the usual smile of greeting.

"I was in town, and I heard what happened here today. I'm sorry I'm so late showing up, but I came as soon as I heard. Is there anything I can do?"

Elsea felt like rushing into his arms to be hugged and comforted as if she were one of her children. "Just come in and talk to us for a bit," she said. "We've just put Dorrie to bed. We could use your company."

Tommy sat still for what he considered to be a polite length of time, listening to the casual conversation between his mom and Corey. During a lull in their conversation, when the hands of the clock had slowly edged past fifteen minutes, he said,

"I'd like to go to bed, Mom. I'm sleepy too."

"So early?" Elsea said with a glance at the clock. "Go whenever you want to, Tommy."

Tommy hurried out of the room, aware mostly of Corey and the way he was watching him. All evening Corey had tried to include him in the conversation, but Tommy just couldn't make himself say more than yes or no, depending on which was more appropriate. The meadows with the yellow poppies, the mountain peaks with their caps of snow, the tall forests, the wild animals all seemed so far away from the horror his life had become. He wished he could talk about it to Corey, but knew he never could. He didn't want Corey to think he was crazy. It was bad enough that Stephanie thought so. It was terrible to think his mother would accuse him of doing things he hadn't done. But no matter what any of them thought, and no matter how scared he was of his own little sister now, he had to get upstairs and make sure the attic door was still locked.

He had to make sure they didn't come down from the attic.

The first thing he saw when he came into the upstairs was Dorrie's open door, and his heart fell. Had she only pretended to be asleep so she could open the door and go back upstairs? She was smart enough to figure out that all she'd have to do was drag a chair to the door and then she'd be able to reach the lock. And belatedly, Tommy realized that if he had stood on a chair, and nailed the lock farther up on the door, Dorrie wouldn't have been able to reach it at all. Too late for that now. At least for tonight.

He tiptoed into her room and saw in the soft shadows from the hallway light that she was still facing the wall, still hugging her teddy bear, and was breathing softly and deeply. Tommy crept out of her room and closed her door without a sound. Then he turned his attention to the attic door.

It was still locked.

But something was different now. There was no light shining beneath the door. Someone, today, had turned out the attic light.

Tommy went into his own room, changed to pajamas, and then with his light out he sat down just inside his bedroom door. From there he could see the attic door, and the plank lock that was ugly and unpainted against the wall.

The house grew still around him.

He wished he could hear the voices of his mother and Corey and Stephanie, but they might as well have been gone, leaving him alone in the house with only Dorrie, and whatever it was that waited upstairs beyond the locked attic door.

They too were silent.

Did they need light to make them move, to let them see?

No.

They were just waiting. He could feel it. Feel them. They were waiting for him to fall asleep, for his mother and sister to fall asleep, and then they would come down to the door and try to open it, but tonight they weren't going to get out because he would stop them. The lock would stop them.

He was going to stay awake and see that it did.

Stephanie came upstairs and went into the

bathroom. He heard her brush her teeth and run water for a bath. Then he heard her go into her room. The house was silent again, and Tommy's head almost fell forward on his chest when his eyes closed. He jerked up, to listen, to stare at the button on the door.

It hadn't turned.

After a while his mother came upstairs, and he heard noises similar to the ones his sister had made. Then again, silence. He held his eyes open with force, and finally got to his feet and stood there, so it would be harder to accidentally fall asleep.

When at last he felt sure both Stephanie and his mother were asleep, he went to their doors and closed them. The lock on the attic door was still just as he had left it, so he went into his room, closed his door, and fell into bed. His small bedside clock told him it was almost midnight, and his brain was begging for sleep. He could not remember, later, when his head touched the pillow.

The time had come. With a murmur that grew and spread among them, they began to move out from all their hiding places, across the darkened attic, down the steps to the door. Like insects building a bridge from one dead tree to another they built their own bridge of bodies and reached upwards to the door knob. It turned, but it did not open. Their murmurs increased to hissings and gruntings of anger. They stirred at the base of the door, their bridge of bodies broken for the moment, confusion reigning. Then they began reaching higher and higher against the door, the bridge going upright, thin claws and sharp fangs reaching out of the crack between door and wall, and eventually, a couple of feet above the doorknob, they came across the obstruction.

Something pressed tight against the door.

In silence they began to work, communal strength pushing at the obstruction, and at last it began to move.

The door opened.

FIFTEEN

Elsea slept a disturbed sleep. Nightmares mingled with sounds that seemed to come from all around her. In dreams she saw her own children lying mangled at the foot of long, narrow, steep stairs that reached far up into dark space. She turned and half woke to the sounds of muffled footsteps in the hallway and scratchings at her door. But when she sat up and tried to listen, to separate dreams from reality, there was nothing but soft murmurs dying away.

The wind, she thought, and pulled over her head not only her summer blanket, but her pillow too, and tried again to sleep without dreaming.

At last daylight made a grayed prison of her room, and she got up and dressed. When she left her room she noticed her door was closed, and she stopped to think. When had she closed it? She made a point of never closing her door, just in case one of the kids might call for her in the night.

She shrugged. The night had been a bad one, and she felt as though she had spent half of it walking and walking. Perhaps she had actually gotten out of bed and closed her own door. The thought wasn't comforting.

The house was still quiet. None of the kids was awake yet, thank goodness. She wanted to be alone, to take a cup of coffee outside and watch the sun rise.

She went down the front stairs and through the parlor into the library. The rooms she passed through were shadowed and dark, the light that came in through the windows still pale and far away, issuing from a sun not yet above the horizon. Here in the mountains the air grew chilly at night, and the house seemed especially cold and damp although it had been weeks since rainfall. Elsea wished for her sweater, but didn't want to go back upstairs. In the kitchen closet she would find something to wear, and of course the hot coffee would help.

Her desk stood in the faint light of the bay windows, and the sheet of paper in the typewriter looked ghostlike in its pure white. Would she ever be able to get back into a story that hadn't been going too well at its best?

She went nearer and nearer, staring at the paper. And finally she gripped the top of the desk chair and read in disbelief the capital letters that covered the page: "ONCE UPON A TIME THERE DIED DIED DIED DIED DIED DIED . . ."

On and on, the paper covered. The words she had

typed, the words beneath these others, no longer mattered. What did matter was that it had happened again, and this time there was no anger in her, only a kind of sick fear. She thought of Tommy, asleep in his bed upstairs. And she could think no further.

She pulled the sheet of paper out of the typewriter, and then hurried from the house. She didn't glance back as she began to run toward the path into the trees, through the trees, out into the cleared space where Corey's trailer was parked.

She stopped, breathless.

Corey might not even be awake yet.

She stood, undecided, yet knowing she had to talk to him.

The door of the trailer opened, and Corey looked out. This time there was a smile on his face. But it died swiftly as he came down the steps toward her.

"Elsea?" he said. "What is it?"

She gave him the sheet of paper and watched his eyes take it in from top to bottom and rise again to meet hers, puzzled. She began to talk, swiftly, telling him of the page that had been typed top to bottom with the first message, and she told him of her worries about Tommy. When she finished, her teeth were chattering nervously and goosebumps covered her arms.

"You're freezing," he said simply and calmly, and pulled her into his house.

It was the first time she had entered the door, and she saw the combination living room and kitchen only superficially. She observed that it was neat. She smelled the fragrance of coffee and food.

He seated her at the tiny table.

"Hungry?"

"No."

"You'll drink coffee, won't you? You need the warmth."

"I don't feel so cold now." But she accepted the cup of coffee with gratitude and warmed her hands on the heat that emanated through the thick sides of the large mug.

Corey sat down across the table from her. "You think Tommy typed that, don't you?"

"He must have." But she was shaking her head. "I know no other explanation. What am I going to do with him? I'm running into trouble, and I don't know how to handle it."

Corey looked out the window at the side of the table, looked toward the stand of tall trees that separated his mobile home from the house where Tommy and his sisters slept.

Elsea said, "What is happening to my son, Corey?"

"I don't know. But I've noticed the change in him. He acts different . . . not like he did when I first met him."

"I can't bear to think what I'm thinking, Corey. Is Tommy having some kind of mental trouble? He's been wanting to move. He's the only one who hates living there. At first he liked it, but now . . . now he seems to hate it."

"Why?"

"I don't know why."

"Maybe he's bored, Elsea. Maybe there just isn't enough for him to do."

"I try to keep him busy."

"Staying busy isn't always the answer. Anybody can stay busy. But busy-bored. Especially if you're a young boy who's been used to friends and activities."

"But is that any excuse for typing such terrible stuff?" Elsea put one finger on the sheet of paper and pushed it toward Corey. "That is terrible! The death of that man yesterday must have sent him over the edge, somehow. And I'm scared, Corey. I don't have the money to go back to the kind of life we had."

Corey looked into her eyes for a long moment. "If I bought a house near your folks would you move into it?"

"Charity! No, thanks. You know I couldn't do that."

"We could make some kind of financial arrangement that would make you feel better, if you insisted."

"Corey, please. That's very thoughtful of you, but I can't do that."

"Well then, why don't I take the kids on that mountain trip I promised them? The snows aren't gone yet, but I'm getting anxious to go anyway. I was planning on a week's trip instead of just three days. We could give it a try, and see if that helps."

"Are you sure it wouldn't be too much trouble for Tommy to go along?"

"You know it wouldn't. I'd love to have him."

"Stephanie wanted to go, too."

"Sure, why not? And you and the baby, too."

"Oh!" She looked dreamily away, seeing the mountains in her mind, and then feeling the cold and the challenges of high country that Dorrie might still be too small to take. "Let me have a rain check on

239

that, OK, Corey? I think Dorrie would be too much to handle for a week on a hiking trip or even in a tent. I mean, she's more fragile than my other two, and I'm afraid the cold weather might be too much for her. But I appreciate so much that you'd bother with Tommy and Stephanie."

"Hey," he said softly, putting his hands out across the narrow table to clasp hers closely within their strong warmth. "Listen, you know it's no bother. Don't you know how I feel about you and your kids, Elsea? I'd like to make it permanent."

She drew her breath in so sharply a pain went through her chest. Part of the pain was built of a memory of Vern, and part from the familiar old guilt that was created by a longing to go into Corey's arms. She pulled back instinctively, and Corey dropped her hands and lowered his head.

"Sorry," he said.

Elsea picked up the sheet of paper that lay on the table between them and crushed it in her hands, rolling it into a tight ball.

"Corey," she said after a moment, "thanks again. Will you be over later today?"

He pushed his chair back and rose, hooked his thumbs in his hip pockets and looked around his small mobile home as though organizing in his mind all that had to be done.

"Will a couple of hours be too soon? It won't take me long to get everything ready to go. I stay ready, most of the time. All I have to do is make sure I've got the stuff for two more people. A couple of extra sleeping bags, a few other things."

"Is there anything I can contribute?"

240

He smiled at her. "Just the kids. And their toothbrushes. Extra jeans, and flannel shirts or sweaters. Something warm. It's still cold up there. I hope they don't object to getting up early, because we'll be getting up before dawn while we're on our trip, and we'll be doing a lot of hiking."

In an attempt to lighten the mood of the day, or her own mood at the very least, Elsea said as she went out his door, "Now I know why I knew I should never try to take Dorrie on a trip like that. I can see her trying to keep up on a hiking trip."

They said goodbye in his yard, and Elsea tried not to see the last look in his eyes, that steady drawing toward her, the now unspoken yearnings. She had a sad feeling that she would not be hearing those words from him again, not for a long, long time. Not until she let him know she was ready. She didn't look back as she entered the trees, but she knew he was still standing there watching her, and she could see him in her mind as clearly as though she had turned to him: a large, broad-shouldered, handsome man with a close-cropped beard and a moustache and kind eyes.

But it was too soon . . . too soon. Vern moved in the shadows ahead of her. But now to her horror he was as he had last lain in his bed, emaciated to a skeleton, broken by illness that couldn't be controlled, unable to help her in this need to help their children.

Not until she crossed through the woods and came out at the driveway of the house did she remember the sheet of paper. She had left it at Corey's house.

It was just as well, she decided. Tommy knew

241

what he had written. He knew she would have seen it. His purpose, whatever it had been, had been served as much as it could be. And she really had no inclination to discuss it with him at all. It was easier to just let Corey take over, get Tommy away for a week. Maybe then Tommy would be back to the boy he had been. Healthy, active, able to handle stress.

Tommy woke with the same sense of urgency he had felt while waiting for everyone to go to sleep the night before. His door was still closed. Early light filtered into his room through the curtains he hadn't pushed back, but the sun was still below the horizon of mountains in the east. A glance toward the window showed him a red streak, cut by the tips of the trees, the promise of a bright, hot sun. But now his room was chilly, and he shivered in the cool air as he shoved away his blanket and ran barefoot to the door.

Dorrie's door, across the hall from his own, was open. He had closed it too when he went to bed. Maybe she had gotten up already. Sometimes she did. His eyes switched to the attic door, and his chin dropped.

That door, too, stood open, and the lock he had nailed on the door facing was gone.

He scrambled to the jog in the hall where the attic door took up the extra space and went down on his hands and knees and began feeling in the near-darkness for the small piece of wood.

Where is it? Where is it? Who pulled it off? Dorrie? No! They did. They.

He sat back on his heels and looked up into the dark tunnel that led into the attic. The light was still out. Dorrie wasn't up there. Some of *them* were, but some of them were also in the rest of the house.

Maybe now they had killed everyone, his mother, his sisters, and were leaving him for last because they knew how much he hated them, how much he knew about them.

He had to see his mother and sisters.

He ran into Dorrie's room and almost fainted when he saw that she was still in her bed, turned now onto her back, her face as pretty as the face of an angel. Beside her, over toward the wall, was her teddy bear, no longer needed in her sleep.

He began to back quietly out of the room, but then, at the foot of her bed, nearly invisible in the shadows of her westside room, something moved in the crumpled blankets.

With his heart stopped, Tommy crept forward, staring hard. From among the blankets came the steady, baleful gleam of eyes. Above the eyes were a strange set of horns that were stuffed with some kind of material that was leaking out a small rip. Tiny ears hung down low on each side of the long-snouted face. It was a stuffed toy no larger than the teddy bear, but it was one of *them*. It was hideously alive, and it edged sideways in a quick movement, like a large insect.

Then it leaped.

Tommy saw it coming toward his face, and in a sudden rage that was built of fear and desperation, he reached for it as he would have a football. He caught it, and felt it twist and struggle in his hands.

243

He dropped it, and stomped it as he had stomped the doll, but his bare feet caused it no harm; it only twisted away, uninjured, untorn. It was making some kind of sound low in its belly, and Tommy was making his own belly-deep sounds of grunting, half-sobbing, as he went down onto the floor after it.

It scuttled away, snarling, but Tommy anticipated its move, and grabbed it again. This time he ran, nearly vomiting with abhorrence as he felt it squirm in his hands. But he made it to the stairway to the attic, and threw it up into the darkness as hard as he could. He heard it strike the attic floor with a nearly soundless thud. He slammed the attic door shut and leaned against it, gasping for breath.

A moment later he ran down the hall, around the corner, and into Stephanie's room. Her door was still closed, and as he shoved it open she sat up in bed and blinked at him.

Before she could speak, he backed out of her room and pulled the door shut with a loud slam. At the other side of the hall his mother's door, though, was open, and he went into that room much more slowly, terrified of what he might find. But her bed was empty. It had been neatly made, the bedspread pulled up and the pillow shams on the pillows, with the little lace-covered cushions scattered here and there the way she always fixed them.

She was alive.

She was downstairs making breakfast.

Tommy stood by the door and looked all around the room. No toys here. Not even under the bed. Nor under the chest with the tall legs. Nowhere.

From behind him, Stephanie's voice, querulous as

it usually was when she first woke in the morning, demanded, "Tommy, what are you doing?"

Startled, his heart jumping and pounding again, he turned to face her. She stood in crumpled pajamas and with her hair going in every direction. But he didn't feel like teasing her about it.

"I was just looking for Mom."

"Under the bed?"

Tommy stood there, returning her stare. He had no answer. He could see in her eyes that this was not the right time to mention the toys again.

"You weren't looking for Mom when you jumped in and out of my room like some idiot."

"No," Tommy said tiredly as he passed by her and went back in the direction of his own room. "I was looking for you, then."

"Why?"

Tommy shrugged. "I got to get dressed."

"Boy, you beat everything, you know it? Sometimes I wonder about you."

Tommy didn't answer. He checked again in Dorrie's room before he went into his own. He looked under the bed, among the blankets that covered her, under and behind the furniture, and even behind the draperies that hung to the floor. And at last, seeing that she was still sleeping heavily, he went into his room to dress.

He stood at the window and watched the sun rise over the mountains. He tried to think, and couldn't. His mind kept going back to what the toys had done. They were getting smarter and stronger. They were strong enough to force the wood lock off the door. And they were smart enough to hide it from him. But he could think no farther. There was this house where he and his mother and sisters lived, and there was the house of his grandparents, which was too small for all of them. Where could they go?

From far away in the house came a shout from Stephanie, and her voice sounded strained, as though she had shouted at him several times before and he hadn't heard.

"Tom! Come down to the kitchen! Mom wants you."

He moved sluggishly, glad to hear her voice even though he didn't answer. The chores of the day would at least partially remove him from thinking of something to which he could find no answer.

He wondered as he went down the stairs: what would Corey say if he told him about the toys?

He didn't want to see the look of disbelief on Corey's face, of maybe disgust that anyone could be so—so nutty.

Toys and dolls didn't move, didn't come to life, didn't attack people, didn't kill.

Sometimes, Stephanie had said, she wondered about him. Well, sometimes he wondered about him too.

When he reached the kitchen he saw that Stephanie was in a better mood. Her face was lit up as if happiness glowed behind her skin. His mother, though, looked a mixture of sadness and happiness. It was a look he had almost gotten used to. A look of hope, maybe. That was all he could think of. Had something good happened? Dorrie was out of it, whatever it was. She sat at the table eating her cereal just like always, as though she lived in another world. Just looking at her made chills go down Tommy's spine. He loved her—but now he was afraid of her. Was she as innocent as she looked?

"Good news, Tommy," said his mother.

Stephanie's smile widened, and Tommy's hopes suddenly bounded into high gear. "Hey," he said, "are we moving?"

Stephanie frowned.

Elsea said, "You're taking that trip into the mountains with Corey. He said the snow isn't gone, but he's ready to go anyway."

"Hurry," Stephanie said, "eat your breakfast and get your stuff ready. We're going today. This morning!"

"Who's going?" Tommy demanded, his eyes taking in Dorrie and his mother.

"You and me," Stephanie said. "Just as we planned. Don't you even remember?"

Tommy stared at her, and then at Elsea. "What about you? And Dorrie?"

"Tommy, you know I can't take her up there."

"You're not going, too?"

"No, we're not going."

Tommy was torn between yearning and terror. More than anything he had wanted that hiking trip with Corey, but he couldn't leave his mother and little sister alone in this house with all the toys.

"You've got to go!" he cried, his face twisting in his desperation. "Dorrie can walk. She's getting bigger all the time. She's not a baby. She went up to the meadow, and she ran all over it! She can go."

Even Dorrie herself had looked up and was staring at Tommy. Milk hung in drops on her lower lip, threatening to fall onto the front of her shirt.

"The meadow where we went is nothing compared to where you'll be going with Corey," Elsea said. "Don't you want to go, Tommy?"

"Yes. But I want you and Dorrie to go, too."

"We can't go," Elsea said firmly. "And there's no use saying any more about it. And if you don't get busy, Corey will have to wait on you, and you know that wouldn't be very considerate of you. After all, he's going out of his way to take you two kids. You're bound to be some trouble, even though he swears you won't. Well, you're going to have to make an effort to make sure you aren't. Now eat your breakfast and get your pack roll together." Elsea turned her back to him and began putting dirty dishes into the sink.

Tommy said, "I'm not going."

Stephanie yelled, "What?" And Elsea turned back toward him and simply looked at her son.

Tommy put his hands into his pockets, tipped his face down and looked at the floor, then slumped out toward the sunshine in the back yard. Without looking at them again, he repeated what he had said, "I'm not going."

"Tommy, come back here!"

When Elsea spoke in that tone of voice, none of her children questioned her. They obeyed, instantly. Tommy came back to stand in the kitchen, but his face was almost a blank, his eyes dull, as though something vital had died in him.

"I think this needs an explanation," Elsea said.

"I'm not going, not unless you and Dorrie go, too." Then he added, "And you can't make me."

"Oh God," Elsea said softly. "What is happening to you, Tommy?"

His mouth tightened. "Nothing."

Stephanie cried, "If he doesn't go, does that mean I can't go either?"

Elsea said, "Of course you can't, you know that!"

Both of them expected a retort of some kind from Tommy, but when there was no word from him at all, Elsea looked at him again, feeling more helpless than ever.

"I don't understand, Tommy. You were looking forward to this."

Tommy's head bowed. "Can I go now?"

Elsea sighed. "Yes, you can go."

She stood in the doorway and watched him go down the back walk to one of the sheds and disappear inside. Behind her, Stephanie ranted and grumbled and wondered aloud what had gone wrong with Tommy. Elsea had no answer for her. She hoped that maybe Corey's arrival would change Tommy's mind, but a few minutes later, when Corey drove into the driveway, Tommy still did not come out of the shed.

Elsea went out to talk to him, to explain to him that her son was continuing his odd behavior.

"Do you want me to talk to him?" Corey asked.

"Would you? Do you mind?"

"Where is he?"

"In that old shed. The buggy shed."

Corey nodded, and Elsea watched him go to the shed, look in, and then enter. She twisted her fingers nervously together and waited long minutes. Stephanie came out of the house and stood beside

249

her a moment, and then left again.

Tommy had never felt so uncomfortable in his life. Eyes, looking at him, from everyone, every direction, it seemed. Eyes that asked questions that weren't spoken, weren't put into words. Corey's eyes bothered him the most. He didn't want Corey to look at him this way. This puzzled, bewildered, betrayed way. He wanted to run to Corey and tell him the truth, but he couldn't.

"What are you looking for?" Corey asked, coming to stand beside him, to pretend to look down at rusty things in the old tool box. "Anything I can help you with?"

"I guess not. Nothing. Just a bolt of some kind."

"A bolt?"

"Yes, sir."

"Any particular reason?"

"I thought I'd bolt the attic door so Dorrie can't go up there."

"Tommy, are you afraid she'll fall, too, and be hurt?"

"I guess so."

Corey's hand touched Tommy's shoulder. "I wouldn't worry about that if I were you. How many times has she gone up and down the stairs without falling?"

"I don't know." He added, "But she could."

"Yes, she could. But maybe you could help her when she wants to go up and come down. Locking her out would probably raise a fuss, right?"

"Yeah, right." Tommy almost smiled, almost

250

forgetting for a moment the real reason he wanted to keep Dorrie out of the attic. "She's got a temper sometimes."

"Sure. Most of us do. Are you sure you won't change your mind and come along on the trip with me? I've been counting on you."

Tommy didn't know what to say. He avoided Corey's eyes as he looked around the shed. He bit his lower lip.

"Maybe I can go next time," he finally said.

"You don't want to leave your mother and sister here alone, do you, Tommy?"

"No, sir."

"Well, I admire your sense of responsibility."

Tommy looked up at Corey with a flush of pleasure, but in Corey's eyes he saw something else, something that denied Corey's words. It was the bewilderment again, the doubt. And that expression of doubt wiped away all pleasure, all feelings of being understood and appreciated. Tommy felt sick.

"I guess I'd better be going," Corey said. He waited a bit longer, and when Tommy did not respond, he walked away, out of the shed, into the sunshine.

For another brief moment he threw a long shadow across the door of the shed, and then he was gone.

Tommy sat down on the dirt in the rear of the shed, put his hands over his face and wept quietly, but with terrible intensity.

He had a feeling he would never see Corey again.

SIXTEEN

Dorrie listened without comment. But she heard it all. Tommy was being naughty again. Mama didn't understand him. Stephanie was mad at him because she didn't get to go with Corey either. Because of Tommy, everyone was either mad or sad. And Tommy was hiding out somewhere, not even coming into the house.

Dorrie washed her hands and face at the sink, with her mother's help, and then she went to the back stairway and began to climb.

The attic door was shut, but that was all right. She could reach the knob and turn it. The ugly piece of wood Tommy had nailed on the door to keep her out was gone. Dorrie began to smile as she looked at the empty nail hole in the wall beside the door. Had her mama made Tommy take the lock away?

Dorrie reached for the doorknob with both hands and turned it, and then she looked up into a tunnel of darkness. The attic light was out.

She hesitated, and then she began to climb the attic steps. She went slowly, the light at the foot of the steps fading away as she went higher into the attic. As her eyes adjusted she saw the faint outlines of the ceiling rafters far above. A tiny bit of light would be coming in from the attic windows, but not enough for her to play. She stood in the dark a few moments, halfway up the steps, and then she started to make her way down again. It was here where the man fell yesterday. Maybe he had turned out the light and couldn't see the steps. She picked her way carefully downward, sliding one hand along the wall for support. She was sorry about the poor man, but just like with Daddy, when she tried to touch him they had pushed her away. When she reached the bottom step she stopped and began yelling.

"Mama? Stephanie? Mama, come and turn on my light."

Stephanie was still complaining. She worked as she complained, putting her fury in her movements, wiping the table so hard the surface was in danger of being wiped away. "It's not fair! Why do you let him get by with acting like that? If it were me—" She stopped, her head poised for listening. From far above in the house came Dorrie's call. Stephanie asked, "What'd she say?"

"I think it was something about her light. The attic light was turned out yesterday by one of

254

the policemen."

"Oh boy. You're not going to let her play up there, are you?"

Elsea gazed out the window a moment, wanting to comply with Dorrie's wishes, and, like Tommy, afraid to let her up and down those dangerously steep attic steps as freely as before.

"If you do," Stephanie said, "Tommy will be impossible to live with."

"He's only concerned with Dorrie's safety, Stephanie. He'd be just as concerned about yours."

Stephanie became gentle in her cleaning of the table. Elsea could see nothing about it that needed cleaning in the first place, but she understood her daughter's need to vent her frustration on something, to keep active, to move.

"I know," Stephanie said. "He's really a good kid. I guess I'm not mad at him anymore."

From upstairs, Dorrie's scream became more insistent. She sounded a bit closer, as though she had come to the head of the rear stairway. "Somebody come and turn on my light!"

Elsea said, "Would you mind going up and pulling the light string, Stephanie? Hold her hand when you climb the stairs, and be very careful when you come down. Maybe we should have a handrail put up there."

"What about Dorrie? When she's ready to come down?"

"Tell her to call first and one of us will help her down the steps."

"Okay."

Stephanie went into the small hallway from which

255

the back stairs rose. When she reached the turn in the stairs, halfway up, she could see Dorrie leaning over the balcony looking down.

"Get back, Dorrie, be careful."

Dorrie backed away and was standing by the open attic door when Stephanie came out into the upstairs hall. Just looking at the bottom step of the attic stairwell gave her shivers.

"Dorrie, are you sure you want to go up?"

"Yes, my toys are up there."

"They are not. Your toys are in your room and downstairs in the TV room."

"I mean my new toys."

"No, you mean those old, old toys, those ugly toys that belonged to people you never knew. Why don't you go downstairs and play with your own toys? You haven't even touched your little piano since we got here. Or your tea set."

"I want to go up in the attic. I want the light turned on again."

Stephanie bent forward at the waist to emphasize her words. To further emphasize, she pointed a finger near Dorrie's chin. "A man fell down those stairs yesterday, Dorrie, and he died because he fell. What if you fell?"

"I won't fall." A worried crease settled between Dorrie's eyebrows. "That man, he'll get up and walk again."

"No. Not ever. He's like Daddy. He's dead, Dorrie. And he died because he fell down the stairs. And we don't want you to die, too."

Dorrie's frown deepened. She merely returned Stephanie's stare now, without another word, and after a moment it was Stephanie who looked away sighing.

"All right," she said, taking Dorrie's hand. "You're not supposed to go up and down by yourself. When you're ready to come down, you call, so someone can help you. Hear?"

"I won't fall. I come down by myself all the time. Every day."

"I know."

Stephanie picked her way slowly up the steep, enclosed stairway. There was light at the bottom, and a far lesser light at the top. Degrees of gray deepened with each step. Going into the attic was like going into a spook house at Halloween, where all but the most shadowy and deceptive light was shut off. It was so dark she couldn't even see the string that hung down from the light bulb that was only a pale spot of white in the gloom, hanging in midair like a bloated, bleached insect.

Piles of boxes and crates loomed like small mountains, throwing pockets of deep black around them. The tiny window in the east end of the attic let in thin strings of sunlight that were filtered by spider webs. Stephanie reached upward and waved her hand around, feeling for the light string. And on the floor, cut by shadows and darkness and a sliver of light, something moved. It was pale, pink, naked, slithering.

"My dolly," Dorrie cried, and jerked away from Stephanie.

Stephanie started to call out to her to stop, to come back, to stay away from whatever it was on the floor, when her hand suddenly touched the string.

She pulled the light on.

Dorrie was sitting on her feet and had picked up the pale little creature. Stephanie gaped, staring. Dorrie was holding the ugly little celluloid doll, cradling it against her breast and up under her chin, and she had begun a singsong lullaby of some kind that Stephanie had never heard before. The doll appeared soft and pliant in Dorrie's hands, and looked as though it turned its face to hers.

Stephanie licked her lips and kept staring as Dorrie's hands caressed the hideous little pink, naked thing. And to her own surprise, she asked, "Dorrie, was that thing moving?" *Of course it wasn't, of course it wasn't,* her own mind told her. She glanced around. Darkness still hung beyond the stacks of furniture and boxes, and it was easy to think she saw things moving there. Mind tricks. Creepy place.

Dorrie twisted sideways so that her back was turned and now the celluloid doll was hidden from Stephanie. The little girl was huddled over it, and Stephanie could hear her whisper something to the doll.

Stephanie said, "I'm going now, Dorrie."

"Okay."

Stephanie stepped backward into nothing.

For a second she was falling, then she caught hold of the edge of the attic floor and sat down heavily on the second step. Her leg was bruised, and she rubbed it, but only automatically. She watched Dorrie's back, the motion of her body as she rocked back and forth, and listened to her crooning voice. Dorrie's attention was focused entirely on the doll. On that

258

hidden, ugly, repulsive thing in her arms.

It hadn't really moved.

Stephanie stood up and picked her way carefully from step to step. She came out into the light of the hall and drew a long breath of relief. She was glad to be downstairs. There was something horribly creepy about the attic, about the ugly old toys there, but she wasn't sure just what it was.

She had an uncomfortable feeling it had something to do with Dorrie.

Elsea stood at her desk and looked down at the typewriter. She felt tired. Drained. Disturbed. Seeing Corey drive away alone, seeing the look in his eyes that reflected her own feelings of bewilderment and worry, had taken even more out of this day that had already gotten off to a bad start. Knowing that he would be in the mountains for a week, maybe longer, added a loneliness and something else she hadn't felt but a few times in her life—a sense of being unprotected, vulnerable to some kind of danger.

Silly, she told herself.

But she couldn't think of writing. She couldn't roll a new sheet of paper into the typewriter without seeing all over again the words that had covered hers: "ONCE UPON A TIME THERE DIED DIED DIED . . ."

She put the typewriter into its case, fastened it, and slid it beneath the desk. Today, she decided with a sudden emotional lift, she would clean house. She would sweep, vacuum, dust, wash, wipe, anything to keep her hands busy and her mind at least half occupied by the mundane things of life. And perhaps somewhere along the way she would touch upon a moment of pleasure.

Corey drove slowly up the mountain road. For the first time in his life he was feeling no pleasure in this kind of trip. His thoughts remained with the family in the green shingled house, with the looks on the faces he had left behind. Something was bothering Tommy, and he wondered how he could persuade the boy to open up and trust him enough to talk about it. It might be a delayed reaction to the death of his father, but Corey somehow doubted it. Whatever it was had started several weeks after they moved into the house. It couldn't have anything to do with school either, or the end of school would have taken care of the problem. Of course the death of the old man yesterday had added deeply to Tommy's problem, but it hadn't been the initial source.

He wanted to turn around and go back, but he kept driving. A few days in the high mountains might clear his mind, help him to see what he could do when he returned.

Dorrie sat still, listening. Stephanie had gone back downstairs. The little dolly knew better than to move when other people were around, because Dorrie had warned her, but the little dolly couldn't be blamed for she no longer had any eyes. She hadn't seen that Dorrie wasn't alone when she came into the attic.

"It's all right," Dorrie whispered into the tiny molded ear on the good side of the doll's head. The other ear was so dented inward that Dorrie always spoke into the only one she considered to be a good ear. "But never, never move when other people see you, or they'll hurt you like Tommy did. Now it's time for your nap. Why do you keep getting out of bed? You have to get well. See, already you're stronger."

The doll's arms curled around Dorrie's wrist and tightened. Its legs reached up, waving blindly, found and touched Dorrie's arm and straddled it and the feet entwined themselves so that when Dorrie tried to lay the doll on its bed she found that it had fastened itself so tightly to her arm that she could not loosen it.

"Let go, dolly, and I'll put you to nap now."

The doll slowly clamped down on Dorrie's arm, tightening, tightening, until it felt as though it were cutting into her flesh. The pain grew, bringing tears to Dorrie's eyes.

"Don't . . . don't . . ."

Dorrie worked at trying to loosen the doll, but the pain grew more intense as the doll tightened.

"No!" Dorrie cried. "It hurts . . . don't hurt me. . . ."

Suddenly something leaped upon her back, toppling her over, enclosing her with arms as strong as steel bands. Dorrie heard sounds, soft, playful, and yet not playful in any way that she had ever heard before. Now she was surrounded by the soft

261

sounds of dozens of them as they rushed out from all their hiding places to crawl over her, walk upon her, pull at her hair, suck at her breath. Dorrie couldn't understand their way of playing with her. Maybe it wasn't play. Maybe it was something else. They were scaring her, making her wish she hadn't come into the attic. When she pleaded with them to stop, their voices rose, chortling, chuckling, and at last she knew they were laughing at her, deliberately mocking her. She rolled on the floor, and struck out with her arms, and her hand hit the edge of the toy box and the celluloid doll lost its grasp on her and fell away. They kept taunting and growling and murmuring in their strange language and their laughter that was turning cruel and demonic. When Dorrie began to cry, when she tried to crawl away from them on her hands and knees, their sounds intensified, and their leaps at her became more tormenting than playful. Claws tore her clothing. The soft, clubby hands of the tall dolls struck her. Fangs snapped in her face.

Dorrie fought her way toward the stairs, crying softly, tears blurring their images in her eyes, fear growing and pushing her onward, a new sickness stirring in her stomach as she realized her toys and dolls were no longer her playmates.

She reached the attic stairs and slid down backwards several steps. Aligned at the top of the stairs, they looked down at her, their faces shimmering through her tears. The tallest of the dolls leaned over the balcony railing and hissed, and Dorrie saw its face was no longer a doll's face, but a thing of nightmare horror with growing fangs and peeling skin and bald patches among the snarled and stringy hair on its head.

Dorrie kept backing down the steps on her hands and knees, looking up. And when she saw they were beginning to follow her down the stairs, she turned and fled, scooting step to step away from them.

When she reached the door, she stood up and shut the door firmly behind her. Sobbing from the rejection of all those she had considered her own, her playmates, she went into her bedroom and climbed onto the bed. She gathered into her arms her old teddy bear.

She would never again go into the attic. They didn't want her anymore.

Elsea found a cloth doll with a china head behind a chair in the library as she vacuumed. She picked it up and looked at it closely. It was perhaps sixteen inches long, and was still wearing its original dress. The lace on the dress was so rotten it tore at her touch. The color, once blue, was now mostly gray. Its body was holding together with the seams still intact. It wore frilly bloomers that came to the ankles ... what were they called? Oh yes, pantaloons, or something like that. It also wore a bonnet. And cute little shoes that buttoned up to the calf. But it was the face that drew her attention and caused her to look at it in wonder. After at least a hundred years it still had the beauty that someone had created, with pink cheeks, white, almost translucent china skin, eyes that looked as deep as the blue sky on a clear day. It had a tiny, curved mouth, pinker than the cheeks. It was smiling. But it was a strange little smile, almost a smirk, as though it knew something Elsea didn't know.

The eyes looked into her own, and the smile remained fixed on the china lips.

Elsea began to feel an odd sense of revulsion.

Carrying the doll in one hand, its head hanging downward, she went to the utility closet in the hallway and got a plastic clothes basket. She dropped the doll into it, and left the basket in the hall.

She found three more toys in the library, all of them in strange places. A stuffed alligator which must have belonged to a much later child than the one who had owned the china doll, was tucked back beneath some books on the bottom shelf of the bookcase section. She would never have found it at all if she hadn't noticed that three books had fallen off the shelf and were lying on the floor. She frowned as she picked up the alligator by its tail. Why would Dorrie pull out the books and put the stuffed creature behind other books? It didn't make sense, and yet obviously that was what had happened.

She tossed the alligator into the plastic basket with the doll.

The third toy was in the corner of the antique settee, its head buried between cushion and back. Two legs stuck out, and Elsea grasped them, and almost turned them loose instantly, for it seemed as though they tried to jerk away from her.

She lifted the cushion, and saw that it was a rag clown, its face a hideous, grinning mask. She carried it between two fingers and dropped it into the basket with the others.

She left the vacuum cleaner and began a search for more toys. It was almost like a game Dorrie was playing with her. An old game she remembered from her own youth, taught to her by her mother, but never passed on to Dorrie that she knew of. Thimble, thimble, where's the thimble? I'll hide it, and you seek and find.

Elsea looked in the desk drawers, under the cushions on the window seat, beneath every piece of furniture that had legs and stood more than two inches off the floor. But there were no more toys in the library.

She went into the parlor and got down on the floor and looked beneath the furniture there. One doll, two. Both of them very old, one of them solid china from the molded yellow hair on its head to the feet with the tiny toes. It was no more than nine inches tall, and wore absolutely nothing. Its round little stomach poked out, its belly button a dimple in its center. The doll fit into the pocket of the shirt she was wearing. The second doll was in the corner beneath a table that was covered by a fringed cloth that hung to the floor all around. It was a larger doll, probably a newer doll, but it was not as well preserved as the china dolls. Its head was made of another kind of material that had lost its glow. Cheeks were pale and pitted, the red mouth was open and the teeth and tongue were snaggled and protruding. The cloth body was packed with straw. Bits of it stuck through the old cloth like needles hidden beneath the ankle-length dress it wore.

Elsea added both dolls to the basket.

In the small room they had taken over and now called the TV room, she found Dorrie's own small toy box, and the few toys they had brought with them. She left them alone. There were no other toys in that room.

She was getting tired of the game. To search every little hiding place in the downstairs would take longer than she wanted to spend.

The back door slammed, and she knew Tommy had come into the kitchen. Stephanie's voice followed the sounds of door and footsteps, and Tommy answered her. Elsea couldn't make out the words of either.

She called out, "Tommy?"

A moment later Tommy looked into the TV room. "Yeah, Mom?"

"How would you like to do something for me?"

"OK."

Elsea saw that he was still subdued, still dull-eyed and withdrawn, and she made her own voice livelier to compensate. If she acted cheerful and happy, maybe she would become so, and it would spread contagiously through her family.

"There's a basket of toys in the hall that I'd like you to carry back up to the attic."

Tommy stood there, gazing steadily at her. His only reaction to her request was a flickering expression of dismay, or fear. It caused Elsea to realize he might be afraid of the attic stairway for his own sake as well as Dorrie's, especially since the accident that occurred there only yesterday.

"On second thought," she said. "I'll take them up."

266

"No," Tommy cried, backing out into the hall, turning and stopping. He stood still then, staring at something on the floor of the hall.

Elsea went to see. The plastic basket was where she had left it, but it was empty.

"Dorrie must have come down and seen the toys and taken them back up with her." Elsea looked at the stairway. There was no sign of Dorrie now, and there had been no sound from her since Stephanie had turned on the attic light so that she could play with the old toys. "I told her not to come down those attic steps alone. She was supposed to call for help."

"Dorrie's in the attic now?"

"Yes. Or she was. Stephanie turned on the light for her. But she must have come down and gone back up again, because that basket was almost full." Elsea picked up the basket and put it back into the utility closet. "Oh well. I guess I don't need your help after all. Unless you want to go up and help Dorrie down. It's close to lunch time. Just be extra careful on the stairs. Or would you rather I go up after her?"

"No."

Tommy's eyes were searching for something. Elsea saw him look over his shoulder, down the hall, into the rooms whose doors stood open.

"Were they the old toys?" he asked. "Or Dorrie's own?"

"The old ones, from the attic. Why?"

"I just wondered. Were they . . . did they . . . I mean, where did you find them?"

"In all kinds of strange places. I think Dorrie is playing a game with them, hiding them here and there, under furniture, even behind books in the bookcase."

"How many of them?"

"Five or six, most of them dolls."

Tommy said softly, "And now they're gone."

Elsea had no answer for her son. There was in his voice an odd sound of dull hopelessness. A kind of acceptance that had no real emotion in it. His words held a finality that disturbed her.

"Gone? Dorrie must have come after them."

Tommy went to the stairs and looked up. "I'll go get Dorrie."

"And I'll start something for lunch. Would you like cold cuts, or something hot?"

"I don't care."

Tommy went up the stairs, turned the corner, and was out of sight. Elsea stood in the hallway listening. Even though he wore soft-soled sneakers, she could hear his footsteps. She heard him go along the upstairs hall, then he stopped and there was nothing more.

Elsea went into the kitchen where Stephanie was already putting together some rather complicated sandwiches. She was working slowly and quietly. She didn't look up at Elsea, nor did she start talking as she ordinarily did.

Elsea did not encourage conversation. Her thoughts had gone back to those words Tommy had spoken with such despair. *And now they're gone.*

The attic door was closed, and Tommy stood for a moment staring at it. He had to go up there and bring Dorrie down, and he didn't want to. His mother didn't know, but he knew, Dorrie had not come down and carried those toys up. Nor had Dorrie been playing a hide and seek game with the toys. They were hiding themselves. They were everywhere now. They had infiltrated the lower stories of the house, and were in every room. Yet when his mother picked them up they had pretended they were just toys, and nothing more.

Only he and Dorrie knew differently.

On sudden impulse Tommy backed up and looked in Dorrie's room. When he saw that she was lying curled in a little knot on her bed, her face toward the wall, he was torn with distinctly different feelings. First was the sense of thanksgiving, of having an unspoken prayer answered. And immediately upon that came the new feeling of fear when he had to be close to Dorrie. He tried to conquer that feeling, to pretend that everything was normal and right again between him and his little sister.

"Dorrie?" He spoke softly. All around him in the silence of the house they were listening. He could feel them. Their eyes looking out through the narrowest of cracks, their ears picking up every little sound made by the humans who were becoming enemy invaders or, maybe worse, powerless game for the wild hunters. And were they not being led by Dorrie, their master?

When Dorrie didn't move or answer, Tommy went closer and looked down at her. At first when he saw she held something in her arms, his heart lurched sickeningly. But then he saw it was only her teddy bear. She was holding tightly to it even in her sleep. Tommy touched her shoulder.

"Dorrie?"

She moved and murmured, "Huh?" and put one fist up and rubbed her eyes.

"It's time for lunch, Dorrie."

"OK."

She sat up, and he saw her knit shirt was ripped and torn, and her bare arms were crisscrossed with pink scratches.

"Dorrie, what happened to you?" he whispered in shrill anxiety as he went down on his knees beside her bed, his fear of her forgotten. Even her legs, he saw, were scratched. Short little scratches, shallow bites, red little holes where claws had sunk in and brought blood to the surface.

Her face puckered, her mouth trembled, and tears filled her eyes. "N-nothing."

"You don't have to lie to me, Dorrie," Tommy whispered. "I know, remember? The toys upstairs did this, didn't they?"

"Y-yes. They don't like me anymore."

Tommy licked his dry lips and hugged Dorrie close to him. So she had been attacked by them. She was no longer their master.

They no longer had a master.

"Dorrie, I want you to dress in a long-sleeved blouse today, and those little slacks that are long-legged and cool. I don't want you to tell Mom, because I've got some thinking to do. And Dorrie?"

"Huh?"

"Stay out of the attic."

"I will."

Tommy went to her closet to find the slack suit that was made of cotton, a matching top and bottom with cute little printed animals. "Take off your shirt and shorts," he told her quietly, "and I'll get rid of them."

When he came back with the pantsuit, Dorrie was standing in her panties waiting. Tommy wadded the ripped clothes into a ball and tucked it under his arm. He took Dorrie by the hand and with a hasty glance up and down the hallway, hurried her next door to the bathroom. When he began to sponge her scratches with alcohol, she objected.

"It hurts, Tommy. I don't want you to do that."

He held tight to her and kept sponging. "I have to. They might be poison. I'm almost through. Here, put these on. If Mom says anything to you about taking the toys out of the basket, just say you did. She'd never believe anything else, and I've got to figure out what we're going to do."

"What basket?"

"Never mind. Just do as I say."

"OK, Tommy."

"I'll hide your other clothes, and don't you say anything about them, either. Not yet. I've got to think."

"OK, Tommy."

He helped Dorrie button her blouse, then with her hand in his they went to Tommy's room where he stuffed the torn clothing under the mattress with his own discarded shirt that had been ripped by the wood horse.

"Now don't you tell," he whispered.

"I won't."

Tommy squared his shoulders and led Dorrie down the stairs toward the kitchen. He kept a lookout for any movement near any item of furniture or any turn in the wall or stairs where one of them might be hiding and waiting, but he saw nothing. *I have to think,* he kept telling himself, but he couldn't. He felt as though he were facing a thick impenetrable wall, a wall that he could not pass through but which would not stop the toys. Yet he also felt he had won a battle, for now he had Dorrie, they didn't. And he would stay close to her from now on. He would watch her every minute, from now on.

Their mother instantly saw the change in Dorrie's clothing. "That's your dress-up pantsuit, Dorrie, why are you wearing it?"

Tommy said quickly, "Her other clothes were dirty."

"She has a dresser drawer full of old shirts and shorts that are good enough for play."

Tommy leaned over the table. "Hey, that really looks good. Are we ready to eat?"

"Yes, sit down."

"Come on, Dorrie, I'll help you up. What do you bet Corey is already up to the mountains? I'll bet he could make a snowball now if he wanted to. I was thinking, maybe we can all go along the next time, or maybe Mom and Dorrie can go down—" He paused to take a large bite out of a sandwich, and continued talking with his mouth full. "Go down to Grandma and Grandpa's, and stay there while . . . Steph and me go with Corey. . . ." Another bite, continued chattering, so that Elsea would forget that Dorrie had changed clothes, so that she wouldn't get a chance to mention the basket of toys, because Dorrie might forget and tell her the truth about the toys. *Because first he had to think.* His brain was muddled. Maybe all the toys wanted was the attic to themselves. But no. If that were the case, they wouldn't come downstairs. Maybe they wanted the whole house to themselves. If that were so, then all he and his mother and sisters had to do was move. But how could they? When he tried to talk to his mother, she didn't listen.

In the afternoon Tommy kept Dorrie with him. They explored the outbuildings, and even climbed up to sit in the buggy and pretend they were driving a horse and going to town in the buggy. Dorrie cooperated in every idea that came to Tommy, so that he began to have fun, and the attic of the house, with its toys, was only a background horror that he didn't want to face again.

But inevitably, night came, and they had to go inside.

Dorrie went to sleep in the beanbag chair watching television, and when Elsea picked her up to put her to bed, Tommy ran along with her, going first into Dorrie's room. He turned on the light.

Elsea laid Dorrie on the bed, and began pulling off the pantsuit that was soiled from an afternoon among rusty old tools in the shed and garages.

"I can put her to bed, Mom," Tommy said, hoping she'd go away, hoping she wouldn't see the scratches on Dorrie's skin.

"You put yourself to bed, Tommy. I'll take care of Dorrie since I'm already here."

Tommy stepped back and waited. Dorrie stirred sleepily as Elsea pulled off the long-legged slacks and long-sleeved shirt. The scratches were still pink and raw looking, still visible.

"What in the world happened to her?" Elsea asked.

Tommy tried to think. Should he tell her the truth? Make her go up into the attic and see for herself? Or would they do to his mother what they had done to the man who was going to buy the house?

Elsea looked over her shoulder at Tommy with a perplexed frown. "Is this why you changed her clothes?"

Tommy nodded.

Elsea examined Dorrie's arms and legs more thoroughly, but gently so that Dorrie went back to sleep. "Where did she get these, Tommy?"

"In the attic, Mom," he said, watching her face closely.

"But how? She looks like she's climbed through a briar patch."

"It was the toys," he said carefully, watching her every expression. He saw her turn her face swiftly toward his, and a disbelieving smile curl the corner of her lips. It was gone almost as swiftly as it appeared.

She wouldn't believe, Tommy saw. Even if the toys would move in her presence, she wouldn't believe what she was seeing. So Tommy came up with an explanation that surprised himself.

"The straw. It's old and brittle, and she rolled around on the floor with a toy, a stuffed animal, and all the stuffing came out of it, and it was straw and it scratched her. It's OK. I already put alcohol on her. But, Mom . . . I was thinking. Maybe we'd better get rid of all the old toys. They're kind of . . . kind of dangerous."

Elsea pulled a light blanket up over Dorrie. "Don't be silly, Tommy. Some modern toys may be dangerous, but certainly not those old things upstairs. Except for the stuffing coming out and sticking. Go on to bed now."

Tommy obeyed. In his room he left the door open and his light out, and he waited and listened. There was silence tonight. Too much silence. Above his room nothing moved, or crawled, or made a sound. But he wasn't fooled. They were waiting, just as he was waiting. He didn't know anymore what they were waiting for, or what they would do next. And tonight all he could do was what he had done before at night: close the bedroom doors of his sisters' and mother's rooms while they slept.

He gave them an hour to fall asleep, while he sat in his doorway and watched the attic door. The thin thread of light was there again, but the white doorknob didn't move, although he stared so hard it sometimes blurred, became double its size, and seemed to move. Yet when he focused his eyes again, he saw it was still. Tonight, it didn't even rattle. And the pale light under the door was not broken by any shadow.

At last he got up and slipped along the hall, closing all the bedroom doors. Then he closed his own, but instead of going to bed, he remained in the hall, leaning back against his door. Tonight he was going to keep vigil.

Tonight, he would see they did not come down from the attic. He would hold the door shut when they tried to open it. He would show them he was stronger than they.

Tomorrow, he would find some kind of lock among the junk in the garages and bolt it to the attic door, so that nothing could open it from either side. The attic door would be permanently locked. At last, he had thought of a way.

Only one night to go.

Only one night.

Tommy leaned against his door, his knees drawn up and supporting his arms. Sometimes his head nodded and almost went to sleep against his will, but he jerked upright again.

The night remained silent.

Hours passed.

Tommy's head touched his arms again, and remained there.

SEVENTEEN

The hour of deepest night had come, and the toys came out from all their hiding places, both in the attic and downstairs, and began to move, to murmur among themselves as they moved, a sound both evil and gleeful. The dolls, the stuffed animals and the clown that came up from downstairs saw the sleeping boy leaning against the door to his bedroom and passed that information through to the dolls and toys that had gathered at the bottom of the attic stairway. The tallest doll in the attic, the doll with the patches of hair, the peeling face, the fangs that had grown from the tiny teeth embedded in the upper part of her mouth, reached the doorknob easily and with hands that were like stuffed mittens, dexterously turned the knob. They fell against the door, clambering over one another like an army of huge ants, pushed it open and gathered in the downstairs hall.

A few of them separated from the group and went over to cluster around Tommy, and their sounds rose to a fever pitch, to a degree too fine for the human ear. But from the larger group came a call, and those around the boy pulled away and joined the army as it fell against the door to Dorrie's room.

They opened the door and crossed the floor to the bed. They climbed, the small ones reaching the edge of the blanket and pulling up, the animals leaping, the large ones going before them all onto the bed to the sleeping child and the sweet breath that issued from between her parted lips. Their murmurs ceased. Small grunts, snarls and growls became their language as they fought one another for Dorrie's breath.

She stirred but didn't waken. A dream that had been sweet with adventure began to grow in horror as a dark cloud came down over her face and smothered her. She tried to throw her arms out against the cloud, but couldn't move them.

Finally there was no dream at all, just a black cloud that smothered her to unconsciousness.

Tommy realized he had fallen asleep and jerked his head upright. His eyes were blurry and unfocused. The light in the place where he was sitting was pale and strange-looking, as though it came from somewhere far away, as though it were filled with tiny, invisible creatures that stirred and floated and fought for supremacy. He blinked and tried to figure out where he was, and what he was doing there. He remembered now. He had turned the hall light on after he'd closed all the bedroom doors. And the hall light was a forty-watt bulb and around the corner from him, and the corner of the wall threw a shadow that cut across his legs and went straight to the attic door. *The attic door . . .*

It was wide open.

Tommy leaped up, every muscle in his body tense. The attic stairs reached up out of sight, and nothing was there, not even the drifting dust, to suggest that anything had walked upon them recently.

Dorrie's door.

It too was open.

And now their sounds reached him, faint gruntings of satisfaction, murmurs of fulfillment. Obscene sounds that brought the taste of gall into his mouth, and the rush of something solid from his stomach into his throat. He forced it back. And he ran.

In the dim shadows of her room, he saw her bed heaped with crawling bodies. Beneath them was his little sister, and he gave out his own primeval grunt as he rushed them. He had no time to be afraid of them. The rage was too compelling, too total. He couldn't even find words for the expression of his abhorrence. His voice kept coming, grunting, growling, as he began throwing them off the bed, throwing them as hard as he could, hearing with satisfaction when a doll's head crashed against the wall. He felt their claws dig into his pajamas, but his skin was immune to their touch in his terrible rage. Their murmurs rose to a communal howl, and as

279

though they had received a command from a leader suddenly they ran, going out of his reach, crowding toward the door and out of the room.

Tommy bent over Dorrie. He lifted her, and she fell back, limp and lifeless. He grabbed her bedside lamp and turned it over, grabbed it up again and set it upright and managed to snap the light on. He saw his little sister was dead, and he began to scream. His voice came as in a nightmare, with effort, low and hoarse at first and then with power.

Elsea heard the scream and was out of her bed before she realized what she was hearing. She stood confused only a moment before she began to run.

Stephanie heard the scream and sat in her bed, paralyzed. And when she heard someone run past her door she knew it was not a dream. Someone in the house was screaming, screaming and someone else was hurt. She too ran.

They came one behind the other into Dorrie's bedroom, and saw Tommy holding Dorrie in his arms. His face was an image in horror.

"She's dead," he cried. "Mama, she's dead!"

Elsea pulled Dorrie from Tommy's arms, and felt her child as limp as though Tommy were right, but it couldn't be. It couldn't be! Elsea willed that it was not true. She laid Dorrie down and bent over her, ear to chest, listening. Her fingers pressed against the child's temples and wrists, feeling for pulse. Finally, she found it. Feeble, slow. Dorrie was breathing almost imperceptibly, but breathing. And as though she had just come up from beneath a great shadow, she gasped and took a deep breath.

Elsea said, "Stay with her. I'll be back in a minute.

We have to take her to the hospital."

Tommy found himself weak with relief, and the tears began. He sank to the floor at the side of her bed and sobbed with his face against the bed. He heard Stephanie say something and run from the room. He tried to get himself under control. He couldn't sit and cry, his eyes sightless with tears, his body weak and trembling. They had almost killed Dorrie, and they were still here, somewhere in the house, and he had to fight them.

He wiped his eyes and stood up. Dorrie was unconscious and pale, her body as limp as her teddy bear, but now at least she was breathing evenly. But would she live?

Elsea and Stephanie came back into the room together, both of them dressed. Without a word Elsea lifted Dorrie, pulled up a light blanket and wrapped it partly around her.

"Let's go," she said.

Tommy followed them downstairs, turning on the lights for them. He waited until they were on the back screened porch before he told them he wasn't going. Elsea barely paused, looking back over her shoulder at him. She had no time to argue.

"I'll stay here," he said again.

"Tommy . . ."

"I'll wait," he said firmly. He had to wait. He had things to do. Now he knew what he was going to do.

They went on. He watched them get into the car, with Stephanie now holding Dorrie. He watched the lights come on, heard the car start and back out of sight. A moment later its tires squealed as it went onto the blacktop and turned the corner toward town.

Silence settled over him.

He stood on the back porch, but now in the quiet he could hear them, far above in the attic, a low murmur that was like the buzzing of a cloud of insects.

The porch light reached a few yards past the driveway, touching the edge of the forest that stood between their house and Corey's. Tommy stared at the dark woods, and saw in it a retreat, a haven. Somehow he would find his way through the woods, and go to Corey, and pray as he went that Corey would be there. He would tell Corey all of it and get him to come back and help him destroy the dolls. *Please God, let Corey be there.*

Tommy ran to the path through the woods, and then felt his way along in a darkness that seemed total. Occasionally he heard the crack of a twig off to his right or his left, and his heart plunged, wondering, had they followed him from the house? Were they at this moment aware of his intentions and able to see in the dark, simply trailing him, waiting for the right moment to attack?

Something was grabbing at his back, pulling at his pajamas. He was too terrified to cry out, to call for Corey. He tried to move, and couldn't. At last he reached around and felt that he was being held only by a tree limb, and he sobbed silently and tearlessly as he disentangled himself.

He reached the edge of the forest. Pale starlight outlined Corey's trailer. But there was no car in the driveway.

Tommy banged on the trailer house door and cried out for Corey, but all the time he knew it was useless. Energy wasted. Corey was gone. He had gone into the mountains after all, and he wouldn't be back for several days, maybe not for several weeks.

Tommy turned his back to the trailer door and looked toward the house of his great-grandmother. Lights blinked far away, beyond the trees. He had to go back, and go alone. He had to conquer them without help.

He entered the path through the forest again and didn't pause. He held his arms out to protect himself from limbs and tree trunks. He kept his eyes on the lights of the house, and they became larger, steadier, and at last when he broke through the forest they were lighted rectangles, windows upstairs and down.

He went to the shed and took down a hatchet he had seen hanging on the wall, a hatchet he had honed until it was sharp as a butcher's knife. Gripping it hard in his right hand, he headed toward the house with a determined walk, not allowing himself to hesitate, not really thinking of what he was facing.

He was going to destroy them.

It was that simple.

He stopped at the bottom of the stairway to the upstairs, and his eyes combed every square inch available to him, but he saw no sign of them. He began to climb. His bare feet made almost no sound on the carpetless stairs. When he reached the upstairs hall he saw the attic door was closed. They had closed it.

He stood against it and listened, and heard nothing. No murmurs now, no movement. Where were they? Gathered at the top waiting?

He opened the attic door, slowly, and its hinges squeaked rustily, for the first time, giving out a warning to those who lived in the attic. He looked up and saw the light was still on. For a moment a thought zipped through his mind—that they might have turned the light out and made it more difficult for him to gain control, for they must know that he could not see as well as they in the dark. But it was on, and so they must have a reason for leaving it on.

He climbed a few steps and looked all around the top of the stairwell. A frail balcony ran around three sides, but there were no faces looking down at him. In the dim light, though, dust motes floated, indicating a recent flurry of activity.

Tommy kept climbing, slowly, deliberately, and he raised his right arm, the hatchet poised to strike.

He reached the top and stepped onto the boards of the attic floor. He stood now on the edge of the place where Dorrie had played, and it had a haunted quality that made his eyes burn. It was as though Dorrie sat there, in spirit, smiling at him, cuddling her ugly, weird, dangerous little celluloid doll.

Only she wasn't there. And neither was the doll.

The doll bed was empty.

The entire attic seemed empty, except for the broken furniture, the wood crates, the cardboard boxes. Yet Tommy could feel the others, the non-creatures, the toys Dorrie had brought to life. He could feel them watching him, waiting, hiding, but watching, watching, watching. . . .

"Come out, you dirty little cowards!"

His voice seemed to echo, as though they had taken up the tones of his call and repeated them; then again came the silence.

"I'll fight you! I'll show you who's the—"

Suddenly they were there, eyes gleaming, glittering, lights reflected from their surfaces, and from some deep source within. They came rushing out from all sides, from all dark little crevices and hiding places. They leaped down from boxes where they had not seemed to be. Now they were everywhere, coming at him from all directions. And they were coming in silence, only the padding of soft feet, the tick-ticking of hard little hooves carved of wood, the clicking of claws on the floor. Tommy swung out with the hatchet, and a head rolled onto the floor. The eyes suddenly dead and dull. He swung again in another direction, and saw he had split a body stuffed with straw squarely in two. But they were grabbing at him from behind, climbing his legs, pulling themselves up by his clothes, coming up to clutch at his hair. He reached round for them, and suddenly the hatchet was jerked out of his hand and carried away and he had nothing left but his hands. They were all over him now, crawling up the front of him, hanging onto his shoulders, reaching into his face.

He fell to his knees.

And then to his face.

He was blinded and couldn't see. He was smothered and couldn't breathe. He felt the light weight of their bodies, and a strength far beyond anything he had imagined.

Their sounds began now, as they immobilized the boy, as they took their turns sucking away his breath. And when at last he had no breath left to give they joined forces and discussed the problem of having him in their attic. Finally they surrounded him, lifted him and carried him down the attic steps, his head bumping each step as his body was half-dragged along. They opened the door to his room, carried him through the door, and then grunting and growling and whining with the effort, laid him on his bed.

Tommy stared sightlessly at the ceiling.

Corey woke and sat up. Above him the night stars were as bright as planets, but there was no beauty nor comfort in them now. He had a terrible premonition that he should be at home . . . no, not at home, but at the house next door. Something was wrong. He couldn't say what, or why he knew. He knew only that he had to hurry, get his things back into the Blazer, and head down the mountain. He worked hurriedly, rolled his sleeping bag, pulled on his boots, threw his gear into the back with the rest of his stuff, got in behind the wheel and headed toward the road. Patches of snow were patches of light in the darkness, and he remembered to turn the car lights on. After that he merely drove, as fast as he could on the twisting mountain roads.

*   *   *

Elsea and Stephanie stood in the hallway outside the room where Dorrie lay in the hospital bed. Through the door they could see a nurse and a doctor who now was coming toward them.

"She now seems to be sleeping normally," he said. "I'm sure it's not a coma. But we'd like to keep her here a few days to run some tests."

Elsea nodded. She longed to stay with Dorrie, but there was no way she could. The doctor appeared to read her mind. He put a hand on her shoulder and smiled.

"She'll be fine, Mrs. Marsh, we'll keep a close eye on her the rest of the night, and of course you can come in as early as you wish."

"I've left one of my children at home," Elsea said. "I have to get back. Are you sure she's all right?"

"I'm sure. Her sleep seems normal," he said again. "Her respiration, her heart, everything is normal. The light coma she was in at first seems to be gone. But we do want her to stay, at least overnight."

Elsea nodded. "Let's go home, Stephanie," she said. "We shouldn't have left Tommy alone."

"He's okay, Mom."

Elsea hurried along the hospital corridor, that brightly lighted hallway that looked so much like all the hallways and corridors in every hospital she had ever seen. She was reminded of the first night she'd left Vern in a hospital, and decided that perhaps the feeling that was now tearing her apart was in some way connected to that experience. For she wanted to stay with Dorrie, and yet she wanted urgently to get home to see, to make sure, that Tommy was safe.

As she drove through the night, the feeling waned. Dorrie was safe. Whatever had happened to her would be discovered and corrected. And they were coming closer and closer to the house where Tommy waited alone.

The lights were still on.

Stephanie said, "What do you bet he's sitting on the back step waiting for us?"

Elsea parked the car in the driveway and turned the switch off. She could see the back step, and Tommy wasn't sitting there.

There was no need to answer Stephanie.

Tommy wasn't in the brightly lighted kitchen either. Elsea paused, listening. The silence in the house was disturbing. Tommy should have come to meet them by now. She looked at Stephanie, and saw that Stephanie was watching her, and her eyes were rounded and puzzled. Together they went into the central hall and up the back stairs, running, and the feeling that something terrible was wrong grew with each step.

"Tommy?" Elsea called out before she reached the top of the stairs, but there was no answer.

The door to his room stood open. She paused in the doorway, with Stephanie close behind her, looking over her shoulder. Tommy's bedroom light was out, but they could see he was lying stretched full length on his bed, his arms at his sides, his face staring at the ceiling.

Elsea was aware that Stephanie pushed past her, but she couldn't move. She knew Tommy was not merely asleep, yet she couldn't accept it. The coma that had almost taken Dorrie now had Tommy; he would wake up, just as Dorrie had. But Stephanie was turning back toward her and saying something she couldn't understand even though she heard the words clearly.

"Mama, Tommy isn't breathing. I think he's dead."

EIGHTEEN

Dorrie hadn't spoken a word since she learned of Tommy's death. She stared at the still, waxlike face of her brother. He was in a coffin that was blue inside and out. His head was supported by a tiny blue satin pillow, and quilted satin was his bed. Just like her daddy had been put to bed forever, so now Tommy had been put into his eternal bed. She wanted to touch him, to kiss him, to make him live again.

She put her hand on the quilted edge of the coffin, within inches of Tommy's face, of his own still hands folded together on his chest. She felt the cool glassiness of the material beneath her fingertips. She moved her hand nearer his face, and then drew it back and left it resting on the quilted fabric as she looked at him. A terrible sadness moved into her as she thought of the calm and gentle looks on the faces of the old toys and dollies before she had made them to living. Would Tommy rise up as they had done with the growing changes? With eyes that saw through darkness and hands grown cruel and hurting? Would her touch make him one of them?

She pulled her hand away and stepped back from the coffin.

She wanted to speak to him, to tell him why she must leave him to death. She wanted him to understand. But she stepped farther back. She had to let him go.

So she remained silent. She waited, she listened, she looked. This time she was going to all the different phases of the funeral. They had left the chapel and were in the cemetery where the coffin was poised over a hole that was covered by a blanket of artificial grass. Stephanie looked pale and sick. So did her grandparents, and so did Corey. But worst of all was her mother. Her tears had started and wouldn't stop. She slumped as though she had no bones in her body. Corey held her, his arm around her waist. Grandma and Grandpa stood silently nearby.

When the funeral was over and the coffin was covered by flowers, Dorrie was led away. They rode in the long, black car that had brought them from the chapel to the cemetery. This time it took them home to Dorrie's grandparents' house.

Just like before, in the weeks after her daddy died, they were staying with Grandma and Grandpa. But Dorrie looked westward, toward the house with the green shingles, and waited patiently to be taken there.

At last Mama stopped crying and began to talk.

"We can't live there anymore. I don't think I can even bear to see that place again. What happened to Tommy? I don't even know what caused his death."

They were sitting at the kitchen table, all of them Dorrie considered to be part of the family. People who had been strangers to her were gone now, even Corey was gone now, and Dorrie waited.

Her grandpa said, "A natural death, Elsea. He just stopped breathing."

"But why? *Why?*"

"There's no answer to that. But the autopsy showed nothing."

Grandma said, "Of course you can't live there. You can live here with us. We'll manage. Don't worry."

"As soon as I can find a place for the girls and me, we'll move out," Elsea said.

"Listen," Grandma insisted, "we want you here. We won't worry about tomorrow."

"I'll have to go get our things."

"Yes. We'll go along and help you pack."

Dorrie raised her head and watched them, alerted for this that she had been waiting for. They were going back to the green-shingled house.

"Tomorrow will be soon enough, won't it?"

"I'm afraid not, Dad. We're running out of clothes. We have time to go today. We have to go."

Dorrie stopped listening. She wandered out into the back yard and over near the driveway. She sat down near one of Grandpa's flower beds and waited. When they came out of the house she was ready

293

to go.

She rode in the back seat between Grandma and Stephanie.

The sun was sinking behind the tall trees to the west when they drove in and parked by the side of the house. Dorrie looked up at the attic window in the high peak of the house, and saw the reflection of the sun. She crawled out of the car behind Stephanie and followed the others into the house.

She heard their voices as they moved through the house, but she was no longer listening to anything they said. She went to the back stairway and up to the second floor. She stood for a while and looked at the closed attic door. There were no sounds of them. They were hiding from her, she knew.

She opened the door and looked up into the attic. The light burned in its dusty socket, and the air was filled with dust. They had been there then, themselves listening, waiting. They knew she had come.

She climbed the enclosed stairway to the attic after being very careful to shut the attic door. With one hand sliding along the wall, she went up.

The celluloid doll was on its bed, as though it knew to obey now. Especially now. Dorrie stared at it.

On the floor around her were arms, legs, heads, all cut away from bodies that lay nearby. And off to one side, in the shadow of boxes was a hatchet.

Dorrie bent and picked up the hatchet. She touched the blade with one finger, and found it sharp as a razor. Tommy had sharpened it.

Dorrie spoke now. Softly. Cajolingly. Her eyes watched every shadow with a sharpness that missed

294

nothing. Occasionally she glanced at the celluloid doll. It stayed on the bed she had made for it.

"Come out, dollies," she said. "Come out and play with me. All of you, all my toys and dolls, come out now."

Her eyes passed again over the bits and pieces of stuffed animals, dolls, toys on the floor. It made a terrible mess in her playroom, with straw scattered, bead eyes lying among the straw like sliced marbles thrown away. The picture was clear to her, as though she went back in time to the night when Tommy had climbed the stairs into the attic with the hatchet in his hand. They had come out to meet him, and he had begun chopping them, chopping, chopping everywhere he could; but they were stronger than he, they were more than he, and at last they had gotten him. He had not known them as well as she knew them. It was she who had made them to living, and it was she who must make them to dying.

"Come out, my dollies, come and see me."

A movement now, in the shadows to her right. She glanced at it, and then quickly looked away and pretended she didn't see.

The murmurs began and grew, over in the darkness to her left. They were gathering now, talking about her. And they were coming closer. She could hear the soft, sliding step of the doll that had one stiff leg and one floppy leg. They were coming, and she held the hatchet behind her back.

She saw their eyes gleaming in the dark. Some of them were green and some red. None of them were blue, the color of their daylight eyes, the color of the beads that made the eyes. In the dark they glowed a different color. But those on the floor no longer glowed. They had gone back to dying.

She saw their faces then, and she saw they had become uglier. Each moment of their lives brought a deeper ugliness, with dripping fangs and mean stares. The light of their eyes was almost too much for her. She gripped the hatchet handle tighter.

"Come on, come on to Dorrie, my dollies, my toys, my little animals. Come now, and I will kiss you."

They stared at her and began to spread out. She turned, keeping them in front of her, but alert to those still in hiding behind her.

"There's a trunk," she said, "that's empty. A nice, nice trunk with a lock, and it's going to be a coffin. Come now, come. Come and see your coffin."

Their movements changed with a suddenness that almost caught her unprepared, that almost made her run instinctively and blindly, seeking only to escape. But she stopped herself and stood still, watching them as they rushed out, fanning out and coming at her from every direction. Their eyes glittered, their murmurs rose to a crescendo of sound that her ears barely caught, their mouths widened in hideous snarls. They paused, just out of reach, and their movements became subtle and calculated as they took short steps toward her, in, back, taunting, tormenting, judging by their own unknown mentality, the best moment to attack.

Dorrie said, "You need me, my little dollies. You can't live without me. Come now, one at a time, and go with me to the trunk. I will make you safe forever."

They edged back away from her, one inch, two. They jostled against one another in the circle around her and their murmurs became guttural disagreements. They did need her. But only for a little while. The breath in her body would keep them strong for a long time to come.

Dorrie watched them. She saw the little wood horse step forward from the group and open his mouth. His eyes had slanted, and were now narrow, evil slits. His teeth were longer, sharper, more dangerous. On the other side the stuffed kitty cat stepped forward from the circle. Now Dorrie knew. The two of them had been sent to attack, first, to grab her attention, and then the others would be upon her, bearing her to the floor, sucking the breath from her just as they had from Tommy.

Dorrie bent, and clutched the handle of the hatchet with both hands. When the horse came within reach she struck out, chopping in a downward stroke, catching it in the center of its body. The two pieces rolled, writhing, and the eyes became as blank as a night sky. With movements as quick as their own, she turned and brought the hatchet down upon the stuffed cat.

"You killed my Tommy!" she cried. "You killed him."

They rushed her, all at once, and she swung around, using the hatchet on every face that came within reach. The clown collapsed, and the rag doll with the china head. Another and another went down under her determination to finish what Tommy had started. Like a beaten army, the survivors pulled back and were instantly gone into hiding again, among the boxes, the crates, the furniture.

Breathing heavily, Dorrie looked at the bed she had made for the little celluloid doll. It was now empty. But the doll was still in sight as it crawled in its sideways motion for the darkness. Dorrie rushed at it and grabbed it up. When it turned and curled itself painfully around her arm she turned the hatchet blade on it. The doll let loose. Dorrie laid it on the floor and bent over it a moment, the hatchet poised to cut off its head. But she picked it up again instead, by one foot, and carried it dangling to the large metal trunk.

She raised the lid and dropped the doll in. Before it could scramble out she slammed the lid shut.

"It's your coffin," she said. "Forever and ever."

She began walking through the dark tunnels, the shadowy aisles, calling, tolling, "I want you, my dollies, my toys. Come now. Don't be disobedient to me."

At the corner of a large stack of boxes she came face to face with the tallest doll. With a snarl and a leap it was upon her, and Dorrie fell to the floor, her head cracking so hard against the wood that she was blinded with pain. The doll was on her stomach, its clubby hands pressed against her forehead. Dorrie lay still, her eyes almost closed. She saw the doll's face come nearer and nearer her own, and when the doll was distracted, when it seemed to have conquered its victim, it began a growling chant, and Dorrie heard the rushing of bodies gather toward her. Still, she waited. She saw more of the dolls, the ⁺ches of stringy, stiff hair, the peeling skin. They were gathering within reach.

Dorrie rolled suddenly. Just as she once had when they played their games, before they had turned on her. And as she rolled she swung the hatchet. The head of the doll upon her rolled into the deeper darkness, and the stuffing of the body spilled out upon Dorrie. She slashed with all her strength in all directions, making contact in various parts of the dolls' bodies. And finally she was on her feet, looking down at destroyed dolls and toys. And then she listened. Movement to her left, somewhere in the pathways of the attic. She went in search of those who were left.

"Dorrie?"

Stephanie stood at the bottom of the attic stairs and called up. She could see nothing but the light above, the balconies that surrounded three sides of the stairwell, and heavy dust in the air. She wondered, how could Dorrie breathe that air? And what made it so dusty, so filled with floating bits of debris?

"Dorrie! Come on down, we're ready to go."

Dorrie didn't answer, and with a sigh of exasperation, Stephanie climbed the attic stairs. She stopped, looking at the floor in astonishment.

It was littered with bits and pieces of the old stuffed toys. Everywhere, it seemed. What wasn't on the floor floated through the air.

Stephanie began walking slowly into the attic, staring around at the continued debris, almost forgetting why she had come into the attic in the first

299

place. She saw Dorrie then, on her knees in front of a very large trunk. The lid was up, and Dorrie was stuffing it full of something.

Stephanie looked over her shoulder. Toys. Dolls. All of them, most of them, chopped to pieces. And on the floor beside Dorrie was a hatchet with a sharp and glinting blade. For a horrible moment Stephanie thought she saw blood on it.

"Dorrie?"

Dorrie looked over her shoulder at Stephanie, a quick glance. "In a minute," she said.

Stephanie watched as Dorrie's small hands pushed the pieces of dolls and toys tighter into the trunk. And she watched too as Dorrie closed the lid and turned the lock.

Dorrie stood up.

"There," she said. "I'm ready to go."

Stephanie took Dorrie's hand, as her mother had instructed, and led her toward the stairs.

She looked back over her shoulder at the hatchet, and she saw that its blade was dark with a substance that dripped onto the floor.

EPILOGUE

Dorrie was two years older. She went to school now, like her big sister Stephanie, and after school she went home to a happy household where there was love and security. She didn't think of it as such. She knew only that she liked her home, the brick house with the fenced back yard that was only three blocks from Grandma and Grandpa's house. She had a baby brother she loved a lot, a mother and dad, a beautiful older sister, a puppy and a kitten, and all the things she wanted. She was happy. But there was a part of her life she could not remember. She knew there had been another daddy once, and an older brother. But they were only pictures in the albums. Sometimes she almost remembered Tommy. She could hear his voice, and yet she couldn't. It was like a dream she had lost once she was fully awake.

Another memory was almost recalled the day she heard the news about the house. She heard only the first words that passed between her mother and dad before the memory struggled to rise and blotted out the present.

Corey asked, "Have you heard the sale of your grandmother's house went through?"

"No, I haven't talked to Mom today," Elsea answered. "After all these years Mom and Dad got a buyer?"

"Yes."

"Who bought it?"

"A family named Cristophen. Large family. Your dad told me they have about five or six kids."

"Wonderful. They'll love it there."

The memory stirred in Dorrie's mind, a dark blot within her consciousness. But then from outside the door came the call from one of her friends, wanting her to come out and play. So Dorrie ran, and the memory was lost.

The Cristophens moved into the green-shingled house on the day the papers were signed and the property became theirs. They were fresh out of the city where even their furniture had been leased, and they felt as though they had inherited a kingdom of treasures because their new house had been sold to them completely furnished. The kids scattered through the rooms, calling to one another, their voices ranging in age from two years to fifteen. Excitement hovered in the air, vibrated in the house

302

from wall to wall, floor to ceiling.

And in the attic their voices were heard, and a doll hidden in its still, dark lair began to move. From across the room, in another hiding place, another doll emerged, slowly, to place itself carefully in sight, where it would not miss being found. They listened, and they waited, and at last the footsteps came, the children came, their voices shrill with excitement, up the stairs and into the attic.